Parasite Girls

Tory Gates

Requests to the Author/Publisher should be addressed to:

Tory Gates Media
1937 Fulton St.
Harrisburg, PA 17102
torygatesmedia@outlook.com

All material is written by the author, except the quoted lyrics to:

"Let Love Get Away," written and performed by Carmen Yates; BMI/Dampcellar Music.

"The Bluest Blues," written and performed by Alvin Lee; Space Songs/Warner Chappell.

Acknowledgements

--This book could not have made it to your hands without a lot of help, encouragement and the occasional figurative kick in the ass.

--To Alice Potteiger, my friend, editor, consultant, web fixer, graphic designer and Jill-of-all-trades, you have put up with me for longer than most, and I love you for it.

--To Mitch Bentley of Atomic Fly Studios, for your wonderful cover design ("Warpaint"), senses of humor and place.

--To Christie Stratos of Proof Positive for her sharp eyes, encouragement and positive outlook.

--To my musical friends and colleagues who allowed me to use their lyrics, my thanks.

--To those who suffer from bipolar disorder, depression or any form of mental illness: I am with you. My hope is by shining a small light on the issue through this story others will know we are not alone, and that help is available.

About the Author

A broadcaster for more than thirty years, Tory Gates has seen and done just about everything in the radio business. He's been a deejay, talk show host, traffic reporter, producer and a journalist. Currently, Tory is the Morning Desk Anchor for the Radio Pennsylvania Network, located in Harrisburg.

Tory's third book, *Live from the Cafe* is available on Sunbury Press Books. His 2016 Sunbury release, *A Moment in the Sun* was a finalist for the Dante Rossetti Award for Young Adult Fiction by Chanticleer Reviews. His self-published debut, *Parasite Girls* is available through Amazon.com and Smashwords.

Tory's works are of young adult/crossover fiction, with exotic settings, but deal with real-life issues and social problems. His future releases include *Sweet Dreams: Searching for Roy Buchanan.*

A native of Vermont, Tory lives in Harrisburg with his five cats. You can find him on Facebook, Twitter (@ToryGates), as a feature writer for BroadwayWorld.com and also online as DJ`Riff, hosting "The Music Club" on the London-based Radio-Airwaves Station, and in the nearest place that serves good coffee!

Table of Contents

1 - Mima's World

2 - Sora

3 - Portrait of the Artist

4 - Layers

5 - The Blade

6 - Kabul

7 - The Tiger

8 - "Just the Games"

9 - Let Love Get Away

10 - Eko

11 - Kaga

12 - Relationship

13 - Incidents One and Two

14 - The Final Disappointment

15 - War

16 - The Bluest Blues

17 - The "L" Word

18 - Stuck in the Moment

19 - Affirmations

20 - Healing Ground

21 - The Call

22 - Crossroads

23 - *Kodokushi*

24 - Recognition

25 - Confessions

26 - What Never Dies

1 - Mima's World

"So you need to tell me," Mima said, "just why you're here."

Aidan lit a Gitanes and leaned against the rail. The sounds and smells of Tokyo drifted up to the second floor apartment, but he did not take them in. Instead, he smiled and gazed through the French tobacco smoke at his host.

Mima regarded Aidan through the bangs of her short hair and rimless glasses. She wore an old sweatshirt, the cuffs frayed from years of wear and washing. The logo was not of a university from Japan, but an American one. Black tights wrapped themselves snugly about her muscular thighs and calves; Mima's build was a shade thicker than the norm when it came to Japanese women. That mattered not at all to Aidan and even less to Mima, who danced to the beat of her own internal drum machine.

"Well," Aidan replied as he carefully flicked the cinders into a smokeless ashtray, "I have a layout in mind for the book as we discussed earlier. I also felt a change of pace was in order." He hoped that would be enough.

"Whatever you have in mind," Mima replied as she took a step closer to Aidan, a smile on her face, "you're welcome here for as long you need. I am so grateful to see you again."

"I appreciate that." Mima, he knew was appraising him behind her sun-darkened lenses. They'd not seen one another in years, and his long-lost friend was taking stock: Aidan's brown hair remained, but there were now streaks of grey, far too soon. His blue eyes were the same, but Mima detected the changes around them. Aidan was not himself, and while Mima picked up on that, she didn't ask.

Mima had changed too, but in her these things were subtle. Only months younger than himself, Mima appeared ageless.

She was a little heavier, chunkier perhaps than Aidan recalled, but from what he saw pass through the apartment earlier that morning Mima was in shape in more ways than one.

"Anyway," she said, "I must get back to work. Got a project to deliver this week."

"No worries." Mima ambled barefoot into the main room of her apartment while Aidan took his time with that guilty pleasure from the first Paris assignment. Skyward, Aidan's eyes passed over the high rises that surrounded Mima's building.

Aidan had experienced many worlds, but Japan was unfamiliar territory. As in any other foreign land, he would immerse himself in it, become part of it and yet remain Aidan Connor.

His cigarette finished, Aidan carefully stubbed it out and slid the butt inside the blue pack. He stuffed this in the breast pocket of his shirt, switched off the curious device Mima provided him and brought it through the sliding door.

"You can leave that out there," Mima commented from his right. "The rain never comes in; it's cool."

Aidan set the ashtray on the black wire table between the matching chairs, and slid the door closed. He turned and again found himself inside Mima's world--or was this her universe?

The apartment was small: one room with a cramped kitchen to the far left, plus a door that led to a tinier bathroom. Against the far wall to the right of the door was Mima's futon, unmade with a nightstand next to it to hold her lamp and clock radio. Before this, a TV rested beside an Xbox with about twenty game discs scattered around the console.

There were also odd gadgets of the kind that could only be dreamed up in this land, including a robotic toy dog. The floor was bare, hardwood and without rugs.

On the other side of the door was Mima's workspace. Beneath an overhead light was a large table that doubled as a desk and drafting board. A USB hub, laser printer, scanner, and router linked Mima's Gateway and Toshiba Satellite laptop plus two external hard drives. The power cords for all of these snaked off behind the table into not one, but two surge protection strips. Two file cabinets and a wall-mounted rack for discs made up the rest of Mima's "office." Mima was hunched over on the high stool, focused on the ad design she'd talked of nonstop since meeting Aidan at the airport the night before.

To Aidan's left was the low couch that became his "guest room," beside which lay his open suitcase. His Sony Walkman, jean jacket and the case that held his ancient Minolta camera rested atop the jumbled pile of clothes.

Aidan sat here now and looked at the wall above the bed. Mima adorned the bare white walls with her original artworks, sketches, doujinshi and anime creations. There also was a pair of wildly colored abstract canvases, not of Mima's hand.

"Those are Sora's," Mima commented. She did not look up as she guided the cursor across the screen. "We'll be seeing her tonight," Mima added. "Sora is excited to meet you; I've told her so much about you."

"Okay," Aidan joked as he unclipped the battered leather case that held his camera, "what have you told her?"

"Only the good things." Mima turned and giggled; this and the screwed-up facial expression that accompanied the sound never failed to make Aidan laugh. "There is nothing bad about you, Aidan," she went on as she turned back to the screen, "but considering some of the scrapes you've been in, I imagine you acquired a few habits."

"Yeah." Aidan tried not to let his voice change, but failed.

Mima turned again. "You okay?"

"There's a lot of stuff to talk about," Aidan admitted as he drew out the Minolta, "but I need to piece it together before I can explain."

"No," Mima said, "I'm sorry. I get the idea what happened in Kabul was pretty rough. You don't have to talk about it unless you want to."

"It's all right," Aidan replied, "I will soon enough. The main reason I'm here I think is to get away from that. Not run from it, mind, but to think about from it from a distance. Then maybe I can go back, you know?"

"I do." Mima slid off the stool and came over to sit beside Aidan. She watched as he broke down the camera for cleaning, and noted the care with which he handled the instrument. "Like I told you," she said, "you're welcome here, Aidan. You were dear to me back then; you still are."

Aidan set the pieces down in his clothes. "You were," he replied, "and are too, Mima. Stuff has to change, and some of it is me; I'm working on it."

Mima slid her arms around Aidan's shoulders. "Take all the time you need, Aidan."

He reached up and felt his friend's thick arm, and the hidden strength within as Mima gave him a squeeze. "Thank you," Aidan said. "I'll try not to be too depressed during my stay; you're good for changing that."

Mima grinned, made an odd but cute, "Nyah" sound before heading back to her table. "I am flattered," she replied as she resumed her work. "Unfortunately, that does not get this finished. I'd like to see the outline down before we hit the streets. We'll go see Sora this evening and find if we can get her out. That cool?"

"It is." Aidan drew out the camera's cleaning kit. "I'm not exactly sure what you mean by getting Sora 'out,' though."

"That will depend," Mima explained, "on which one of Sora is available when we get there." She continued to sketch across the extra-large mouse pad with a slow, deliberate hand, and said no more.

The statement made Aidan pause. Mima's comment about Sora was a fleeting one and sounded like she said it fairly often.

As he carefully wiped the Minolta's lens, Aidan wondered what was up with Sora. She was a talented artist, easy to see by the depth and originality of those paintings.

Aidan then reminded himself that when it came to people, everyone had a story, and there was always more than what they thought they saw.

2 - Sora

The Metro was packed with commuters and travelers this evening. Aidan silently took note how the trains lived up to their reputation for being fast, efficient and clean.

The ride from Mima's district to this neighboring one was short, and Mima now led him through the neon inner city. Past bars, nightclubs, restaurants and shops they went; then down into the lesser but properly lit sidewalks of the suburb. Mima's pace was fast, and her bike rides about the city kept her curvy physique fit.

Aidan looked out the corner of his eye at Mima. Her body type was not typical here, but Mima long ago accepted her true form. Aidan recalled their college days in Boston, and of stereotypical Asian students there were plenty. Mima stood out, not only due to her build but her personality. She was for the most part a ball of bubbly, happy energy then. She seemed the same, to Aidan's relief; her work ethic surely was.

Their meeting was one of those chance moments, between the Butera School student of graphic design and the one of photography at Suffolk. Both were in line at the Rat, Kenmore Square's hole-in-the-wall club where a cocksure punk band called The Police once played a gig.

Sting, Summers and Copeland since moved up in the world, but *Rathskeller* was the place to go for bands known and unknown. Aidan didn't remember any of the no-names on the bill that night; he and his drinking buddies fell in with the girls from Butera, and that was all there was to it.

Aidan and Mima became fast friends as they drank and listened to the music, but soon found themselves attracted to one another. It wasn't about trying to get laid; Aidan plain liked this girl--the promise to see him again was kept, and the two years Mima spent in the city were a reward to Aidan.

He was the shutterbug from Everett. From an early age, Aidan was fascinated by photography and knew it would be his life. His parents gave him his first camera, a secondhand Nikon while still in grade school. Aidan photographed everything: his friends, wildlife, outdoor festivals and events. Later he contributed photos and stories to his high school paper.

While there, Aidan sold pictures ranging from sporting events to car crashes to the *Globe*, *Herald* and *Phoenix*. The enterprising shots landed Aidan freelance work, and more jobs followed after college. Then Aidan made the jump to photojournalism and international travel. Though never on anyone's payroll, Aidan's work appeared on network news sites, national magazines, plus political and social blogs.

The Kabul assignment, and what went down after was fresh in Aidan's mind--and raw. As they walked, Aidan again thought of his companion: like he, Mima had a way of setting things aside in her own mind.

"Here we are." They'd walked some distance; Aidan didn't notice, a recent habit of his. He followed Mima's arm through the dark towards a large home, at least by this neighborhood's standards. The roof was of that particular tile which made such houses storm-proof. Aidan guessed it was built on the traditional corner stilts plus some reinforcement. There was a lawn with a neatly laid walkway, which led to a flight of three steps. The overhead porch light was on, and additional ones shone through the picture window beside the door.

Mima rang the bell. A moment later the door slid back to reveal a small woman of about fifty with a trace of Korean descent in her features. She was dressed in a heavy sweater and dark slacks, her black hair cut short. The woman's actions were warm as she greeted "Mima-chan." Sora's mother graciously accepted the tin of green tea Mima and Aidan brought as a gift. He was then introduced, and Aidan remembered to bow politely.

"So this is Aidan-san," the woman responded with a huge smile. "Welcome, and please call me Suemi."

Over his thanks, Aidan and Mima removed their shoes. Aidan noted a pair of sneakers and brown suede boots a size larger. He assumed these belonged to the unmet Sora. Jackets disposed of, Suemi then led the way up another short flight of stairs into an open kitchen; the smell of some dinner recently consumed remained in the air.

"Yuzuki is still at work," Suemi said, "and I have coffee on, should you like some."

"Thanks, *Okasan*," Mima replied as they paused in the kitchen. "How's Sora doing?"

At this question, Suemi's face took on a resigned look, but not one that displayed sadness. "She has not been out lately, but your being here will help."

"How long?" Aidan turned to Mima as she asked. Mima looked concerned, but not dramatically so; this was a regular occurrence.

"Two days." Suemi turned to attend to some remaining dishes in the sink. "One of those periods, I'm sorry to say."

"Come on," Mima said to Aidan, "we'll get her up." She led Aidan out of the kitchen, and cautioned him to mind his head on the low overhang of woodwork. They then turned down a narrow hallway. Four sliding doors opened out into the corridor, two on either side. Mima rapped on the first of the left ones.

"Sora," she called softly, "it's Mima. Aidan and I are here."

There was no answer. Undaunted, Mima slid the door open a crack. The dim light from the hallway sent a knife-like shaft into it, but Aidan couldn't see anything over Mima's shoulder.

"They took the lock off," Mima commented. "Wait here for a minute."

Aidan nodded, and Mima disappeared inside the room. Through the door, Aidan watched has Mima picked her way over and around a number of items on the floor to a platform bed in the corner.

"*Sora-chan…*" Mima called again as she sat on the edge of the bed. There was a form lying under a heavy comforter, but Aidan could not detect any features.

A voice, which sounded as if its owner was roused from a deep sleep, replied to Mima. Aidan couldn't hear the words. He watched as Mima gently pulled the cover away from Sora's head and stroked the woman's hair. She continued to speak softly to Sora in Japanese.

The voice mumbled something back, and Aidan now observed the language of Sora's body. From a fetal pose, the body slowly uncoiled and dragged itself in Mima's direction.

Mima responded by pulling Sora into her arms. The woman rested her head on Mima's lap as Mima began to whisper to her quietly. From the light, Aidan could see a tangle of long hair; a small, slender hand reached out to find Mima's.

Aidan stepped back. Sora was Mima's oldest friend; she on occasion remarked that Sora had "issues" but never elaborated. He noiselessly retraced his steps and returned to the kitchen.

"Please sit, Aidan." A large, steaming cup of coffee was on the low table at the seat nearest him. Suemi sat across from him, her hands wrapped about her own.

"Thank you." Aidan carefully made himself comfortable under the table and hoped his knees would not knock against the underside of it. The coffee was left as prepared – black, which Aidan preferred.

Suemi smiled. "That may take some time," she said. "You seem cognizant of such matters."

"Well," Aidan stumbled to answer, "there appeared to be a bit of a moment going on. I didn't feel I should intrude."

"Yes," Suemi said after a sip of her coffee, "Sora and Mima are like sisters, and Mima is as much a daughter to me."

A taste of the black brew – the coffee wasn't as strong as the stuff he'd been served in Istanbul, but a contender. "This is very good," he complimented.

"I am pleased you like it."

"Anyway," Aidan continued, "Mima has only told me a few things. I believe she lived with you for some time. Mima always spoke highly of you all."

Suemi nodded. "That is so. Yes," she continued, "Mima was under adverse circumstances for a time. That was as difficult, if not more so in some ways, as what my daughter contends with."

Aidan thought for a long moment. He liked Suemi, but weighed in his mind as to whether or not he should ask the next question. That consideration was brief. "What does Sora 'contend' with?" he asked. "Forgive me," Aidan was quick to add, "I am not trying to pry."

"Of course not." Suemi chuckled and shook her head. "Mima has told me of your work, but I am certain this is not one of your assignments. Sora," she explained, "suffers from Bipolar Disorder. It is also called Manic Depression. For Sora, the illness causes divergent mood swings, and they are hard to contend with. She can become euphoric, then deeply depressed, almost from one moment to the next."

Suemi's expression during this statement remained the same; she was collected, Aidan thought, but not in a passive way. Sora's mother accepted her daughter, and her condition, as read.

"The highs and lows," Aidan commented. "I know a little about them. I have a couple of friends who deal with it. For you and your husband, it must also be hard."

"It can be." Suemi sipped her drink again and said, "Sora depends upon Yuzuki and me for nearly everything, her medication included. Those must be monitored as well as altered. Sora is what would be termed by medical professionals as 'high functioning,' but she cannot live on her own, at least for now. She has tried in the past."

Aidan was paying full attention to Suemi, the way he would any subject he was interviewing or taking pictures of. The woman fascinated him, as Mima had when they first met. "I saw two of Sora's paintings," he replied, "and while I'm no expert, they were well done. There was real emotion in how Sora painted them; that's what stood out for me."

"You have looked into those works, then." Suemi's smile widened. "Sora is a wonderful artist," she said. "She has always loved to draw and paint. Sora has also sold some of her works; it is her passion. Sometimes it is all she has."

"You mean," Aidan ventured, "Sora's art is her life?"

"You do understand," Suemi replied. "That's right. For Sora, her creative outlet is also what steadies her. There are periods, such as now when Sora cannot create – those are the worst of times for her. Sora feels worthless if she cannot make her inspirations come to life."

Aidan had to respond. He understood a lot more than Suemi imagined. "It's difficult," he admitted, "to make a life for oneself beyond that which drives your survival. I know the feeling, perhaps not as Sora does, but I think I do."

"That's good. Please understand," Suemi went on, "my husband and I support our daughter, and Mima, wholeheartedly. The lot we have drawn in life is one that cannot be predicted, and we must consider each moment as it comes. Sora and Mima's happiness are the most crucial things. We are secure in our own lives, and parents must love their children and acknowledge them for what they are." There was a gentle knowing in Suemi's eye. "Warts and all, as you westerners might say?"

The two laughed, and Aidan raised his cup to Suemi's at the moment hers rose. "Thank you," he said, "for saying something that has great meaning to me, Suemi-san."

"Something, perhaps," she inquired, "that you needed to hear?"

The cups clinked together across the table. "Indeed."

"Here we are!" A young woman bounded into the kitchen, Mima in her wake. Aidan extricated himself from the table and stood up to meet Sora.

Aidan knew Sora was the same age as himself and Mima. The woman was tall – five-six, Aidan's practiced eye measured. Her hair was long down her back and shiny, with streams of reddish-brown highlights in them. She was dressed in tight designer Capri jeans and a black t-shirt, which showed off the curves of her thin shoulders and arms, plus her bared, flat midriff.

Sora was introduced to Aidan. "I'm sorry," she said, "I didn't intend to make you wait. Anyway, I'm so happy to finally meet you."

Sora was the exact opposite of what Aidan viewed before. The woman whose voice and body were weary to the point of exhaustion moments ago was now bright and ecstatic. Sora's two sides were indeed opposites.

He also noted how Mima looked at Aidan with a sly smile. It was her way of saying, *I warned you.*

3 - Portrait of the Artist

The four sat around the low table. For the first time in too long Aidan was enveloped by the ardor of family and good friends.

Open for inspection were the contents of a thin volume of Aidan's photographic works, part of his planned book. They were not of any specific collection, merely Aidan's favorite shots from his assignments over the years. "The reason I'm here," Aidan explained over a second cup of coffee, "is to take photos that reflect aspects of Japan. This is a country I've spent little time in and I think some from here will help round it out."

The pictures attracted praise from Sora and Suemi. Both complimented Aidan on the depth and sharpness of his work. Sora was particularly interested in one of the recent shots from Kabul. It was a street scene, and she noticed its subtext.

"This is excellent," she praised, "you've not only captured the road, the buildings, but also a cross-section of the population." Sora pointed out those in traditional as well as western dress, and those of more conservative Muslim faiths: the women in burkas and their husbands (presumably so) sharing the street as if there were no differences between them.

"Does it remain a dangerous place?" Suemi asked. "From what we have seen on the news and in the papers, it appears that way."

Aidan gave a gesture of agreement, but hoped they didn't catch the sudden blink of his eyes. Mima had. "It varies," he replied. "Certain parts of the city are safer than others, but someone like me has to remain on guard."

"Why were you there?" Sora asked.

Mima shot her friend a look too late, but Aidan found he could answer. "I was on assignment," he explained, "my last one. I was to interview and photograph some of the secure areas of Kabul, and also to get a look at more progressive aspects of the city and its people. The changes since the ouster of the Taliban have not come without some real stress; change is difficult to accept there."

"As it is in most places," Suemi agreed as she examined another of the photos. "Sora," she added as she turned to her daughter, "I'm sure you wish to show off your own works."

There was laughter and Sora replied, "Mama-san, as much as I want to, Aidan is the guest. I'm not sure that's proper."

"Oh, it's fine," Aidan said as he carefully restored the pictures to their sleeves in the volume. "I actually would love to see more of your paintings, Sora. I need to look at other people's work or else I get hung up on what I've done."

"Well, give me just a minute to clear things up!" Sora was on her feet, through the kitchen and down the hall at full speed. Aidan had to chuckle, but the others did not.

"Sorry, Aidan," Mima said. "With Sora, what you see is what you get."

Suemi shrugged as she began to clear the cups away. "We have all become used to it," she commented. "Sora is at times like a typhoon: once it gathers strength, it must reach its destination, no matter the consequences."

As Aidan rose, his eyes were attracted to another article: stuck to the refrigerator by a series of magnets was a printed list in Kanji characters. It seemed out of place in this homey atmosphere. He said nothing, but Mima read Aidan's mind.

"Sora's medications," Mima explained as they rounded the corner and stopped. "Sora," she continued in a quiet voice, "is on at least eight different ones right now."

"Eight?" Aidan saw the worried look in Mima's eyes. "That's quite a few," he remarked, "does she need them all?"

Mima nodded. "She does, but she hates to take them. Sora probably won't want to talk about it, so I'd not say anything. However," Mima finished with a shrug, "this is how it is."

She removed her glasses and ran her free hand through her hair. "Sora and her family were a Godsend to me," Mima continued. "She's been my best friend since grade school. I take her as she is because she's always been good to me. Without her family, I would have been on the street."

Aidan watched the sad expression grow behind Mima's replaced glasses. "I knew you had problems in your family," he said, "but I never knew about that."

"I didn't feel the need to discuss it." With her index fingers, Mima traced two parallel lines from below her eyes and down her cheeks.

"Tears," she whispered. "I would cry them, not thinking of what I went through, but over what Sora deals with every day."

"The rollercoaster effect, right?"

"Yeah. I've seen Sora at her best, her worst, and every level in between," Mima said. "Suemi and Yuzuki are two of the strongest, most loving people I've known. For Sora, but also for me; we're kind of stuck with one another."

Aidan had to smile, and Mima permitted herself a weak one. They were now aware of the tumult in Sora's room. It sounded as if she were doing a quick cleanup to make the place presentable.

"You often spoke," Aidan observed, "of the closeness you two share. I would say you are like sisters. I never had a close relationship with my family either. Though you know yourself," he admitted, "we New Englanders aren't always good with emotions."

Mima deepened into her sweatshirt. "We can be," she replied, "as people, but Sora is all over the place. Sora didn't have a lot of friends growing up; me, one or two others -- that was all. Sora's never been able to have a boyfriend or a steady relationship for too long because when men see how things are, they break it off."

Mima then gave what Aidan called her "little smile," the tiniest upturn of her lips. "Sometimes," Mima finished, "they run!"

"Okay!" Sora's voice called through the open door. "You can bring him in, Mima."

Chuckling again, Mima and Aidan stepped into Sora's bedroom. The room was larger than Aidan guessed, now that the lights were on. Aidan realized he could have stepped back into Mima's apartment without knowing it.

The difference came in what sorts of things populated this room: Sora's bed was in the far left corner; there were piles of clothes next to this on the wood floor. The walls were jammed with paintings of varied sizes, both framed and unframed. Drawings, notes and clippings from newspapers and magazines, some yellowed and curled with age covered almost every other open space. On the other side of the room were a dresser and desk, the latter of which held Sora's computer.

An easel stood beside these, a paint-spattered drop cloth beneath. The easel was empty, but a series of virgin canvases were stacked behind it. Shelves took up the rest of the wall: supplies, paints, brushes, oils, plus jars, markers, books and other materials filled these. It looked like an art supply shop was built into one wall and compressed, there was so much.

"It's like a studio," Aidan commented as he regarded some of the abstract works.

Sora laughed hard. "It's not quite like that," she replied, "but these are the few I'm most proud of." Sora went on to explain in detail the aspects of individual paintings, her inspirations, what she was going for and how she felt about them. Mima tended to discuss her own projects in this way, but with Sora there was more detail. She clearly enjoyed having someone to talk to about it.

Sora then went to her computer and showed off her website, which she credited Mima for. "Mima designed it," Sora said, "and she's showed me how to keep from messing it up."

"Not really," Mima replied. "Besides, I made it easy to update."

"Easy for you," Sora sighed, "but you know me."

Aidan examined the site, whose primary colors were black, magenta and bright yellow. He found the page well constructed and easy to navigate, with the links blocked out in large print. They were all in Kanji, but Sora translated them for Aidan. Sora then took over the navigation to show some categorized pages of her works, their prices and related information.

Now in full flow, Sora flounced about the room as she spoke. Aidan shifted into journalist mode to keep up. When someone was rambling, best to let the subject run. One never knew; they might see or hear something of importance.

Eventually, Mima stepped in. "Sora," she said jokingly, but with a serious undertone, "you're going to knock Aidan out with all that."

"Oh! I'm sorry." Sora turned, and Aidan watched as the brown eyes, so wide with delight, suddenly fell. Her face did as well, and she went to Aidan. "I didn't mean to go on," she said. "It's how I am, but I don't mean that as an excuse."

"No, do not be sorry," Aidan assured her. "You're into what you do, there's nothing wrong with that."

Mima moved to Sora and placed a sisterly set of hands on her shoulders. "I didn't mean it like that either," she added, "I wasn't trying to upset you."

Sora shook her head vigorously. "It's all right," she said as she embraced Mima. "You understand the way it is." She looked again to Aidan. "I guess Mama-san and Mima told you about me?" she asked.

"Only a bit."

Sora shrugged as she went to her bed and sat down. Mima sat alongside her while Aidan took the floor before them. "My illness," Sora explained, "gets the better of me at times. The reason I didn't come right out is because some days it is so hard to leave my bed. Getting up to get a drink of water or use the bathroom is an effort."

She sighed, and Sora's hair covered her face as she lowered it into her hand. "Any task," she said, "becomes monumental, including the ones most take for granted. On top of that is the way society looks upon people like me."

"How do you mean?" Aidan asked. He watched as Mima put her arm around Sora's shoulder, and the woman's head rose up again.

"It's not the sickness itself," Sora said, "but how I and others like me are looked upon. Unless you have what I have or something like it, no one gets it. You can't understand the feelings."

Sora's hands, which Aidan since noted were long and extremely thin, now moved to express what Sora wanted to say. "You've seen both ends of it tonight," she went on. "I am glad one minute, depressed and wishing to die the next. My medicines don't work for long before I must go to the doctor and have them changed again. I also have a therapist whom I see every week. Then," she added, "there is something much worse."

"What's that?" Aidan asked. He leaned forward to let Sora know that he was listening, trying to understand.

Sora looked to Mima, in askance of her friend that it was all right, and Mima nodded. "You're not from here," Sora told Aidan, "so I don't suppose you ever heard of this: I'm considered by some a 'Parasite Single.'" Her voice turned bitter. Sora continued, "It is an unkind term made up by some idiot who wanted to come down on people who don't get married when he thinks they ought to."

"I've never heard of the saying," Aidan replied, "what does it mean?"

"It's attributed to single women, but some men as well," Mima explained. "It targets those who choose to continue to live at home for longer than is usual. Most people in this country live alone if they're unmarried, or they live with family. Living in Tokyo is expensive, and a lot of people can't make it by themselves."

"That's true in most cases," Sora added, "but there are those who have good jobs and could make a go of it, but they don't. They stay at home, live off their parents and spend their money any way they want. The men are seen as slackers, the women as gold-diggers."

Sora then motioned to herself. "Me? I'm seen as a parasite," she snapped, "because no one gets that I'm sick. It's all I can do to keep myself together and try to help my family, but living alone? I can't do it; I've tried, and I failed. But people, even some of our relatives think I'm just sponging off Mom and Dad until I can find a rich husband. That's not it – I'm not a parasite! If there's one in our circle of friends, it's Eko!"

Mima took a tighter grip on Sora with her hands. "Sora, no one sees you as that," she said. "Some might think like that, but it's none of their business."

Sora buried her face in her hands. "I know," she replied in a muffled voice. "But," she continued, "it hurts me! And I don't wish to pick on Eko; she has her reasons."

Her head snapped up, and Aidan saw the light band of mascara around Sora's eyes going liquid. "Aidan, I'm sorry," she said, "you are a nice guy. I'm sorry you have to see me like this."

Aidan moved to his knees and placed himself in front of Sora. "Sora," he said, "you must not be sorry. What you have for an illness is not your fault. You do have to work with it, but Mima's right, it's no one's business but yours. That label is a mean one and should not be used."

He reached out and took Sora's hands. "Being around you, even in this short time," Aidan said, "helps me see things. Mima is a friend I value highly, and I know why she has such love for you and your parents. Don't worry about the others. If society as a whole paid less attention to what a few people say, we'd be in a better world."

He watched as Sora's eyes welled up. She smiled and pulled both Aidan and Mima to her. "Thank you," she said, "both of you. I know I'm not a parasite, and I'll never be, but it helps to hear people say I'm not, you know?"

"We do know," Mima replied as she continued to hold Sora to her. "I love you, Sora, no matter what."

"Warts and all?" Sora asked, and all three had to laugh.

4 • Layers

"I hope Sora wasn't too much for you," Mima said on their walk back to the Metro.

"Not at all." The rest of the evening passed easily; Sora's father Yuzuki finally arrived home from work. A stocky individual, his neatly trimmed mustache and goatee were quite the anomaly from the stiff, clean-shaven businessmen Aidan came to expect here. Though possessed of a gruff voice, Yuzuki was affable and exhibited an open and loving affection for his family and Mima.

Over a late dinner for himself (more coffee for the rest), Yuzuki asked many questions of Aidan and also took a keen interest in his portfolio. His energy level, even after a workday hours longer than most Americans could stand was amazingly high. Sora, he thought, was a woman who took after her father.

Aidan did his best to stay quiet and watch. The kindness of Sora and her parents was genuine towards Aidan and especially Mima. He took note of the warmth each gave Mima, the kind any parent or sibling would give. She was without doubt a member of the family.

He noticed something else, too: while Mima addressed Suemi and Yuzuki in the proper *Okasan* and *Otousan* at first, Mima later more affectionately referred to them as "Mom and Dad", a habit she brought back from the States.

Sora, on the other hand, called her folks *Mama-san* and *Papa-san*, as a child would call their parents. This appeared to be more out of closeness than any lack of maturity on Sora's part. Aidan reminded himself to be careful; the misconceptions needed to go.

A mistake reporters, as any visitor could make was to go to a foreign country and assume things. Mima at least paved the way for him during his time with her in Boston. He'd picked up numerous sayings from Mima, what they meant and how one phrase could have different meanings. Even armed with these insights, Aidan would be a stranger here without Mima.

Aidan lit a Gitanes. Once he received his first injection of nicotine in four hours, he said, "Mima, I'm glad you brought me here. I like Sora and her parents. I can see how important they are to you."

Instinct made Aidan change the subject. "Sora does have a lot of energy," he added, "at least when she's up."

"That's Sora." They turned the corner, and the dim lights of the Metro came into view. Mima kept her pace slow so Aidan could enjoy his smoke. "Sora struggles every day with her bipolarity," she said. "Other than Eko and me, the only people close to her are Mom and Dad."

"Who is Eko?" Aidan recalled Sora's harsh statement about her.

Mima sighed. "Eko is an old friend of ours from high school," she explained, "you'll likely meet her. She is closer to Sora than to me, but we are good friends. When it comes to parasite girls, Eko is the poster child."

"In what way?" The two stopped at a bench near the perimeter of the station. Shielded by an overhanging tree, the seat gave them a dark, private place to talk.

"Eko is a very smart, sweet and engaging person," Mima said, "and most attractive. I think you would like her, Aidan, and I don't mean that in a bad way."

Aidan chuckled, and fortunately Mima did. "No offense taken," he replied, "but I gather she still lives at home?"

"She does." Mima shrugged. "It is her choice and her business," she said, "but Eko is sometimes rather blatant about it. You see," Mima went on, "Eko has a job, and she does well for herself. Now I've told you about how hard it is to live in Tokyo, the cost of living?"

Aidan stubbed out the cigarette in his fingers. "Right."

"Well," Mima said, "I must be fair about that. In this city, two-thirds or more of one's income tends to go to living expenses – rent, food and so on. When I returned home, I moved back in because I had no money, and I had to get my business started."

"That's understood." Aidan leaned against the bench and watched Mima as she spoke. Mima huddled into her fleece jacket and leaned forward, her bangs hanging over the top of her glasses.

"I was welcome to stay as long as I required," she continued, "but Aidan, I needed to be self-sufficient. I had to get out on my own."

Mima adjusted the collar of her jacket and stuffed her gloved hands back in her pockets. "I love Sora without condition," she said. "Things were much the same when I got back: we drew and painted together, we went out together, we did all things as we had before. What was missing was one thing I picked up in America, outside of my training: my independence. I needed that."

"From your emails," Aidan recalled, "it sounded as though you were doing all you could to get the money together for your apartment."

"The key money doesn't come back, either," Mima replied.

"Huh?" Aidan thought he'd missed something. "You mean you don't get your security deposit back?"

Mima shook her head. "No," she replied. "What you call a security deposit, we call 'key money'. It is a tribute and payment to the landlord. It's six months' rent."

"I see why it took so long."

"Exactly," Mima said. "Even so, I remember it being so hard to leave. Sora became depressed about that--not that I was leaving but that she could not go herself. She tried to live on her own after she got out of school, but it didn't work out. Sora can't handle the everyday things you and I would not think twice about."

Mima stood up, and Aidan joined her in the walk to the Metro's main entrance. "My mother would have called Sora flighty," Aidan commented.

"That's an accurate term. Sora only made it about a year in her own place," Mima explained. "She continued to paint, but her illness made it too much for her. Sora drifted in and out of part-time jobs. She was perpetually late with her rent, and she ran up her credit cards. Finally, Yuzuki and Suemi had to bail her out and convince her to return home."

Mima pulled out her Metro pass. "As you noticed, Sora gets intensely focused," she said. "When Sora's painting or sketching, she vanishes into the wormhole."

"Kind of like you," Aidan commented as they passed into the station's bowels, "though I would say you focus your energy better; you have some direction over it."

"Well, thanks," Mima replied sarcastically, and she playfully punched Aidan in the arm. "You do the same, traveling about in war zones to get the story, right?"

"Right." Aidan realized his voice had gotten testy again.

"We remain a lot alike, you and I," Mima redirected.

Aidan didn't answer as they joined a handful of riders waiting for the train. Down here the sounds were no different than those of the T, Aidan thought. The cavernous underground echoed with footsteps, voices and loudspeaker announcements; only the language changed.

"How do you mean?" Aidan now asked.

"Sora and I are passionate," Mima replied. "We are passionate about our art, and I am as well about my business. I have to be, Aidan--to make a living, to keep my head above water, but also..."

Mima's voice trailed off, along with her gaze. It went down the track and into the dark tunnel.

Aidan slowly put his arm around Mima's shoulder. "Also what?"

Mima was silent, and she leaned against Aidan. "I have to be self-sufficient," she finally repeated. "I know I've said that already, but I must stress it. Not to compete with Sora, but so as not to end up like I was years ago, when I lost my family."

A rush of cold wind assailed them as the train made its way into the station. Mima shivered. Aidan held her close, and Mima's arms slowly found their way around his waist. Mima was not about to say more at this point; the closeness they shared took Aidan back, thirteen years...

* * *

Fall had come to New England, but the winds in the Back Bay made it seem like December. Aidan wound the wool scarf about his neck and re-buttoned his old sailor's pea coat over it. He lit a Marlboro and leaned against the wall as he waited for Mima outside the front door of the Butera School.

He looked the long way down Beacon Street. Two lanes of vehicles merged into a long, unending stream as they battled for position. Some would make the turn onto Storrow Drive at the corner of the building that housed WERS, the Emerson College station. Others struggled onward toward Mass Ave, Kenmore and the Fenway.

Aidan shifted the case around his shoulder. The weighty, sixties vintage Minolta was a hand-me-down from his sister, who long since upgraded to a lighter and more modern rig. Whereas Katie took pictures for fun, for Aidan it was another matter. The afternoon shoot had gone well, and the eight rolls of film in his bag would be a test of his skill, when the time came for development.

A deep drag; Mima should be done with class soon. Since they'd started hanging out, Aidan was barraged with questions about her from fellow students. These were always the same: were they "going out" and, of course, had Aidan nailed her yet?

Aidan laughed the last one off, but for some reason he couldn't look at Mima the way he looked at other girls or women. Mima had a way of disarming him; Aidan could never put up a front with her, and in her presence, found he spoke and acted in the most sincere manner. He'd never been that way with anyone in his life, even his family.

The door swung open, and Aidan turned to see Mima click down the steps in her ankle-high Doc Martens, jeans, a sweatshirt (no matter the weather), a heavy wool jacket, cloth bag over her shoulder. She also had a thick scarf around her neck and looked more like a bundled up high schooler than a college student.

"Hi!" Mima hopped down from the second step to Aidan and the two embraced. Mima's arms were surprisingly strong, and despite his attempt to be ready for it, Aidan exhaled involuntarily. He had to grin, as did Mima.

The two headed down Beacon for Kenmore. They discussed classes, one another's current projects and what they might do after hitting up Crossroads for a round.

At one point along the walk, they stopped, and Aidan, not being good at these things pulled Mima to him.

At first, Mima seemed all right with it; she'd always been touchy-feely and an affectionate person. "Mima," Aidan said, "I hope you don't mind…"

He leaned over to kiss Mima. Immediately she pushed Aidan away and with force. The look on her face was one of surprise, and Aidan hurriedly withdrew.

"My God, I'm sorry!" He blurted out. "I didn't mean…"

"…no, it's okay." Mima's hands went to his arms and held them at length from her. She then smiled with requisite apology behind it. "Aidan, I appreciate that," she said, "but I'm not interested. Nothing against you; I love your company, but it's not what I am."

Aidan was embarrassed, and he could feel the heat in his face. Fortunately, Mima was forgiving. She took his hands in hers and said, "Don't feel ashamed, Aidan. It's lovely you think that much of me, but I'm not interested in sex. It's just not in me."

"It isn't?" Aidan was now confused. "Um, okay," he stammered, "how is that?"

"It's a long story," she replied, "but I'll give you the basics: I had a girlfriend in high school and it didn't work out. It's not that I'm a total lesbian; I don't actually see myself as one thing or another. It's how I was in those days, and," Mima quickly added, "I'm not a LUG, thank you very much!"

Aidan laughed at the term, a collegiate euphemism for *Lesbian Until Graduation*. "I had a relationship with a good friend, Kaga," Mima continued as they resumed walking. "We're friends, and it's cool. But right now, I don't feel anything for anyone, sexually. I know that must go against the stereotype of Asian women, right?"

Aidan had to smile. "I don't actually know what that is."

"Oh, come now, Aidan!" Mima countered, "You know, us Asian women are supposed to be horny all the time, exciting in bed and all that stuff. You must have watched some porn in your lifetime."

Aidan joined her in the laughter and had to bend over to keep his balance. "All right," he said at length, "I've looked at my share of porn. I must admit Asian women are certainly appealing under any circumstance, but I never put you in that lineup."

He took a deep breath, looked down at Mima and said with all seriousness, "I'm sorry about that, Mima. I do like you a lot, and I respect you too damn much to think of you as anything but who you are."

Mima grinned. "Apology accepted, Aidan. Thank you." She wrapped her arms around Aidan's body, and she almost took both of them right off the sidewalk, but they recovered and kept going.

"Aidan," she declared after they reached Clarendon, "I do love you as a friend, I honestly do. You're not like most Americans, and the Bostonians I was warned about."

"Are we talking Irish?" Aidan shot back. "You know I am."

"Yes, and no." Mima hooked her arm into Aidan's and said, "You are a gentleman, and," she continued with emphasis, "a gentle man, Aidan. I like that, and you. Now stop feeling sorry. Each of us has our way, but we fit. I appreciate that more than all the sex in the world."

Aidan smiled as he and Mima crossed Mass Ave. He felt guilty about hitting on Mima, but thankfully she'd let it go. More and more, Aidan found his friend was a puzzle, one with a number of layers. Like an onion, they needed to be peeled away, one at a time.

5 - The Blade

"Tell me about Kaga."

Aidan and Mima were huddled over their drinks at Crossroads. The dark, yet welcoming Irish pub on Beacon was one block and an underpass away from Kenmore, their destination for the evening.

Mima considered Aidan's request as she sipped her Amstel Light. The bar was smack in the middle of the Emerson sphere of influence. Emerson was a renowned performing arts school: knots of chattering girls ("Musical Theatre Muffins", one of Aidan's exes called them), cliques of frat brothers, plus the odd, artsy types occupied the tables and booths. The latter were the musicians, painters, builders, techies and other like-minded sorts Aidan and Mima identified with.

"What would you like to know?" she responded.

Aidan was in the midst of quaffing a good draught of Guinness. He wiped his mouth first, which made Mima smile in that cute way, then replied, "Well, it's probably not my business, but I guess Kaga was your first?"

Mima nodded as she drank. "That's right. Her given name is Kagura, but Kaga was what everyone called her," she said. "I went to high school and played soccer with her. Suffice to say, Kaga was someone I looked up to, really liked, and fell for."

"Interesting how you say that," Aidan replied.

Mima peered over her glasses in mock seriousness. "Interesting, how?"

Aidan leaned forward as did Mima to keep the conversation private, though the noise of the other patrons and jukebox would have prevented even the people closest to them from eavesdropping. "Your eyes," he said, "they misted over a little."

Mima giggled. "How can you tell that in here?" She demanded.

"I could see a change," Aidan replied with a grin. "You still care for her, but that's good, isn't it?"

"I suppose so." Mima sighed and took another drink, belched quietly, then went on, "I became kind of obsessed with Kaga," she explained. "We were in the same grade, and we played juniors on the soccer team our first two years. Kaga was a devoted friend. As we trained and played together, we came to know one another."

"But you say obsessed," Aidan pointed out. "How so?"

Mima laced her fingers around the glass as she held it on the table in front of her. "Kaga became my ideal," Mima said. "She was the girl I so wanted to be like, Aidan. Kaga was tall, athletic and had a beautiful body. She was pretty, at least to me; Kaga had some masculine features, which made her stand out. You might call her a tomboy. From our first acquaintance, I found my thoughts were of Kaga."

"I see." Aidan examined his glass, which had a third of Guinness to go. "So Kaga was a love interest?"

"Not right away." Mima shook her head and drained her Amstel. "You see, I couldn't imagine Kaga being inclined toward girls, and I had no idea which way I went. I was so into my art and school, I didn't have time to think about it. Gradually though," she continued, "I found myself looking in Kaga's direction, a lot. I wasn't stalking her, I just watched. I watched her on the pitch, in the locker room, in class; wherever she went, I watched her."

"To pick up on something?"

"Yes." Mima nodded, in relief that Aidan understood. "I think I wanted to capture a bit of her aura, you know how I mean?" she asked. "Kaga had a fascinating one; there was this strong, standoffish, physical exterior. She intimidated, even scared people who didn't know her, yet she was always polite to others. Except when there was a match, of course."

The two laughed, and Aidan finished his drink. "Want another?"

Mima checked her watch and shook her head. "No. If we want to get in," she said, "we'd better go now."

"Right." Each threw in a couple of dollars extra for a tip, and Aidan slid the bills under his glass. As they pulled their jackets back on, Mima said, "Actually if you don't mind I'd rather not talk about Kaga right now. It's a fresh wound if you follow me."

"I do." As they exited back onto Beacon, Aidan said, "I'm sorry if I ask too many questions. Cut me off, will you?"

Mima laughed again, and it sounded like a genuine one. She put her arm in Aidan's and added, "It's not like that, Aidan. You are like me, curious about things. You want to know more, but it isn't for a bad reason. Kaga and I remain friends, though I haven't seen her in a while. But it's alright, I'm on a new stage of my life, and I'm fine." She then looked up to Aidan with a pointed expression. "Okay?"

Aidan smiled as Mima leaned against his shoulder. "Okay."

* * *

The clatter of the train as it went over a switch shook Aidan back to the now. Mima was seated to his right, the two scrunched together in the crowded car. A few people, mostly younger passengers chose to stand, and clung to the handholds.

Aidan thought again of that particular night because of two specific incidents.

They made their way to the Rat in time to catch the opener, some strange folksinger whose name they never got. He looked like a refugee biker, all in black with a leather vest, and his arms were covered in tattoos. The guy plugged in an old acoustic/electric guitar, sat on a borrowed bar stool and proceeded to pour out a series of rare songs. The speakers competed with the loud talk of the patrons, and most of them weren't listening.

The singer's voice was okay. His guitar work was mostly chords, but Aidan and Mima agreed he wasn't half bad. He was certainly no worse than anyone else they'd seen here. But there was one song that caught Aidan's ear. The singer sounded like Lou Reed on this one, singing from his throat with a guttural, almost sneering tone.

> *"She lives in her shell*
> *Protected by fear*
> *Can't move away*
> *From those who attack..."*

A few turned toward the stage as the singer leaned over his guitar and droned out these lyrics, about a young woman and her peculiar habit.

> *"When she uses her blade*
> *Does she feel pain*
> *Is the physical better*
> *Than the mental..."*

Aidan knew about bladers. He'd recently attended a performance art show that was written by and starred an

Emerson student. Throughout the play, he simulated the act of carving his forearms with a straight razor. Some of the audience found this excessive and gross, but others saw the value in the play and what the lead tried to get across. One person's obscenity was another's art.

His eyes shifted toward Mima. She was fully focused on the singer. Her mouth dropped open, enough to make Aidan think Mima was caught up in the song and its words.

"She won't cut the vein
The one she knows will kill
She's saving that one
For when it gets too much..."

The song earned the obscure performer the best hand of the set. Eventually, the soloist left the stage to polite applause and made way for a three-piece punk outfit. They stayed a while longer, then left to go back to Mima's apartment.

On the way, they discussed the varied performers, but when it came to the first fellow, Mima only said, "He was good." Aidan got the impression that particular song hit too close to home for Mima because she changed the subject to one of the other bands. He let it pass.

Mima's apartment was a loft in one of the old brownstones on a side street between Berkeley and Clarendon. Rents here were exorbitant, but Mima's scholarship took care of that. The central room was a square, with a kitchen and bathroom. Secondhand furniture, a desk and her art supplies were crammed into the space, with her bed in the rafters.

On her easel in the center of the square room was a new work, which Mima wanted to show him. "It's not finished," she said as she flicked on the overhead light, "but take a look, and tell me what you think."

While she hung up their coats, Aidan examined the painting. It appeared to depict a thin, naked human, stretched, drawn and emaciated. The primary color was a deep red.

Aidan felt his skin crawl. He took a breath. After the initial split second, Aidan exhaled, but slowly as possible. He looked closer, and hoped Mima would view this as examination, and not what Aidan was trying to do. The dark red was spattered against the canvas, then brushed and smeared into the human form. There was some black, but that was more for an outline. The work evoked in Aidan one thing, and it scared the shit out of him.

Aidan turned to find Mima beside him, her face impassive. "What's it about?"

"A lot of things."

* * *

The train pulled to a hard stop. Again awakened from his reverie, Aidan rose and walked with Mima through the doors. He didn't remember passing through the station; only when the cold hit him did Aidan know he was outside again.

"You are silent, Aidan," Mima observed. "Is something the matter?"

"Oh," Aidan replied as he reached for his cigarettes, "just thinking back, you know, to our time back home."

Mima's arm again slid into Aidan's. "I know what makes you feel that way."

Aidan took his time in lighting up, then exhaled. "Do you?"

"Those days are over," Mima said, "though we live through some of them today. When I left America, the home I returned to after school was the same. Only the calendar changed."

"I guess." Aidan took another drag and continued, "It's foolish of me to think that we are as we were. We have changed, grown up, evolved perhaps."

Mima leaned against Aidan as they crossed the street and made for Mima's neighborhood. "Sora is the same," Mima replied, "though she is a shade or two better. I suppose I have progressed, too."

"You never told me in so many words," Aidan said, "why you did what you did."

She shrugged. "A combination of issues." Mima's hand moved in a throwaway gesture. "Loneliness; the pain of being so far away from my family, the problems in my real family, and the loss of Kaga. Then there was the fear of not knowing my future. I liked feeling secure in knowledge, but I didn't have it then. I like to think I do now."

"None of us knew where we were going then," Aidan said, "I sure didn't." Again, Aidan's mind drifted back to the discovery. Mima brought it up, so it was okay to think about it...for now.

* * *

Aidan stepped into the foyer of Mima's apartment building. He wasn't expected; Aidan was in the neighborhood and decided to drop by. He was about to press the button to Mima's unit to be buzzed in, but a tenant on her way out opened the door. Thanking her, Aidan passed through and climbed the stairs to the third floor.

The hallway was narrow, lit by a couple of 60-watt bulbs. The walls and ceiling were yellow, but this did little to offset the dingy nature of the building. Anyone walking by the brownstone would have admired the old-world architecture, but if they could see inside...

There were two units on this floor, with Mima's on the right. As he made for it, he heard a noise.

Aidan slowed his steps. He now walked as quietly as his boots would let him. There was that sound again: a moan, and it came from Mima.

Silently, Aidan tried the door handle. His first instinct was to rush in; perhaps Mima was in trouble or being attacked. But he could hear no other voices or sounds that would have led him to believe Mima was not alone.

The door was unlocked--Mima always bolted her door when home. Tensed, Aidan pushed the door open, ready for anything.

He was not ready for this.

At first Aidan thought Mima was painting on the floor, like Jackson Pollock. She was in the middle of the room on her knees in sweat pants and a t-shirt. Before her was a large, rectangular canvas. Mima's glasses and a thick paintbrush lay to the side.

Aidan couldn't move. He stared as he watched Mima. She wasn't painting.

A stream of red sprayed across the canvas. Mima then leaned forward, her bare right arm extended over it, and she again dragged the carving knife across it. Blood streamed from the limb, and it dripped down onto the canvas, now half white and half red. Mima's body shook, but she made no sound. The knife came up again...

Aidan knocked the knife from Mima's hand and wrapped his arms about her from behind. "Mima, stop it!"

Mima's response was a cry that sounded more like an animal than a human. She struggled. Mima was stronger than she looked, but Aidan was able to hold her from behind, and the two went to the floor in a tumble of arms and legs.

"Mima," Aidan shouted, "get hold of yourself!" He managed to pin Mima down, but the blood pouring from her right arm made him lose his grip. Mima swung at him, and while she missed, a warm stream of blood struck him in the face.

That stopped him. The liquid was hot, and Aidan threw himself back.

"Aidan," Mima cried, "I'm sorry!" She picked up a dishtowel that lay on the floor and crawled to him.

Aidan yanked it from Mima's hand. "For Christ's sake Mima," he snapped, "what the bloody hell are you doing?"

Oh, fuck… bad choice of words! Fortunately, Mima had come down. She let Aidan wrap the towel around her arm. As he did so, Aidan saw the telltale scars. There were several of them on both of Mima's forearms, crisscrossing at several angles. Small wonder she always wore long sleeves.

Aidan tugged his handkerchief from his coat. Mima took it and began to wipe off his face. "Aidan, I'm sorry you had to see this," she said. Mima was back to normal again, calm and composed.

"What is this, Mima?" he demanded again. "What are these? Wait, I know what they are! Why… why are you doing this to yourself?"

"The pain I'm in," Mima replied. Her eyes were dry but large and betrayed shame at having been caught. "I can't deal with it any other way."

"There's got to be." Aidan pulled Mima to her feet and guided her to a battered easy chair. His mind racing, Aidan went into the bathroom. He grabbed the towel that hung by the sink. In the cabinet beneath was a first aid kit, and Aidan took that.

Mima allowed Aidan to clean her wounds, which were not deep, and bandage them. "I hurt, Aidan," she admitted as she hid her face in her left hand. "You can't imagine how. I do this because it expels the hurt I feel inside."

"What is it, though?" Aidan kept his voice calm as he wrapped Mima's arm. "Look," he went on, "you know I'm not gonna say anything, Mima. We've always been straight with each other – you can be with me now."

Mima looked up. With the index and middle fingers of her left hand, she drew the familiar traces from her eyes downward. "Tears," she said softly, "the ones I can't cry, and the ones I never will."

"What?"

Mima swallowed, gave a deep sigh and looked down at the floor. "This is your home, Aidan," she said, "you've lived all your life here. I've never been so far from mine. Being away from my friends, my family, living here; it has consumed me."

The bandaging done, Aidan slid his hand along Mima's face and lifted hers level with his own. "Mima," he replied, "I get you, believe me I do; but why turn a knife on your body?"

"The pain that I feel when I do it," she whispered, "is better than the suffering I have inside me. You don't know all of it, Aidan – you don't know about my people."

"That's part of it, right?" Aidan moved onto the chair beside Mima and put his arms about her. "Go ahead, what is the deal with your family? You've said you and your parents were estranged; that's right?"

Mima nodded, her head again lowered. "We had a violent disagreement," she mumbled. "I lived with my friend Sora and her family since then."

"I'm sorry." Aidan continued to hold Mima to him. He wished he knew what else to say or do, but couldn't think of anything.

"Not your fault." Mima shuddered. "I should feel so lucky," she said. "I have Sora's family to turn to, and that's good. I'm on scholarship, I have enough to live on while I study, and I can go back to Japan when all is said and done. But right now…"

Mima huddled against Aidan. "What I feel is so bad, Aidan," she continued. "I can't expect you to understand; all I know is, I hurt. I hurt inside, despite all this. I know what I'm doing is wrong, but it's the only way."

"There's got to be another way," Aidan cut in. He seized Mima's shoulders and turned her to face him. "Listen, Mima," he said, "I'll do what I can. If you need to talk, or you need more than that, I'll do it. You're my friend," he went on, "and I love you, Mima. I know we'll never be like that, but that's not the point. You're my friend, and I've never had a real one like you. Please, will you let me help?"

Aidan was losing it; he was ready to break down, something he hadn't done since he lost that fight to Stephen when he was twelve. From that day, Aidan kept his coarsest feelings inside; Mima was letting hers out this way.

Mima's eyes looked into his. "Yes."

* * *

"Yes." They were back on the apartment's deck.

"Yes to what?" Mima responded.

Aidan told her his thoughts. "I guess you triggered it," he admitted, "but that incident has stayed with me."

"It would," Mima replied in the flicker of his old Zippo. "It had to do with one of your friends," she explained, "in a situation you didn't expect and weren't prepared for. I didn't want to explain, but I had to."

Mima then stepped forward and put her arms about Aidan's waist. Her nose wrinkled up because of the Gitanes smoke, but she continued, "You helped me then, Aidan. I presume you are here for more than the reasons you've stated. Either way, know I'll help you, too."

The two embraced. Despite the late-night traffic from below and the low-flying jet that passed above, the strains of that odd song from the nameless singer penetrated Aidan's consciousness. He couldn't remember all the words about the pain his subject felt…it was not a dream… or something like that.

6 - Kabul

There were two lights in the room, from the monitor and overhead. Aidan's left eye opened a crack; he shifted his position on the couch and rolled to his right to face inwards against its back.

"This isn't bothering you, is it?" Mima asked from her work.

"No." Aidan wrapped the blanket about himself. "Not sleeping," he mumbled, "but it's nothing you're doing."

"Are you sure?"

"I'm sure." Aidan was going there, whether he wanted to or not.

* * *

Aidan climbed into the passenger seat of the four-wheel drive and buckled up. It was hot, probably 100 degrees again, and inside the vehicle Aidan began to sweat.

"Ready, boss?" Mansur grinned from the driver's seat and fired the engine. The SUV dated back to the Soviet invasion, but still had balls as Mansur wheeled it into the street.

The assignment was different from what Aidan expected. "Right up your alley," Philippa commented the week before as she pushed the folder across her cluttered desk at the network office.

Aidan smiled as he eyed Philippa from her tightly permed, red-dyed hair, the pale skin, geek glasses and curves well shown off by the dress she'd snagged on one of her thrift store crawls. Aidan could picture every other aspect of his girlfriend, but he opened the file and examined that instead.

He scanned the main page. The network wanted an account of a section of Kabul rarely if ever seen on American TV screens. Video would have been friendlier to the medium, but the network wasn't releasing any of its regular staff. No other independents such as Aidan had bitten, either.

"The other side of Kabul?" Aidan mused. "Interesting."

"Yeah." Philippa peered over her glasses. "This is the aspect of the capital most don't see: that there is a safe side to it, but also the people who want to see that side exposed and spread."

Aidan nodded. "Got some top-level contacts here."

Philippa turned to examine her computer and the web link to the TV show she produced. Over the top of the file, Aidan noted Philippa's expression of disgust at the host's airbrushed headshot. "Callie hasn't given up the Mary Tyler Moore look, I see," he cracked.

"Yeah," Philippa said at length, "such a wench. Anyway, she didn't like the idea at the start. Then all of a sudden, Callie came around. Her spin of course is gonna be that the elites of Kabul are not really on our side in this war, and they want economic and political control of the nation for themselves."

Aidan shrugged. Callie Fontaine-Smith pulled decent ratings in her primetime talk show slot, and paid her dues to get there. Unfortunately, that was the point when Callie's journalistic skills went on permanent hiatus.

"Why do you stay as her producer, Phil?" Aidan asked. "You could get a job anywhere in TV you wanted. Callie's a self-centered camera slut. Why deal with her?"

Philippa sighed as she turned back to Aidan. "I don't like to quit," she replied. "I think you know me well enough."

"Touché." Aidan smiled and placed the information in his shoulder bag. "I'll take it," he said. "When am I off?"

"Tomorrow." Philippa passed an airline ticket across the desk to him. "I'll see you off at National," she added.

Aidan raised an eyebrow. "And shall I be ensconced at an appointed place tonight?"

Philippa grinned. The stud in her left nostril flashed under the office light, and her large teeth showed two almost perfect white rows. "Yeah, but while we're at it," she replied, "we gotta talk."

It turned into quite a night at Philippa's apartment on the Hill. After all was said and done, the two did have that talk, one Aidan expected for a long time.

"You know," Philippa said as she wound her body about Aidan's, "we've been trying to figure this out for a while. I think I know where we're at."

"I do, too. It doesn't seem as though we're going to work, are we, Phil?"

"No." Philippa pressed her body closer to Aidan's, her head on his chest. "Your life and mine, Aidan, they're way too different: you live for travel, and I live for what I do here. I'd have no problem letting you base yourself here, but then again," she sighed, "I'm not here more than I need to be. I sleep here, and that's it."

Aidan nodded as he held Philippa. "We both work ourselves to death," he admitted, "but it's what I do. I have to do it to get what I'm trying to find."

"And that's what it's about," Philippa finished for him. "I'm the same way." She leaned on her elbow, and Aidan admired her curves as they disappeared beneath the covers.

"You're still looking for you, Aidan. You're restless like a lot of us. Me, I have a job to do, and I love it. I live for that, and I've found it. I want to keep doing it."

"I'd never stop you," Aidan replied, "as I know you'd not stop me."

There was little more discussion that night, and Aidan felt they didn't say anything at all. Philippa said even less after an early breakfast at the airport, and the goodbye was even shorter. Despite the outward appearance, Philippa was not one for drama, and the embrace and kiss were perfunctory. Aidan slept for most of the flight westward; he wouldn't get a lot in Kabul.

The SUV's horn brought Aidan back as Mansur swung the vehicle past an old minivan and shot through an intersection. Mansur put on speed. They were headed out of the city and up a paved road.

Aidan now listened more carefully to Mansur. An Afghan national, Mansur was a tall, wiry fellow with a thin moustache and a good sense of humor. Attached to the U.S. Embassy as a driver, Mansur had opened doors for Aidan all week. "Thing is boss," he said, "these changes being called for are ones that most of our corner of the world do not understand. You've seen that."

"Right." So far Aidan had conducted interviews with a number of Afghans who lived and worked lives more suited to the west. Mansur's cousin, who operated a clothing store, that looked like it belonged in an American shopping mall; an uncle and aunt, the curators of an art gallery; and the sister-in-law who worked at an exchange market. Yet another friend of a friend was the moderate head cleric of a well-appointed mosque.

They now traveled into a more suburban, and largely unseen part of the capital. This portion of Kabul was markedly different: the roads were well maintained, the cars late models and a fair number of the populace walked about in western dress. It was a western world within a nation long torn apart by war and the battle over what values, both politically and spiritually, would prevail.

Aidan's recorded interviews were emailed back to Philippa. His photos remained undeveloped due to Aidan's insistence on using the Minolta. The camera was more than forty years old. Aidan personally oiled, repaired, replaced and tweaked every part of the old girl. It in return never failed him. The Minolta was a good luck charm, even a talisman.

He kept a protective hand on the case as they rode. The camera documented and survived the firefights between insurgents and Army MPs in Tikrit, the street battles in Cairo and bomb attacks on Buddhist monks and government forces in Bangkok. It may have even captured a glimpse of what the Congolese called Mokele-Mbembe, though even Aidan didn't think he'd shot Africa's version of the Loch Ness Monster. They were the tag team.

Aidan owned four other cameras, including a fair digital one. The latter at least felt like a real camera but was not the same. Aidan now pulled the Minolta out and again checked the new roll of film he'd put in at the hotel was ready to go.

Today's visit was to one of the larger homes in the suburb. Behind a thick stone wall, the house rose three floors. Picture windows gleamed in the sunlight and outside decks ringed the home with ornate railings and balustrades. Admitted entrance through the wrought iron gate by a servant, Mansur pulled up alongside a black, late model BMW.

The interior of the house was a combination of traditional and western decoration. Aidan felt like he was at one of the colonial Sirdar's homes in India as they sat on the veranda. Another servant brought coffee to Aidan, Mansur and the subject of the interview.

This was one of the "top-level" people on Aidan's contact list. His name was known, but Aidan had agreed that it and this man's picture would not be used in the story. He was about 45, Aidan guessed, and directly involved in the growing political sphere of Afghans who went west for education, then returned home. He sat before Aidan and Mansur in a white polo shirt and slacks, more ready for a round of golf than a discussion of geopolitics.

"You must realize," the man now said in perfect, unaccented English, "that what we seek to bring to our homeland is something very difficult to accept, let alone comprehend for most of our countrymen."

Aidan scribbled responses on a pad. "You speak of the larger population as a whole," he asked, "not only the religious conservatives?"

"Correct." The man sipped his coffee and carefully laid the china cup in its saucer on the table. "Afghanistan is a conduit," he explained. "The Soviets invaded to use our country as a semi-direct line to the Indian Ocean, to commerce and economic development. It of course meant going through Pakistan as well, but that was to be a separate arrangement. That matter is now irrelevant. Currently, the gas pipeline that passes through our nation represents an opportunity for limitless growth."

He leaned forward for emphasis. "This is a nation," he continued, "that must rise out of its provincial, territorial and tribal ways, Mr. Connor. We have suffered far too long. My colleagues and I want to see an industrial Afghanistan, one that is ruled by western, not Sharia law. One where women are educated equally to men, and where Democracy can exist and thrive."

The man sat back. "It is fair to say," he went on, "change like this is radical, and will not happen soon enough for me to experience it. But we can carry it forward. There is significant potential for the full population, not merely a privileged few."

He paused. "I am sure," the man said with a sly smile, "this must seem mighty strange to you. Here you are in a neighborhood such as this, in a land where most Americans only see mountains, sand and people out of their time. One day, it will rise," he added with an expanse of his hand over the scene, "to this."

Aidan was permitted to take photos of the house and surrounding views, though not the subject's family or his servants. The fellow was indeed sincere in what he was saying, though experience taught Aidan that while others might share his views, they would be seen as an extremely small minority in this land.

"Achmed," Mansur commented once they were back on the road, "is a decent man. Unfortunately, boss," he continued over the roar of the engine, "the changes he speaks of will not be accepted in this nation, not for many years. Change occurs, but it can also be slow, and my people are resistant to it."

"Who wants this change, Mansur?" Aidan asked.

"The people," Mansur replied, "who have tasted your kind of life. They know it, but bringing that here is not possible. Achmed is the visionary of the group," he went on. "The majority of those who wish to move this country, the social, cultural and political ones do want it spread, but only so far.

It is to be spread like wealth in America. Only so much is released, with the rest concentrated in the hands of the few."

Aidan listened. The windows were open, yet that didn't do a thing to reduce the heat. "It seems like madness, doesn't it?" he asked. "To create change in a world that since its beginnings has not known any other way. Changes like that won't happen overnight."

"Like in Iraq, eh?" Mansur grinned and motioned to Aidan's camera case. "You see, Aidan," he continued, "we view the world through a different lens. I am a Muslim, but I am an Afghan, too. You notice how I put my religion first? That is how many of us do; the spirituality comes first, the nationality second. Understand this and you understand everything. The man we saw today? Achmed is true to what he believes, but even within his circle, they do not see things in the same exact way."

They were back in the city. Mansur turned down a narrow side street and pulled off before a marketplace where motor vehicles were not permitted. Aidan pulled out his Gitanes and offered one to Mansur. "I'll get it," Aidan said after they lit up.

"Thanks, boss." Mansur leaned back in his seat to enjoy the smoke. Aidan exited the vehicle, slung the Minolta over his shoulder, and turned the corner. He passed into the market. Animal carcasses hung from meat racks at one kiosk while a fruit vendor poured freshly squeezed juice for a customer at a second. Next to these was a purveyor of coffee; an older man scooped beans into a scale and haggled with the buyer while the seller's son took orders for the liquid kind. It was Aidan's turn to treat. He'd picked up the local saying for the number two and for "coffee".

The sight of westerners in this part of the city, soldiers and otherwise was not uncommon. Even if someone bothered to look Aidan over, there was not enough time to consider his presence.

What came out of the sky took care of that.

7 - The Tiger

The blast threw Aidan, both physically and mentally out of his body and left him temporarily deaf. Slowly, his eardrums allowed him hear the screams of the wounded and the shouts of others around him.

Aidan ended up on his side, a chunk of cement under his ribs. He coughed for several seconds in spite of the pain it caused. Aidan next did a body check: his limbs were all there and nothing was broken. In the distance, he heard the wail of sirens.

He disentangled himself from a motionless body and staggered to his feet. Dazed, Aidan stared about him. The marketplace was gone. All that remained were piles of rubble, and flames shot from a broken gas main. Bodies, whole and dismembered lay in the street and protruded from the wreckage. Very few seemed alive; those who were struggled and cried out for help or shouted to their deity.

Aidan's next thought was for his camera; the Minolta was still in its case. In an action done so many times it was automatic, Aidan whipped out his camera, removed and stowed the lens cap and began to shoot. All the while, he thought of Mansur; he had to get back to him.

The sun was at his back before the explosion, so Aidan stumbled towards it. There were no pathways; residents of the area, injured and not swarmed over the debris.

At the top of a pile, Aidan stopped. He looked down into the crater where the missile struck. At the bottom was a smoldering piece of twisted metal.

Aidan raised his camera and took one shot. Now he had to get out of here.

About four blocks over, the streets and buildings resumed. The roads were clogged with vehicles. Ambulance sirens screamed in protest of the blockages. There were two lines of human traffic: one surged toward the scene of the blast, the other rushed away from it.

Aidan joined the latter. He darted in and out of the slower moving people; some were only shell-shocked, but others trailed blood or assisted others. Aidan didn't have time to think about them; his inner voice told him to get away. Around another corner, Aidan tucked the Minolta back into its case. He looked this way and that. Mansur was his guide, and Aidan cursed himself for not taking a more careful view of landmarks. He was lost.

Open space presented itself, and Aidan ran down an undamaged street to a corner, where an ancient taxi was parked. The back door closest to the curb was being vacated by two men, and Aidan timed his movements to slip into the rear of it two seconds after they left. The driver, a young man in traditional dress blinked at this stranger.

Aidan didn't give him a chance to speak. "US Embassy," he ordered. "Go!"

The driver at least understood that much English, and he hit the gas. While he seemed unaware of what just happened a few blocks away, the taxi operator guessed this was a fare that would pay him well.

Aidan's fists balled around the camera strap, and he braced himself in the back seat. He'd escaped death, this time closer than any other. He shook from the adrenalin, and his mind raced from one thought to another.

He first thought of Mansur and felt sick for the man. Then about the attack: it must have been a Taliban strike, and Aidan thought about the type of armament they were known to possess. Aidan was not a weapons expert, but he'd heard numerous missiles in flight before. This one had no telltale warning; was it a new kind?

There were no other strikes or a follow-up attack. Was it a hit-and-run? Or was this an air strike? Aidan didn't notice any planes overhead, but in the loud old vehicle, he and Mansur wouldn't have heard them anyway.

Aidan didn't know the answers, and couldn't process more. He had to get back to the embassy and find Jack, his contact.

The driver pulled up in front of the Embassy, which was ringed by heavily armed US Special and Afghan forces. Aidan paid with a large bill of the local currency and jumped out.

He then realized he was a mess. Aidan was covered in dust from head to foot. He brushed himself off as he approached, but that wasn't going to do any good. Aidan then became aware of the extra troops, more than he'd seen on the grounds the day before. They weren't going let Aidan pass through.

Then he saw Jack rush down the walkway. A head taller than the biggest man, he stood out. His blond hair, tropical suit and shades were straight out of Belize, Jack's previous posting. He shouted a command; the officer in charge gave an order, and the soldiers made way.

There were no pleasantries. "Come on," Jack said and he grabbed Aidan's arm. They hurried past the guards and up the walkway to the Embassy doors. Jack's status was a pass for anyone with him; there was no challenge, no ID checks and no questions.

"How did you know?" Aidan asked. Jack didn't answer right away; their shoes echoed off the tiles as they walked through the brightly lit foyer, past Embassy personnel, and more guards.

Jack steered Aidan into a restroom. "I knew before it even happened," he replied. "Wash up and I'll give you the skinny."

The water ran hot and steamed up the mirror. Aidan looked as though he'd stepped off the set of a horror film, minus the blood: his face was covered in a layer of dirt, and his hair could use a good washing, but there was no time for that. He scrubbed his hands and did the same with his face. "Tell me what you can."

You were headed into hostile territory, Aidan," Jack said. "They knew where Mansur was taking you; they didn't want you to come back."

Aidan looked over. "Me? And who's 'they'?"

"Certain people," Jack explained, "the ones who want to call the shots. This job of yours cut too close to home. You were to be a warning, but we're too embedded here. You shouldn't have been involved, but now you are, and we gotta get you out."

Aidan pulled a sheaf of paper towels from the dispenser and began to wipe his face and hands. "Out? You mean now?"

"Yes, right now." Jack motioned for him to follow. "I've made arrangements," he explained as they walked back into the hallway. "We've got a routine flight to Jakarta -- you're on it. After that, you're on your own."

"Jack, what the fuck is this?" Aidan demanded. "What is going on?"

"I can't tell you anymore," Jack shouted back, "I shouldn't have told you this!" He took the sleeve of Aidan's jacket in hand as he quickened their pace. "You need to go. Don't worry about your stuff, you can always get more – but don't let your story go untold. You hear me?"

Aidan caught the squinted blue eye Jack used on others when he had a point to make. "Yeah, I hear you."

"Got your passport, right?"

Aidan nodded, and Jack took him through a side door into a low-ceilinged garage. There were three bulletproof retractable doors to the outside. In the two outer lanes rested a troop truck, an armored personnel carrier and a Jeep. These faced the closed doors, but the garage's main activity took place in the lane nearest them.

The two climbed into the back of a Humvee, which had Jeeps parked before and behind it. The garage door clattered up, and all three rolled out.

They weren't alone in the darkened vehicle: two Marines sat in the rear seat, fully armed and armored, as was the one who rode shotgun. Jack went silent; Aidan was left to listen to the radio traffic between the vehicles, the language a jumble of code words and military slang.

The motorcade drove through the streets at top speed, then turned into another military area. They were waved through a series of guard posts. Once on the tarmac, the vehicles again accelerated. Through the windscreen, Aidan saw a waiting C-130 Hercules. The rear ramp was down; a half dozen men and women stood around the aircraft's entrance.

The doors opened, and all but the driver disembarked. Jack led Aidan to the rear ramp and motioned to one of the flight crew standing there. Before the handoff, Jack told him, "You're gonna meet someone to help you back in the States, and you'll be put in the picture there. Sorry I can't do more than this."

"Thanks, Jack." The two shook hands before Aidan hurried up the ramp behind the crewman. Moments later the cargo door swung up and closed behind them.

Aidan followed the officer through the interior, past stacks of cargo until they reached the area before the flight deck. The man motioned to one of the benches used by paratroopers and shouted over the engines, "Have a seat, sir. Strap in and hang on!"

He would be the only passenger on this flight. Aidan's companions were crates, boxes, and containers. The engines wound up to full power and moments later the C-130 headed down the runway.

Aidan leaned over, closed his eyes and buried his face in his arms.

* * *

"Aidan? Hello..."

Aidan jerked and turned on the couch. Mima was kneeling in front him, her hands on his shoulders. She was in her favored sleepwear, a long t-shirt. "It's okay, Aidan," she said, "I'm here."

Aidan sat up and pushed the blanket off him. He was covered in sweat and felt feverish. "What time is it?" he asked.

"It's morning," she replied. "Were you having a nightmare?"

"I don't know." Aidan took a series of deep breaths to try and calm himself. "I wasn't at first," he added, "but I was back in Kabul again."

Mima moved beside Aidan on the couch. At a time like this, he noticed how different Mima looked without her glasses.

"Aidan, what happened there?" Mima asked. "I haven't wanted to pry," she added, "but I think you need me to."

"I know." Aidan ran his hands through his hair and along his unshaven face. "This was part of it," he explained. "What happened after is kind of like act two, but I'm dealing with all of it at once."

Mima rose and headed for the kitchen. "I'll make some coffee," she said, "unless you want to go out?"

"No." Aidan got to his feet, unsteady. He felt hung over; his t-shirt and sweatpants were visibly damp like he'd just come out of a workout.

Aidan joined Mima in the tiny space where she was filling her coffeemaker with water. "I think," he said, "I do need to talk now. My turn, I guess."

Mima turned, her expression sympathetic, but knowing. "I knew you would have to," she replied. "You've listened to me; I owe you the favor."

Aidan headed into the bathroom. He turned on the cold water, picked up a washcloth and soaked it under the faucet. As he brought it to his face, Aidan saw it: he looked as he did in the Embassy bathroom. The fright, exhaustion and experience were etched into his face, and his psyche.

He felt old, and disgusted.

* * *

The flight to Jakarta was a long one. Aidan put his feet up and did his best to get some sleep, but the Hercules was not built for comfort. No one communicated with him but for an African-American officer in fatigues who came back and offered him coffee in a steel mess cup, which Aidan gratefully accepted.

"Need your passport, sir," the man said. "Gotta work it so you check through okay."

Aidan tugged the document out of his inside coat pocket and handed it over. The man took it back to the flight deck while Aidan held his hands around the cup and warmed them. He sipped the steaming drink and felt the hot liquid slowly heat his insides. It was black and damned strong, the taste a bit too familiar.

The officer came back a few minutes later, Aidan's passport in hand. "You're signed and sealed, sir," he joked, then added more professionally, "thank you."

Aidan nodded and paged open the book with his thumb. Near the back, Aidan noted a Customs stamp was entered under the one he received when he arrived in Kabul. Over the pink ink, a scrawled signature was affixed, the name unreadable. Aidan wondered just who up front had that kind of authority.

It was nighttime when the C-130 finally touched down in Jakarta. Aidan was escorted out the back to a Jeep that whisked him off the base and into the city.

There was no armed entourage this time. Aidan rode alone beside the driver, a Marine sergeant. He guessed the vehicle was being followed at a discreet distance by at least one other as the Embassy staffer did not ride with them. Other than standard radio communications, his driver wasn't talking.

The Jeep pulled up at Jakarta International several minutes later but around the corner from the main entrance. The sergeant let him off with a brief, "Good luck, sir", and he was gone.

Aidan was no stranger to this airport. A brief walk through the terminal, and his American Express card secured him a seat on Garuda Indonesia, the national airline. This was not by choice; it was the first flight out of the country, bound for Sydney. The agent didn't bat an eye at the dirty, disheveled American in front of him, or that his ticket was one-way; Aidan was just another passenger.

He bought an English language copy of the *Jakarta Post* from a newsstand and joined the short queue for Customs. Surprisingly, Aidan cleared; the officers barely glanced at this Caucasian with only a camera as luggage.

Aidan's ticket placed him before the wing in the right-hand section of the 747, on the aisle. The plane was only a third full, and the well-dressed Indian businessman with the window seat chose to go to sleep the moment he buckled his seatbelt.

Aidan proceeded to down three more cups of coffee as he read through the *Post*. The attack made page one of the late edition. Sixty was the death toll with more than twice that number wounded. Government officials were blaming the Taliban, whose nebulous spokespeople denied responsibility for, or even knowledge of, the incident.

Aidan read slowly and methodically through the paper to kill time. He also considered his next move, a specific one.

On the off chance he might have to deal with someone who wanted to examine his film, Aidan resorted to his favored method of concealment. In the lavatory, he carefully manipulated the tabs of the used rolls to make them look new. He then re-sealed each one in their containers; a glance by any busy Customs or security agent would lead them to think they'd never been opened.

To deal with the possible question of why a foreign tourist would have a camera and all these rolls of film (but not taken any pictures), Aidan had an answer. Two used rolls of the same brand were tucked into the strap of the Minolta. These particular photos were old and not of this trip, but they would serve to lower the suspicion level of anyone who might take notice.

Aidan remained wide-awake and apprehensive. He was used to traveling light, but not like this. Jack pulled strings to get him out of Kabul, but Aidan couldn't figure how he knew about the attack before it happened.

He also wondered why Jack was so intent on getting him out of the country. Aidan ran it over in his mind: Jack said I got too close to something. That could be Achmed and his people, or at least their ideas. Those would be a reason for many, not just the Taliban, to take action. Then Jack also said those who want to make the decisions were involved in this. Did he mean people on the ground there, or someplace else?

This led to an overriding question: could Aidan have been the target?

That made no sense. Aidan was known, but more to his colleagues than politicians or news junkies. He certainly wasn't famous; Aidan was no blogger, he didn't frequent the talk shows. On politics, Aidan was moderate to the point of ambivalence.

If he was the target, then the missile attack was coordinated. Jack told Aidan enough; he was tipped off, but not in time to prevent the attack and Mansur's death. Aidan then reminded himself about all the others who'd been killed, but it was hard to think about them right now.

Aidan next wondered whom he was supposed to meet in America; whatever happened, he had to get back to Washington, and Philippa. He was sure to end up on Callie's idiotic program; he never cared for that style of journalism, a talk show where the host did most of the talking, and opinions weighed more than facts. Aidan couldn't think about that, either. He had to get into and out of Sydney next.

He signaled the passing flight attendant for another refill. *One tiger at a time*, Aidan was once counseled, *one tiger at a time*.

8 - Just the Games

"I have to admit, Aidan," Mima said, "I'm fascinated by this, in spite of what it has done to you."

The two were seated on the deck. Mima lifted the carafe off the table. "Another?"

"Thanks." Aidan slid his cup over. "I'm PTSD'ing all over the place, aren't I?"

"No," Mima replied in all seriousness. "You are telling me a story. I get the feeling this runs deeper, doesn't it?"

Aidan leaned in Mima's direction. "There is," he replied, "but I haven't reached the depths of it, not yet."

Mima filled Aidan's cup, then her own. "Do," she said and looked him in the eye. "That's why I'm here."

* * *

The Sydney leg of the trip passed without incident, and Aidan searched the airline boards to find the soonest and most direct way back to the States. His Amex card got him onto a Qantas flight to LAX via Honolulu. Once on the mainland, he'd have to book a third one to DC. At least Aidan was out of danger, or so he hoped.

He killed two more hours by staring at CNN International in an all-night lounge, went through the drill of Customs once more and boarded the flight. This one was full, mostly due to a package tour of Americans. Surrounded by a crowd who nattered about Aussies, the Outback and their timeshares in Acapulco, Aidan actually felt safe. He even got some sleep.

It would be early afternoon by the time he arrived in Hawaii, and Aidan wondered whether he should call Philippa. He decided against it. Aidan shut down his iPhone in Jakarta and resisted the urge to turn it back on in Sydney. At this point, Aidan ruled out making any contact to guard against pinging.

At Honolulu Aidan disembarked, cleared Customs and headed straight for the Qantas departure gate. He checked his flight was on schedule. With that confirmed, he went to find a quiet hiding place.

Aidan would not have minded seeing more of Hawaii--and getting in a badly needed smoke--but the view through the airport windows would have to do. He found a secluded seat in a restaurant and devoured a club sandwich and a platter of fries along with a frosted glass of Primo. He also read through discarded copies of the *Honolulu Weekly* and *The Sporting News*.

Then things got strange.

While debating whether to have dessert, a loudspeaker announcement blocked out an automated flight call: "Would Mr. Aidan Connor, please come to the Visitor Information desk, located in the Central Lobby? Mr. Aidan Connor..."

Shit.

Aidan waited five minutes, and then casually called for his check. During this, Aidan thought fast. Who could have known he was here? Jack might have sent a message to someone in DC--Philippa might also be trying to contact him. Perhaps someone was waiting for him again? After all, he was back in America...

He paid with cash. Aidan looked past the rims of his shades as he left the restaurant and headed down the escalator to the first floor of the airport. The terminal was full of the typical travelers, flight crews, car rental agents and baggage handlers. No one seemed out of place.

As he approached the desk, Aidan carefully looked that over. There were two uniformed Hawaiian women behind it. A man loaded down with three bags attached to a rolling rack and a set of golf clubs was being served. No one stood or loitered nearby.

Aidan gave his name to the idle clerk and showed his passport. "Yes, thank you, Mr. Connor," the woman replied. She consulted a portable stand that held a number of file folders and withdrew a Telex envelope. "If you would please sign here..."

He signed and walked away. Opening the document, he stared at the message: *"Got your boots on? See you in Hollywood, Bro."*

For the first time in too long, Aidan grinned.

∗ ∗ ∗

Aidan and Mima were into their third cups of coffee, augmented by a microwaved breakfast pastry. "This is getting crazier by the moment, Aidan," Mima said. "It's like a spy thriller, something Morimura or Heinlein would write."

"Or Ian Fleming." A devoted reader of the Bond series when he was a kid, Aidan found himself in 007's position of having to get out of town fast as the opening chapter of *Goldfinger* necessitated. "Needless to say, I was paranoid as hell by that point," Aidan went on, "but once I got that message, the pressure was off -- or so I thought."

"So what happened next?"

"It went like this..."

* * *

Most of the same travelers from Australia were on this flight along with some Hawaiians and a contingent of Japanese businessmen. Aidan picked out most of the first group by face and clothing; he was searching for outsiders, beside himself.

There were none Aidan could detect, and he was able to relax on the flight to Los Angeles. Several hours, a plastic meal, more coffee and a package of stale cocktail pretzels later, Aidan hoped he'd escaped the worst of it. The only question was what awaited him when he reached the mainland.

Disembarking at LAX, and with barely a glance from U.S. Customs, Aidan was through. His next thought was to book the last part of his run to DC, but Aidan needed a look about first.

Aidan saw him as he entered the concourse. He was seated in the Starbucks, back to the wall. A tall, brawny individual with a full, reddish-brown beard and skin to match, he didn't fit the scene. Dressed in Wranglers, Red Wing boots and a flannel work shirt, the man stared through his own darkened shades. The lips of his mouth turned up slightly as Aidan took his place in line.

Two minutes later, a Pike's Peak Roast in hand, Aidan walked with careful casualness through the crowded tables and sat opposite the stranger. "Hi, Stephen."

The man raised his cup to Aidan's. "Good to see you, Bro. Have a nice flight?"

Aidan had to laugh, and Stephen joined him in it. Aidan hadn't seen his brother in over two years.

"Yeah," he replied. "L.A.'s been good to you, I see."

"Good as most things, I guess." Stephen sipped his drink and pushed an American Airlines folder across the table. "For you," he said, "non-stop to the District. Business Class, my man."

"Cool, thanks." Aidan examined the boarding pass. "Who's my contact?"

"Philippa," Stephen told him. "She knows what's up, and my people in Washington say you'll be free of it once the final chapter plays out."

"So you had a man in Kabul," Aidan replied. He put the ticket in his passport and secured it inside his jacket.

Stephen nodded. "Jack and I were in the same academy class back in the day," he said. "Great guy, put me in the loop. Not to change the subject so abruptly now, but you've got film, right?"

Aidan nodded. "Six rolls, the assignment and the site."

Stephen stood up. "Development time," he declared. "You've got a while before the flight. Let's go."

They passed through the terminal. "Have 'em out and ready," Stephen said, "once we get in the car."

The walk from the air-conditioned airport into the heat of L.A. was tolerable for Aidan compared to Kabul. They took a shuttle bus down to Park One. Ten minutes later, they were in Stephen's black Impala.

He turned onto Sepulveda. Aidan removed the six plastic containers, which looked like pill bottles to the inexperienced. He enclosed them in a small plastic bag Stephen handed him and knotted the top.

A few minutes later they turned into the nearby Post Office parking lot as a featureless silver Saturn made its way out.

Stephen grabbed the bag, passed it out the driver's side window to a blonde woman in shades. She made the grab and was onto Sepulveda. The handoff took barely a second to complete.

Stephen swung the car around and backed it against the rear brick wall of the office, between two trucks. "Company car," he commented, "we'll be cool here."

Stephen lit a Marlboro while Aidan fired up his first Gitanes in what felt like ages. The two smoked, drank their coffee and viewed the planes that took off and landed. They spoke of the family, what their sister was up to, Katie's kids and other mundane matters like two workmen on a break.

"So what's going on?" Aidan asked at length.

Stephen kept his gaze forward, but his eyes shifted this way and that, one ear on the two-way radio that crackled in the alcove above the stereo. "A complete and total fuckup," he replied, "that's what's going on. You were targeted, man. That missile wasn't fired by some shoulder-packing yahoo – it was one of ours."

"Ours?"

"Yeah." Stephen removed his shades to reveal his own blue eyes. "The target was too well protected," he explained. "The deal's this: those people you went to see in Afghanistan? Most of them are connected to the NATO mission in one way or another. Some of it is political, but mostly it's business. The pipeline, that kind of thing."

Aidan pondered this as Stephen continued, "Someone informed individuals based in Kabul that you'd be interviewing those people. That someone is connected to a group in Washington that wants the whole mission to fail in order to continue the war."

"Continue it?" Aidan blurted out. "But why? Isn't the point to end it, get our troops out, whatever the policy is?"

"Would be, you'd think." Stephen drank more of his coffee and tossed his smoke outside. As he brought the window back up he said, "There's this think tank in DC, and it's got its tentacles into the military-industrial complex. Their goal is to prolong the war and maintain a US combat troop presence there for as long as possible. Osama bin Laden was a blip on the radar screen to them; they just want the show to keep going." He again looked pointedly at Aidan. "They also have access to the hardware that allowed them to try and rub you out."

Aidan stared back at his brother. "What does that mean?"

"One word," Stephen replied, and paused for emphasis. "Drones."

Stephen nodded when Aidan didn't answer. "You heard me right," he said, "that was a drone strike. They're called UAS, but you already know that. Most of these operations are in the hands of indie contractors. The military doesn't have enough of the technology or the skilled users yet. Not a lot of checks and balances either."

Stephen's voice became a growl. "They don't care about the Afghans," he went on, "and they don't give a fuck about our troops, either. They want their hooks into the pipeline, and the resources of that God-forsaken country. It's another Iraq -- they want all they can get out of it, see?"

"Who are these people?"

"That's what you will soon find out," Stephen replied, "but the person in question that is your springboard is very close."

Stephen grabbed the bag, passed it out the driver's side window to a blonde woman in shades. She made the grab and was onto Sepulveda. The handoff took barely a second to complete.

Stephen swung the car around and backed it against the rear brick wall of the office, between two trucks. "Company car," he commented, "we'll be cool here."

Stephen lit a Marlboro while Aidan fired up his first Gitanes in what felt like ages. The two smoked, drank their coffee and viewed the planes that took off and landed. They spoke of the family, what their sister was up to, Katie's kids and other mundane matters like two workmen on a break.

"So what's going on?" Aidan asked at length.

Stephen kept his gaze forward, but his eyes shifted this way and that, one ear on the two-way radio that crackled in the alcove above the stereo. "A complete and total fuckup," he replied, "that's what's going on. You were targeted, man. That missile wasn't fired by some shoulder-packing yahoo – it was one of ours."

"Ours?"

"Yeah." Stephen removed his shades to reveal his own blue eyes. "The target was too well protected," he explained. "The deal's this: those people you went to see in Afghanistan? Most of them are connected to the NATO mission in one way or another. Some of it is political, but mostly it's business. The pipeline, that kind of thing."

Aidan pondered this as Stephen continued, "Someone informed individuals based in Kabul that you'd be interviewing those people. That someone is connected to a group in Washington that wants the whole mission to fail in order to continue the war."

"Continue it?" Aidan blurted out. "But why? Isn't the point to end it, get our troops out, whatever the policy is?"

"Would be, you'd think." Stephen drank more of his coffee and tossed his smoke outside. As he brought the window back up he said, "There's this think tank in DC, and it's got its tentacles into the military-industrial complex. Their goal is to prolong the war and maintain a US combat troop presence there for as long as possible. Osama bin Laden was a blip on the radar screen to them; they just want the show to keep going." He again looked pointedly at Aidan. "They also have access to the hardware that allowed them to try and rub you out."

Aidan stared back at his brother. "What does that mean?"

"One word," Stephen replied, and paused for emphasis. "Drones."

Stephen nodded when Aidan didn't answer. "You heard me right," he said, "that was a drone strike. They're called UAS, but you already know that. Most of these operations are in the hands of indie contractors. The military doesn't have enough of the technology or the skilled users yet. Not a lot of checks and balances either."

Stephen's voice became a growl. "They don't care about the Afghans," he went on, "and they don't give a fuck about our troops, either. They want their hooks into the pipeline, and the resources of that God-forsaken country. It's another Iraq -- they want all they can get out of it, see?"

"Who are these people?"

"That's what you will soon find out," Stephen replied, "but the person in question that is your springboard is very close."

He put back on his seatbelt, and Aidan did the same. "I'll take you back," Stephen continued, "but roll your window down. You get to receive."

The warm breeze passed through the car as Stephen turned back onto Sepulveda. In the distance, Aidan saw a bicyclist.

"Get ready." Stephen kept the Impala at 35 as they caught up to the helmeted, dark-skinned woman in the spandex outfit of a competitive rider. At the last moment, she reached behind her back, and a small package flew into Aidan's lap.

Stephen put on speed. Aidan looked at the thick envelope, sealed by tape with his initials on it. "Don't open that," Stephen told him, "not till you're back in DC. Philippa can see 'em. Use whatever you want for the show. You two have the next part of the job; she knows the deal. All you guys gotta do is follow, target and shoot."

"Not kill someone, I hope you mean."

Stephen laughed. "No, with your camera, brother! Look, I can't say any more than that, okay? I'm in enough trouble doing this, but the chief owes me more than a few favors, so it's all good."

"Okay." Aidan's fingers felt the envelope's contours. "Negatives here, too?"

"Of course." He folded the edges of the envelope and stuffed it into his jacket while Stephen popped a CD from the overhead visor into the player. "We made copies," his brother added. "Got a good lab here."

"Vertigo" blared out of the stereo system as Stephen tore down the short stretch and swerved into the American Airlines terminal area. Stephen was the world's biggest U2 fan. "Sorry this had to happen, Aidan," he said over the Edge's guitar riffs, "but we need your help now. We need to get this under control, but we can't act yet. Don't feel guilty about this, okay? It's just the games."

Aidan nodded. He was now unofficially undercover, at least for the next part of this insanity. He couldn't blame his brother but didn't like it one bit.

"Thanks, Stephen," he said instead and offered his hand.

"Come here." Stephen grabbed Aidan and gave his brother a bear hug. "Love you, man," he said, "and thanks."

Aidan returned the affection. "Gotcha," he replied as he jumped out, shouldered his Minolta and headed inside. There were two steps and Aidan heard the car pull away. He didn't look back.

9 - Let Love Get Away

Aidan lowered the window as the Land Rover made its way down M Street. Two cars ahead a silver, late model Mercedes cruised, one well known to his current driver.

Philippa navigated around the vehicle between them as it turned off, but took pains to keep her distance. Minolta in hand, Aidan prepared for the next round of shots.

The producer was the welcome wagon at Dulles. The two embraced, and Philippa planted a kiss on him, more friendship than what they once had. "I can't believe this shit is happening," she said during the ride, her agitation obvious. "Your brother sent one of his colleagues to my apartment at eleven last night. I had no idea I was gonna be caught up in some kind of damned espionage caper."

"Neither did I," Aidan replied, "but we've become the strike force. Stephen's people can't make a move yet, and a job is too risky. They decided the people least likely to be suspected would be best – that's us."

"You know how this makes me feel," Philippa continued.

"Think I feel any better about it?" Aidan was exhausted and didn't want to hear it, even from Philippa. "I went there for an interview and to take pictures," he returned. "I didn't plan to get myself killed."

Philippa sighed. "I know," she said, "I'm not mad at you, Aidan, sorry. I just would like to know how the hell a straightforward story about Kabul turned into this! We're not counter-terrorists, for fuck's sake."

Aidan didn't have anything to say; Philippa knew what he knew.

After a stop at Aidan's apartment, the two drove to Philippa's. Over an extra-large pizza and a six-pack of MGD, they formulated their end of the operation.

Philippa spread a floor plan of the network's broadcast studio on her coffee table while Aidan opened a box about the size of a video game console. "Guy left it here," she explained, "said you'd know how to use it."

Aidan examined the equipment inside while Philippa went over the outline. "I've booked you for Callie's show tonight," she said. "You should dress up a little, but you don't need to go with the whole suit and tie thing. We know how you work, and that'll lend to the show."

"Got it." Aidan listened as he tested the device. He'd used similar gear before, but would have only one shot.

"Let me remind you of Callie's routine." Philippa ran her long black fingernail over the document. "Makeup comes first. Then she'll go past the Scream Room to here." Philippa indicated a small square at the end of the corridor.

Aidan grinned at Philippa's nickname for the "Green Room." Such places often did turn into the former, based on the attitudes of host and guest alike. "Understood," he replied. "I make my move, and the rest follows."

"Predicated on Callie following routine," Philippa noted, "which she does, but it's a very tight window."

Aidan returned to real time as Philippa slowed. Ahead of them, the driver of the Mercedes executed a perfect parallel park, between two other luxury cars. They could not pass; the driver most certainly would recognize the Rover. They stopped, and Philippa took the risk of switching on her flashers. To anyone else, it would look as though they were waiting for someone to come out of one of the other homes on the street.

The door of the Mercedes opened, and a shapely, nylon sheathed leg emerged, preceded by a dark blue high heel. The rest of the woman in the suit, matched perfectly by the shoes, got out. Purse over her shoulder, the woman brushed her long brown hair back and keyed the car alarm. Callie Fontaine-Smith swung with self-assurance along the sidewalk, up the steps and into the exclusive home. She did not notice them.

"Okay," Aidan said.

Philippa put the Rover back in gear and slowly brought the SUV down the street. As they approached, Aidan lowered his window and took a series of photos of each car on this side of the block with particular focus on the license plates. Most were DC tags, the "Taxation Without Representation" message on each. There were two from Virginia and one diplomatic plate, all of which Aidan captured.

Philippa drove around the block while Aidan changed to a telephoto lens. Back down M Street once more Philippa stopped directly in front of the home Callie had entered.

Aidan aimed through the main window, saw what he needed and clicked the shutter. "Got 'em."

The window slid up, and Philippa guided the Rover out of the suburbs. Aidan spun off the film while they turned onto to 14th Street; they passed through Seaton Park and onto New York Avenue. "Got a nice little shot of that reunion," Aidan commented.

"I'll bet," Philippa replied. "I recognized a lot of those cars, too--good friends of other good friends." She shook her head. "This is going to be one hell of a scandal, Aidan," she continued. "That's one thing, but you realize this is tantamount to blackmail as well."

"I know," Aidan said. He put the Minolta away and leaned his seat back as Philippa glided the Rover past two slow-moving cars. "We should be able to get these developed at Photo, right?"

"Right," Philippa replied, "and I'll run you back to your place so we can see about your clothes," she added with a chuckle.

Like with Stephen, Aidan had to laugh. The story was beyond surreal at this point.

* * *

"So let me get this straight," Mima asked as they walked the streets of Tokyo, "your brother knew about the attack, who was involved, and somehow got you and your producer to go after this Callie? Why? It doesn't sound like your line of work."

Aidan gave a derisive laugh. "I'll get to how Stephen knew in a moment," he replied. He lit a Gitanes (Mima brought him to a tobacconist in Shibuya Ward who specialized in foreign brands) and looked around. Mima had suggested getting out. Aidan was glad for this, and he tried hard not to look over his shoulder.

They were in a fashionable shopping and commercial district. The midmorning weather was sunny, but with a chill in the air. As school was in session, there were few young people about. Aidan saw the typical shoppers and a scattering of salarymen and women, corporate and otherwise.

Aidan's shaded eyes analyzed the first group, then stopped himself. It was over.

"Technically," he continued, "Phil and I would not be involved in such a thing, but by then it became too delicate for official hands. The connections Callie had with some of those people made it too close for any direct action."

Mima considered this while they waited at an intersection. "What did Callie have to do with it?" she inquired. "She's a talk show host."

"On the face of it, yes." The light changed, and they joined a dozen others in crossing the street. "Callie's web of colleagues, friends, guests of her show and the like have led to other, more powerful contacts," Aidan explained. "Once her show became popular, Callie was less discreet about her political views. The journalistic community would have frowned upon her hobnobbing with these types years ago. Not so anymore."

* * *

"Hey! Get the brows even, damn it!"

Callie sat up in her padded makeup chair, or "throne" as Philippa called it. She gave an overdramatic sigh, swept her hair back and let the makeup artist have another go at her face.

Aidan tried to conceal his grin. He sat in the chair beside Callie. Fortunately the young woman working on him didn't have a lot to do. Aidan hated makeup, but this person had "done" him before.

The other woman wasn't having so easy a time. Callie was nervous as hosts often were before a show. "Aidan," she asked, "has Phil gone over the plan with you?"

"Yes," Aidan replied, "you'll work through some of the photos, plus video that was grabbed by the network."

"Actually," she sniffed, "we had to pirate it from al Jazeera. We'll probably be threatened with a lawsuit, but people steal from us all the time." The two student interns from American U. who stood by giggled. One did so ingratiatingly, the other because she enjoyed seeing Callie riled.

Makeup complete, Aidan stood up. He was wearing a black sport jacket, one Philippa had to brush off at the apartment, but it looked okay. That and the gray turtleneck didn't go with Aidan's jeans, but he would be sitting at the news desk.

Philippa leaned in. She was in one of her black Goth dresses, plus her ever-present fishnets and boots. The skull tattoo, outlined in black, was visible on her right shoulder. "Fifteen minutes to air, Callie. You ready?" She called, with an anxious look at Aidan.

"Yeah." Callie nodded to the makeup girl, who backed away. She rose, turned and examined her face in the mirrors that ran the length of the makeup room. She checked her dark green suit and silken, off-white blouse were correct, along with her string of pearls. A quick glance at her Rolex and Callie said, "Be right back." She passed between Aidan and Philippa and headed down the hall.

They leaned out and watched Callie walk down the tiled floor to the private washroom. She went inside; they heard the lock snap shut.

"You ready?" Philippa asked. She looked and sounded scared.

"Go time." Aidan walked down the hallway and reached inside his coat pocket as he did so. At the door, Aidan used his American Express card for another purpose, and effortlessly slipped the lock. He looked back once more. Philippa, the makeup girls and interns were all watching.

He winked and went inside. Aidan silently closed the door, but left it unlocked. The restroom was done in a white tile to chest level with peach drywall to the ceiling. To his right in a small alcove was a sink, across from this an automatic hand dryer. The stall was closed. Aidan could hear Callie finishing her business, and the toilet flushed.

Aidan waited. He was no longer worried. A dark calm had come over him.

The door opened, and Callie stepped out. Her surprise was genuine. "Uh...Aidan, what are you doing in here?" Callie asked. She wasn't angry, more stunned than anything.

"Seeking answers, Callie," he replied. "Before we go out there, I want to know what you were up to today and in the days before."

"Up to? Aidan, what are you talking about?" Her cheekbones, highlighted by the makeup, flushed. Callie tried to play dumb; it wasn't working.

"The drone strike," Aidan replied, his voice level, but expressionless. "I was set up in Kabul. Someone wanted me dead, but instead they got my driver, and quite a few other innocent people."

Callie's body twitched. "And you think I had something to do with that?" She asked, fake surprise in her voice. "Aidan, I think you've been flying high for too long."

She was about to pass by Aidan, but his stiff arm shoved her back. Callie managed to keep herself upright by backing against the sink. Before she could respond, Aidan put a finger to his lips. "Quiet now, Miss –– you have a lot of explaining to do. The only people who knew I was going to Kabul to interview those individuals were Philippa and you. The Embassy knew as well, but my contact didn't squeal, and Phil doesn't have the connections you do."

Like his brother, Aidan's anger rose in a slow burn. Callie was cornered, and she knew it.

"What are you talking about, Aidan?" She shot back. "Where does this conspiracy theory come from?"

The door opened. Aidan didn't have to turn to know that his brother had stepped into the restroom. Stephen was dressed as he'd been in L.A., plus a battered leather jacket. Behind him were two men in dark suits.

Callie's eyes darted amongst the new arrivals. "Who the hell are you?" She demanded.

Stephen displayed his ID. "Special Agent Connor, FBI," he said in his clipped, law enforcement voice. These," he added as he motioned to the others, "are two of my colleagues, but their names aren't necessary unless you need them. You've left quite a trail behind you, Ms. Fontaine-Smith. Why not let's get all the complicated stuff out of the way?" He checked his watch. "Ten minutes to air time."

"What?" Callie looked ready to have a nervous breakdown, but she recovered. "What exactly is this interrogation about, Mister?" She demanded in her haughty, on-air voice. "If I'm to be questioned, I want my attorney present."

"Let's get to the point," Aidan replied. "You set me up, Callie. Philippa said you were rip-shit about the assignment, and that your boss approved it. The people who were gathered at that house in Georgetown this afternoon are among a lot who don't like the idea of peace of any kind in Afghanistan. You tipped them off, and they tipped their people off. At least an educated guess would have it that way."

Callie's jaw dropped. "I saw you go into that house on M Street this afternoon, Callie," he continued. "We've got photos. We also have a fabulous shot of you standing in the middle of the room in a most intimate position with one of those men. A certain Mr. Jonathan McClellan, am I right?"

A gasp. The name dropped was well known: a low-level Reagan Administration official, McClellan rose to become an influential political advisor. He was also a columnist, a blogger and regular talking head on a certain news channel. Add to it: Callie wasn't married, but McClellan was.

"Mr. McClellan," Stephen now took up the tale, "is also one of the chief executives of GoldHawk Enterprises. They have extensive contracts with our defense industry, including one for their UAS, or Unmanned Aircraft Systems. Otherwise known as," Stephen paused, "drones, one of which carried out an unauthorized attack in Kabul the other day."

"Just because I was in Georgetown, that doesn't mean I committed a crime!" Callie snapped. "How could I call in an air strike on you from thousands of miles away, Aidan? Answer me that!"

"You passed on the information," Aidan replied, "and McClellan ordered someone to do the job. It's easy to make things happen when you're one of the owners of the company. As an added attraction, McClellan has a fascinating little group of right-wingers in his crew, the so-called Foundation for American Freedom."

"An organization," Stephen continued, "that has been under investigation for more than a year. Several members, including McClellan have moneyed interests in Afghanistan, Ms. Fontaine-Smith. Your movements and contacts with them are no secret, and we've plenty of documentation on that." Stephen's voice turned harsh. "You better start talking--why was my brother targeted and for what purpose?"

Callie shook again, partly from rage, but mostly fear. "I didn't have anything to do with it," she said in a low voice, "I didn't know that would happen. Aidan was getting close," she went on as her pitch rose, "too close to people who are going to turn that nation over to a bunch of one-world elitists, who will show no thanks to this country."

"That's not exactly America's call, is it?" Aidan countered. "It's the Afghan's country; it is theirs to govern as they see fit, whether we like it or not."

"But that nation has resources that will keep America in its rightful place in the world!" Callie shot back. "We need bases for the war on terror, and to secure the gas pipeline. Those people have no mandate; it's a matter of time before they nationalize the companies that operate the line. There will be nothing for us!"

"They haven't done that part yet," Aidan noted, "but let's focus on trying to kill me. What did you tell McClellan and those others?"

"Only that you were going!"

"And whom I would be interviewing." Aidan made it a statement, not a question.

"I told them that, yes!"

"They knew my whole itinerary," Aidan went on, "and my schedule. You had access to my movements, based on what I reported to Philippa. GoldHawk had me under surveillance from the moment I got there. So it came down to a matter of timing," he added with a smirk, "apart from my turn to go for coffee."

Callie's long nails dug into her hands. Her face was crimson through the makeup, but that was secondary to her audience. She'd cracked, and Aidan enjoyed watching it.

"Now that's settled," Stephen said, "allow me to enlighten you about the identity of one Mansur al-Sajadi, the driver of the vehicle who was killed, along with nearly a hundred others."

He produced a second identity card. It bore Mansur's face, but even Aidan was surprised at the information on it. "Mr. al-Sajadi was Assistant CIA Station Chief in Kabul," Stephen explained, his voice growing louder by the syllable. "He was also an American citizen. You are now under arrest, Ms. Fontaine-Smith, for complicity in the murder of a federal agent."

Stephen nodded to his fellows, who stepped forward. One snapped a pair of handcuffs on Callie's wrists behind her back while the other read her Miranda rights. After being asked if she understood them, Callie replied, "Yes, of course I do." She then turned and glared at Aidan and Stephen. "You guys have no case," she sneered, "I'll deny everything!"

"Like you could." Aidan reached into his inside coat pocket and drew out the recording device, which he handed to Stephen. "I think you have a lot of explaining to do, Callie," he added, "downtown. Don't worry, that guy who does weekends will cover for you. So if you'll excuse me, I've got to go do some TV."

"Thanks, Bro," Stephen said as he left the room. Aidan could hear Callie's screamed obscenities all the way down the hall to the studio. He also heard the additional wild threats cast in his direction, but he didn't care. Aidan walked onto the set, rounded the desk and settled into the seat opposite a twenty-something man in a pinstriped suit that didn't look right on him.

As he made the young man's acquaintance, Aidan clipped the wireless mic to his lapel and did a quick level check. He set the ear monitor in place and looked over toward the two cameras and the Floor Manager. Standing beside the latter was Philippa. She gave him thumbs up, but she wasn't smiling.

The FM made the countdown to air, and Aidan turned his attention to the host as he opened the program. "Good evening; tonight, an inside view of Afghanistan you never knew existed…"

* * *

"My God." Mima stared over her can of Vivo Coffee while Aidan put his to use. They were seated on a bench near a rank of vending machines. They stopped for drinks, and so Aidan could smoke.

"A lot stronger language than that was used." Aidan sucked deeply on his Gitanes. "The story got lost in what followed, though Callie's network did their best to downplay it. The shit hit the fan with the scandal that followed, though. There was the intrigue, not to mention Callie's involvement with McClellan on the personal level."

Mima eyed Aidan, attentive but in search of more than his expression. "Where do things stand now?" she asked. "What happened to Callie?"

"She's free on bail," Aidan replied, "and she's singing to anyone who'll listen. No jail time I guess, but her broadcast career is done." He took another drag. "I'm not bothered," he said. "Callie dug her hole, but she'll find work elsewhere. There've been no arrests yet, but a number of Foundation members were questioned. McClellan was one of them; his wife has already filed for divorce. GoldHawk's involvement in the UAS program was suspended. There's a second investigation going. I probably will be subpoenaed, and I may even have to testify before Congress. I'll do it, but..."

Aidan's set his can down on the bench beside him and looked away.

"But what?" Mima's hand took his. Aidan looked back at her for a long moment, then sighed and leaned over. Another type of stimuli entered. He heard a song by a New York folk duo in his head, and Aidan didn't want to hear it now...

> *"Well, I'm standin' here, tryin' to figure out what I'm after*
> *And I seem so far away from my dreams*
> *There's only one good thing I know now that matters*
> *And my pride won't let me take what I need..."*

"Phil and I," he said, "we're friends, but she was spooked by the whole thing. We were on the outs anyway, but this finished us. We were made to play dirty. Philippa's a lot of things, but she's not that kind of person. She didn't blame me for it, but any chance I had of getting her back was gone."

"Do you still love her?" Mima asked.

Aidan sighed. "Yes," he admitted, "very much. If ever we work together again, it's business, that's all. I don't like borrowing phrases from songs because I'd like to think I can do better than that," Aidan added, "but I've let love get away. I let her go, Mima, but it wasn't us --it was me."

> *"And I been takin' my time, keepin' my distance*
> *Then tellin' myself, I won't make those same mistakes*
> *I been so afraid of fallin'*

I may have gone and let love get away..."

The words tumbled out. "I don't like what I've turned into, Mima," he said, "I got used, by the system, by my own brother. I'm a journalist, Mima, not a spy. I know why things went the way they did, but I became a tool. That's one thing I've hated more than any."

Aidan squeezed the still-lit cigarette in his fingers. "Callie is a tool of the network," he went on, "and especially of her own politics and image. We're all tools in some way, but I want out of that."

He threw down his smoke and hid it under his boot. "I feel like, despite all the wonderful things I've seen, the people I've met," he continued, "I've been used for my talents, Mima. I didn't go to Kabul to get myself or Mansur killed. I went for a story, and there was one there, one some people didn't want told. I had to do my job, but then it became something else.

"Mansur was my friend," Aidan went on. "I should have been the one to die, Mima. I wouldn't have had to know why, and he'd be alive."

"Aidan," Mima said as she now held his hand in both of hers, "Mansur knew the dangers. He knew he could get killed. You mustn't blame yourself for his death or the deaths of the others. You were just there; that's not your fault."

"I know." Aidan sat up and put his other hand over Mima's to try and keep them from trembling. "I only wanted the story," he said, "but therein lies my problem. I've been all over the world, but I don't think I've ever actually seen it. I chase what others want me to chase. I push open doors the people on the other side don't want to open. I'm as rotten as Callie in a different way; there are human beings behind the stories, and I've had to forget about them in pursuit of what I thought I wanted."

He sighed. "I guess I lied a minute ago," he said. "I do feel guilty over Callie--we entrapped her. The wire job was at the least unethical, if not illegal. Stephen calls it, 'the games', but I don't like those games, Mima. That's not what I am, and that was the last straw between Philippa and me." He sighed. "I became what she despises."

Mima put her arms about Aidan's shoulders. "Is that why you're here?" She asked. "To get away from all that, and from what you feel you've become? Perhaps to get away from Philippa, too?"

"I may have gone and let love get away..." Aidan rested his head on her shoulder, and she held him.

"Yes," he whispered.

10 - Eko

"I know you have work to do," Aidan said as they climbed the stairs to Mima's apartment, "sorry to take you from it."

Mima's response to his apology was to whack him on the shoulder. "*Baka!* Stop apologizing, Aidan," She shouted, but with a grin. "You have nothing to be sorry for. You had to let that out."

"I did," Aidan replied, "and thank you, Mima. I have a lot to sort out, and I couldn't do it at home."

"You came a long way to do that," Mima observed as they entered the hallway, "but you do feel better, right?"

"I do," Aidan said. "Like you intimated, I had to let go."

Mima slid her key into the lock. "I wish I could do that sometimes."

The statement was odd because of how Mima said it. "Well, you do," Aidan replied, "but in your own way. You're on a different method, though."

They entered the apartment. Mima's glance was inquisitive. "In what way?"

"You let your emotions out," Aidan explained, "through your work. Sometimes it doesn't seem to be the work itself, but rather how you do it."

Mima kicked off her shoes by the door, threw her jacket onto the bed and headed to the computer. "I suppose you mean," she replied, "by my ethic of sitting before this thing for hours at a time like a geek?"

"In a way," Aidan replied, "but 'geek' doesn't seem a kind word for it." He returned to the couch and checked his iPhone. There were no messages of concern, apart from a text from Stephen. It included a brief update on the case, and his brother's regards.

Aidan texted a response; he had no news to report, at least nothing Stephen needed to know about.

"Oh," Mima called, "want to go drinking tonight? I feel you could use it."

Aidan chuckled. "Who with?"

"Sora wants out of the house." Mima indicated an email on her screen. "Since we'll be with her, Suemi isn't so worried." She paused. "Eko is coming along, too."

"You don't seem so enthused, all of a sudden," Aidan noted.

Mima brought her project up on the screen and began to edit with her mouse. "I am very fond of Eko," she replied, "but she is at times too much for me."

Aidan leaned on the side of her worktable. "How's that?" he asked. "I can see Sora being that way to some."

"Eko," Mima replied, her eyes fixed on the screen, "is a genuine, good person, but she is concerned with herself. I'm sure all she'll talk about tonight is her latest boyfriend, what she's bought, where she's going for vacation, that kind of thing. It's all about her, you might say."

"Wears you down, huh?"

Mima picked up a microfiber cloth and cleaned her glasses. "To be fair," she said, "there is nothing Eko wouldn't do for us if we needed her. You will like her, though," she added, "and I should not prejudice your opinion. I'm sorry."

"*Baka!*" Aidan playfully slapped Mima on her shoulder. "Who's sorry now? Don't worry," he added, "I'll draw my own conclusions. But," he continued as he leaned closer to Mima, "thanks for the warning."

The two shared the joke with a laugh. Aidan needed one, but Mima needed it more.

Harajuku lived up to its name, Aidan discovered. It was the place to be heard and seen as evidenced by the numerous musicians, street performers and especially cosplay characters. Aidan brought his Minolta, and the locals were more than happy to show off their style for him.

The club he and Mima entered was a microcosm. From their high, round table off the bar, they could see its length, dominated by the young, hip and casual of Tokyo. Down a short flight of stairs, past the video game terminals was the dance floor, where the aforementioned mingled with *otaku* of both sexes under the flashing neon lights. A techno DJ presided over the enclosed space. Partially hidden by his laptop, turntables and related gear, he cranked out a series of bass-heavy mixes.

"Having fun?" Mima asked.

"I am," Aidan replied as he finished off his first Asahi of the night. "I'll get this one."

Mima nodded, and Aidan moved through the crowd to an open spot at the bar. Over the noise, he managed to order two more Asahi's, which made the female bartender smile. The Japanese loved a *gaijin* who made an effort to speak the language.

Bottles in hand, Aidan turned at the sound of a familiar voice. Sora had arrived. All in black, she wore a shirt that exposed one shoulder and the tank top beneath it, with a long lace skirt to match. With her was the woman who had to be Eko.

As Aidan watched them share hellos with Mima, Eko turned and looked directly at him. Their eyes locked.

Eko was everything Mima described: she stood no more than five-one, not counting the chunky heels of her boots. She wore a dark-colored sweater dress, which cut off around mid-thigh with black tights beneath. Eko also had on a denim jacket, expensive by the look of the decorative studs that adorned it.

He slowly approached. Eko's long hair was dyed blonde, or at least the attempt had been made. The result turned out "blorange," a term coined one of Aidan's Japanese-American friends. Her eyes were large and brown, and there was one hell of a light coming from them.

Aidan got an overly loud hello and a hug from Sora, and she then introduced Eko. The young woman was as vivacious as Sora, but more controlled.

"So this is Aidan-san," Eko appraised. She offered her hand, which Aidan took, and they exchanged polite bows. "A pleasure to meet you," she added.

"Nice to meet you, too." Aidan retook his seat. Eko chose the one beside him, which placed Sora across from Aidan.

Sora hung her coat over the back of her chair. "I'll get the drinks, Eko," she said. "What do you want?"

"Cosmo," Eko replied, and Sora bounced off to the bar. In spite of Mima's intimation that Eko was "too much" for her, she did speak with her old friend the same as anyone else. The conversation was spirited, though Mima proved herself right about Eko being about Eko. The first topic was of her customer service job, and the display of her jacket.

Sora returned during this exchange and passed a martini-shaped glass to Eko. Sora raised her bottle of Asahi and said, "To good friends, *Kanpai!*"

"Cheers," Aidan replied as the others responded with the native version of the toast.

So far, Mima was correct, Aidan thought. Eko was talking about her life up to the moment, but Aidan thought everyone did that to some extent.

Then Eko turned to him. "How about you, Aidan-san? Mima and Sora have made you sound most attractive," she said. "It's your turn."

Aidan brought Eko up to date on why he was in Japan, but left out the personal details. Eko was attentive as she sipped her drink. She listened, made eye contact, and occasionally asked questions. It wasn't an interview, but Aidan found himself being drawn in the way he would do with a subject. When turned on him Aidan resisted that approach; but Eko had some skill of this kind, and she was using it.

The conversation soon shifted back to the women. Mima got in some updates on her project and the deadline she faced. Sora discussed her latest artwork, and Eko again veered off into her life, plus the ongoing situation at home.

"They're not giving you trouble, are they?" Sora asked. Aidan assumed that meant Eko's parents.

"Oh, no," Eko replied, "they're fine. I am waiting for the right man, one that interests me in all ways." She cast a direct glance toward Aidan and continued, "I know what you mean though, the 'Parasite' thing. I so could not care less what people say about that. It's my business, and nobody else's."

"I've been told about that expression," Aidan cut in. "Everyone has given me a different view of it, Eko--what is yours?"

Eko considered the question as she finished off her Cosmopolitan. "Should I even say?" She asked her friends. "I don't want to bring everyone down."

Mima shook her head, and Sora did the same, partly on the former's cue. "It's no different here than any other time, Eko," Sora replied.

"Very well." Turning to Aidan, Eko said, "We are cast as 'Parasite Singles.' A university professor coined the term several years ago. The concept insinuates we women stay at home and leech off our parents so we can enjoy our lives."

Eko turned serious. "For the record," she continued, "I have never lived off my family. I work, I pay rent, and I take care of my side of the duplex they own. My mother and father are supportive of me; they want me to find a good man. I also want someone that can look after both of us. And he has to be smart, you see? I'm not wasting my life for just anyone."

The explanation was not difficult for Aidan to read. While not taking her family for a ride, Eko had a high standard for any potential husband to meet.

"There's another thing," Eko added as she pushed her glass to the side. "I do want to get married, and yes, I want children one day. The idea that we must all stop working, catch a husband and open our legs at the slightest indication he wants sex is garbage. Times have changed; Japan is a country that adapts to the world around it, yet we have such views on women? I don't accept that."

She sighed. "I am sorry." Eko placed her hand on Aidan's wrist for emphasis, "I didn't mean to go off, but that's how it is, at least in my view. These two right here," she indicated Mima and Sora, "are among the best friends I could ask for. We've lived each other's lives since middle school. That's one thing I'll never let go of."

Sora put her arms around Eko and kissed her. "We love you, Eko," she replied. "Don't think we're judging you."

"None of us do, Eko," Mima added.

"I'm not either," Aidan said. "You have made your case, Eko, and you're right, that is your business."

Eko smiled gratefully and nodded. "Thank you," she replied, "I appreciate that." She indicated the now-empty bottles about her. "I'll get the next one," she offered, "I think I owe you a round."

She was up and off to the bar, and Aidan could not stop his eyes from following her. Eko's slim frame filled the tight dress and her boots nicely.

Aidan turned back to his friends. Sora smiled in an effort to make up for the dark cloud that formed over Mima. "What is it?" Aidan asked.

"You just got Eko," Mima replied. She polished off her beer and added, "You got her as she is, Aidan; can't say I didn't warn you."

"I hope you don't feel sorry about that," he said. "I do like her, and Eko certainly can stand up for herself."

"True," Sora replied, "and you know, the parasite thing? I mean, we're all in our thirties, and we don't have anyone in our lives to speak of, apart from ourselves. I know I'm unlikely to go anywhere past my parents' home, but I have a reason."

Mima nodded agreement. "I have my work," she added, "and you've seen that, Aidan. It's all I can do to make a living on my commissions. Eko at least has a cushion to work within."

Eko returned, another Cosmo and three Asahi's in expert hands. "Here we are," she called and set down the drinks for each, her own last.

As she sat again, Eko looked once more at Aidan. He was being hit upon, and out of the corner of his eye, he could tell Mima was not impressed.

Aidan wondered what to do. He felt a stirring within, one he'd not had in a long time. In hadn't happened since he first met Philippa…

"Hey!" Eko exclaimed. "Sorry I forgot, but I got an email from Kaga. She's coming back to Tokyo for a visit in a couple days. She wants to hook up with everyone."

Sora was instantly excited, and while Mima smiled, Aidan got the feeling she wasn't totally thrilled at this prospect, either.

Sora began to discuss with Eko what they should do when Kaga hit town. Aidan leaned over to Mima. "You all right?"

"Yeah," Mima replied. "I want to see Kaga too, but it's hard."

"Should we go?"

"No, it's cool. Besides," Mima added with a chuckle, "I think Eko likes you."

"That gonna be a problem?"

Mima shook her head. "No," she said matter-of-factly, "I knew you and she would get on, and I'm not your mom."

Aidan left it at that. The four drank, and the bar continued to fill up. Near the end of the round, Aidan excused himself for nature's call. He carefully passed through a four-deep line of people at the bar for the men's room. Inside, Aidan completed his mission, washed and headed back out. In the alcove, he found Sora.

"Oh, hi." Sora looked worried.

"Waiting for the others?" He asked.

"No." Sora shook her head, and then stepped close to Aidan. "Listen," she said, "I should not ask, but is Mima all right?"

"You're asking me?" Aidan replied.

Sora shrugged again, and she shifted from one foot to the other. "I'm sure it was the mention of Kaga's name," she said, "I don't know what she's told you about that."

"Some," Aidan replied, "but there's more to it, isn't there?"

Sora nodded vigorously. "Please, Aidan," she said, her voice worried, "don't tell Mima I'm talking about this. Mima is still hurting over Kaga, and it's not just the relationship. It's a buildup of all that's been tearing at her the past fifteen years."

It was hard to tell if Sora's emotions were a product of her bipolarity, concern over Mima or both. "Can you tell me?" Aidan asked. "Mima only said the relationship with Kaga caused problems in her family. Is that so?"

Sora nodded again, and Aidan, even in the dark corner of this place saw Sora's eyes widen. "Yes," she said, "Mima lost her family, she really lost them! She never talks about them anymore. Part of me," she admitted after a furtive look around, "thinks it was for the best, but I could never say that to Mima."

"How so?"

Sora shook her head. "Mima's father," she replied, "was not a likeable man. When we were girls, he would put Mima down in front of others, which you shouldn't do."

Sora's expression grew sadder. "In what way?" Aidan asked. "You mean like a loss of face?"

"Exactly." Sora reached into her bag for a tissue and carefully dabbed her eyes. Her hand shook as she checked her mascara had not run. "He was never satisfied with anything Mima did," she said. "I think he was embarrassed by Mima because she was heavier than most girls, and he almost never showed affection toward his family."

Aidan could sympathize. "My father wasn't exactly open with his praise, either," he admitted, "but if he had anything serious to say to us, he did that in private."

"Normally that is what one does," Sora replied, "but not that man. He was hard, and his heart was that of a stone."

People were working their way in and out of the alcove to use the facilities, and Sora said, "We should go back. Aidan, Mima speaks with such respect for you--she needs you right now, as her friend. I know what she went through in America, what she did to herself, and what she's doing now."

Sora's words now came rapidly, as if they might be taken from her. "She's driving herself to succeed," she went on, "to not be seen as a parasite. Even living independently, for Mima it is a struggle. Mima is like my sister; I love her so. I do my best to support her, but I have my own issues."

"Sora," Aidan promised, "Mima's already given me the support I've had to have. I'll do the same while I'm here; she's my friend too. I will give it my best."

Sora was relieved as the two returned. Mima and Eko had ordered another round. As they approached Aidan looked to Mima; through her lenses (and his own), he saw the eyes of a woman elevated by alcohol. Behind it, however, was the sadness he'd seen in Boston, and now here.

His arrival was timely, Aidan thought, but not only for him.

11 - Kaga

The group hit two more clubs in Harajuku but drank less with each stop. After a late meal at a Ramen shop near the Metro, they called it a night.

Eko, who quit drinking after the two Cosmo's, was driving Sora back to her place. Through the good wishes, Aidan got a polite hug from Eko. "A pleasure, Aidan-san," she said, "I hope to see you again while you're here."

She seemed genuine about it, and Aidan couldn't help but smile. "I hope so, too."

After a final farewell, he and Mima entered the station. Mima was in a pensive mood, and Aidan asked about it.

Mima didn't answer at first. They passed through the turnstiles and descended the stairs for the platform with a dozen other late-nighters. "I wish I knew why," she responded as they went. "I guess Eko drains me, but it's not anything she does deliberately. Eko's energy level takes more out of me than other people."

They found seats on a bench before the tracks. "You seemed saddened by some other matter," Aidan continued. "Did it have to do with Kaga?"

Mima gazed up at Aidan. "Yes," she replied, "and I would suppose that sometime tonight Sora told you about that relationship."

Aidan's start could not be controlled. Mima's reaction was noncommittal. "It's okay," she added, "Sora is a dear; she's looking out for me."

The train pulled into the station with an ear-rending screech. A hiss of hydraulics and the doors slid open. A surge of travelers exited through the doors. Those on the platform plus late arrivals rushed to get inside with the aid of Metro employees. Moments later, the train was again on its way.

Footwear of various types clicked, thumped and clattered along the walkway, up the stairs and through the building. The voices of travelers and workers faded away with the steps. There was an announcement, and all was quiet again.

Two people remained on the platform. "The story does have more chapters," Mima said. "You have told me about Kabul, Philippa and Callie – may I tell you of Kaga and myself?"

"Certainly."

"Then this begins when I was 16, as was Kaga." Mima held her hands in her lap and looked down at them as she took Aidan back in time…

* * *

There was no shade on the athletic field; players and coaches alike sweated under the hot sun. The black and gold of the practice jerseys and shorts, plus the pads and socks the players wore of the same colors didn't make conditions any better.

A scrimmage was underway, and Mima was in the defensive backfield of the second team. She and her mates wore yellow nylon vests over their jerseys to indicate which side they were on. Through her prescription goggles, Mima viewed the ground as they moved to thwart an attack down the left sideline, and especially the girl who wore number ten.

Kaga moved forward from her midfielder's spot to make the run. As she set up her defense, Mima watched Kaga and her graceful, fluid movements.

She was a head taller than Mima. In fact, Kaga was taller than almost all the other girls on the team. Her lithe, muscular body was darker than most Japanese due partly to her descent, and from being out in the sun. Kaga's bare arms were toned. Her legs, exposed from her knees to upper thighs were supple and muscular. Her brown hair went to her collar, thick and worn in a spiky, punk cut. In uniform or out, Kaga attracted attention; she had Mima's.

Kaga rushed down the sideline, back heeled the ball, spun and rushed around a defender. The star player of the junior squad the past two seasons, Kaga was a lock for varsity.

After a cross, Kaga moved up to apply pressure. Mima focused on her job. Though thicker in the body and legs than most of the girls, she was in good aerobic shape. She'd made the scorer's column only once, but being the next Shinsuke Nakamura (the footballer, not the wrestler of the same name) was for Mima beyond dreams.

Mima's chances at making varsity were not good for another reason. She was assigned number 27. While most didn't see anything remarkable about that, there was a pecking order. On Coach Usami's teams, the number one was always assigned to a goalkeeper. Number ten usually went to a striker or the team leader. Beyond this, the higher the number, the lower the status of the player.

A whistle, and the top squad set up for a corner kick on the far side. Mima placed herself to the right of the goalkeeper's box and jockeyed for position against one of the first-teamers. Soccer was a rougher game than most imagined. There was plenty of pushing, shoving and elbowing along with the trash talk of other sports. Mima was intimidated at first, but Kaga counseled her to ignore it and outthink the talkers.

The ball arced left, out in front of the box. A pair of headers and the ball sailed to Mima. She took it off her chest, gained control, shifted to her right and cleared upfield.

"Good one, Meem!" Kaga waved and grinned at Mima as she ran back into position. Mima's smile was a hidden one. It felt good to get a compliment from her.

It was not only two seasons on juniors that drew Mima toward Kaga. From the start, Mima had a "girl crush" for Kaga. Everything about her was attractive to Mima.

The two shared homeroom each of their years in high school. Kaga came off as aloof toward any but her teammates, but once she knew someone, Kaga warmed up to them.

One day early in their first year, Kaga made a deal with a classmate in order to sit next to her in homeroom. Mima could not hold back her smile. "So do you like me," she asked, "or do you need a study partner?"

Kaga laughed at the joke. "Don't worry," she assured Mima, "I'm not gonna cheat off you, but I'd appreciate having someone nearby who knew what they were doing."

The friendship began there. As time went on, Mima and Kaga found they were together more often. They ate lunch together, practiced together, and when Mima struggled on the pitch, Kaga worked out with her and offered tips to improve her play.

Mima was well aware of her fascination for Kaga and feared it. Mima altered her daily routine, but never in a way that anyone, especially Kaga would notice. She did this to see Kaga, to be in her presence and to have her as more than the girl she sat next to and played soccer with.

It should never have worked. The two were opposites. In addition to her athleticism and looks, Kaga had plenty of male suitors, or least a lot of boys who were interested in her.

Mima, on the other hand, was the nerd who happened to play sports. An honor student, Mima was proficient in all her subjects, but superior in art. That was fortunate, for Mima faced the same scrutiny from her parents most high school kids experienced. She did not, however, have the body of the standard expected for young Japanese women.

Mima was always heavy--not overweight, but "big-boned," as her mother often said. That didn't help, yet Mima was realistic enough to know she could not transform into a stick figure girl.

There was in the back of Mima's mind that maybe, just maybe, Kaga did like her. Kaga was encouraging of Mima, in soccer and her artwork. She often asked to see Mima's sketchbook. Awed by her skill, Kaga often wished aloud she could create such things.

The situation changed a few days into their third year. Practice was off, and Mima was headed home when she saw Kaga. She was leaned against the brick wall by the main entrance, school bag over her shoulder.

Mima took the image in as she approached. Kaga hated the school uniform, but she looked so good in it: the black blazer that covered the white, short-sleeved blouse and the black miniskirt accentuated everything good about Kaga; her thighs were bare to her knees, where the black legwarmers took over. Even the gold neck ribbon female students wore looked right.

After pleasantries, Mima invited her home and Kaga accepted. "I don't feel like going home, anyway," she said, "there's nothing to do."

Mima smiled, but inwardly it was a bigger one. She had an ulterior motive, and Mima was glad Kaga didn't catch on.

The bus trip from school to Mima's house was a short one, and on the way the girls talked about classes and who might make varsity. "You're in, Kaga," Mima commented. "Usami-Sensei would not have given you number ten if there was doubt."

Kaga blushed and looked out the window so Mima couldn't see. "I don't know," she replied cautiously, "I'd like to think I'll make it, but it's a new position." Kaga played forward on juniors, but Usami felt he had enough strikers. He was trying Kaga out in the midfield with an eye toward bringing her up as an extra attacker.

"Oh, come on," Mima said, "you led the juniors in goals two years running. There's no way he will leave you off it, Kaga. Me," she continued, her voice lowered, "that's another matter."

"Hey, don't talk like that." Kaga took Mima's hand and said, "You're good, Mima; just play your game and you'll make it. Besides," Kaga added, "I'd miss you if you weren't with us."

Now it was Mima's turn to blush. Kaga laughed as she saw it and put her arm around her. "I'm sorry, Meem," Kaga said (she often used Mima's nickname), "but you are a good player. And well..." There was a pause, and Kaga added, "you're a good friend, too."

Mima looked up. The girl's smile was modest but heartfelt. "You mean that?"

"Sure I do," Kaga replied. "Look, don't take this the wrong way," she went on, "but Mima, you're like the best friend I've got. Do you know what I mean?"

"How?" Mima tried not to show her excitement. "Tell me, Kaga," she added, "I need to know."

"Well..." Kaga took a deep breath, then said, "The whole time we've known each other Mima, you've treated me the way you wish people would treat you. You see me as a person, not an athlete. So many guys are after me because I play soccer and they like my body. Girls want to be around me, too, and I don't mean our teammates; it's like a status thing. I don't care for that, and I don't even know who most of my friends are."

"Can you explain that?"

Kaga thought for a moment. "Yeah," she replied, "you know how in the lunchroom, there's the team table?"

"Yes." Most of the sports teams congregated at the same tables for lunch. The varsity players would sit together (boys and girls separately, however) with the invited juniors seated further down at one end. As one of the latter, Mima never felt comfortable sitting there because it left Sora alone.

"I have friends on the team, sure," Kaga continued, "but for a lot of girls, I think it's because I can play that they accept me. I don't have any contact with most of them beyond the game. I have no idea what they honestly think of me."

Kaga tightened her arm around Mima's shoulder. "That's where you come in," she said. "You are one to me. Sora and Eko are terrific friends, too, but you're the true one."

Mima drew a shallow breath. "Kaga," she replied, "that's so sweet of you." She then added, "I like you too Kaga, very much. You are the same to me, and I admire you for everything you are."

"You do?" Kaga's eyes widened, but she understood what Mima meant. Her hand gripped Mima's more tightly as she said, "That's lovely of you too, Meem…"

She pulled Mima close; Mima felt those toned, muscled limbs surround and take her. They'd embraced on the field after a goal or a victory before but never like this. This was different.

Mima's body trembled as she reached around Kaga's shoulders. Neither heard anything else. Even the short walk from the bus stop to Mima's home went unnoticed.

As they removed their shoes in the foyer, Mima saw the space for her father was empty. That was no surprise; he worked until early evening most days, and Mima was glad he wasn't home.

Her mother was here. The small, slightly overweight woman got up from the low couch in the living room and welcomed her daughter home. She greeted Kaga with equal friendliness. After a short discussion, the girls entered Mima's bedroom.

Like all the rooms in the suburban home, the one where Mima slept was small. Her futon was in one corner, her dresser and desk in another. The rest was given over to Mima's painting. Today, a canvas the size of a large poster rested in the easel covered by a drop cloth.

Kaga removed her jacket and set it on the bed, her bag on the floor beside it. "What do you have there?" She asked.

"I've been working on this for a while," Mima replied. "I have wanted you to see this, Kaga, but first you need to close your eyes."

Amused, Kaga turned away and brought her hands to her face. "Okay," she said, "I'm not looking."

Mima slowly removed the cloth, and nervously called, "You can look now."

Kaga turned back, and Mima watched her expression change from a smile to stunned silence. The girl's eyes widened, her mouth slowly dropped open. "Oh...."

The painting was of Kaga in the soccer team's black and gold "home" kit. She was in the act of shooting, her long, lean body extended with her right leg drawn back for the kick. Featured was Mima's unique style when it came to painting the human figure: a little blurring, a minor amount of distortion, but the depiction remained sharp.

Kaga approached the easel and stared at the work. Mima grinned; she knew her friend approved.

"Mima," Kaga finally said, "this is awesome. Even if it wasn't of me, I'd say that."

Mima moved to Kaga's side. "It's for you," she declared.

"No way," Kaga replied, "I couldn't take this. It's too good, Mima. This should hang in a gallery or someplace."

"That wasn't the point," Mima told her. She took Kaga's hands in her own and faced her. "I made this for you," she said, "because you're my friend, too, Kaga. You're one of the best friends I have."

Mima no longer felt afraid. "I need you to know," Mima continued as she looked up, "that I care for you, Kaga. I am not sure how to say it, but you are someone I have looked up to all this time. You've helped me so much, Kaga, and you've given me a good feeling about myself. I've needed that as I've needed you."

There was a silence as Kaga looked down to their joined hands. It took several seconds for Kaga to find her voice.

"Mima," she finally whispered, "no one's ever told me that. Thank you; for the painting, and for what you've said."

The arms slid around Mima's body again. She slid her own up Kaga's back and peered into those eyes. "Kaga," she whispered, "I love you. You are the one friend that I love, and I don't care how that sounds. I need you to know that I'm sincere in what I say."

Kaga could barely speak in response. "You… love me?"

"Yes," Mima replied. "I can't say if it's like that way because I don't know," she admitted. "I don't know what that is."

"Neither do I," Kaga said, "but I want to know."

She pulled Mima to her tightly. "Can I," Kaga stammered, "may I?"

Mima's eyes welled up, and Kaga's face blurred before her. "Yes," she replied, "yes."

Awkwardly, two pairs of lips met and pressed against one another. Two sets of arms held to the body of the other, if possible, for dear life.

12 - Relationship

"That must have been an amazing moment," Aidan commented.

"Yes." Mima's hands were in her jacket pockets, her chin tucked down into the collar. Instead of boarding the train, the two left the Metro and took the long way home on foot. Aidan didn't protest; the walk helped clear his head.

He lit another smoke.

"Everything I'd dreamed about regarding Kaga became true," Mima continued, "though I never expected it. The first time you've ever been held by another, kissed and known precisely that this person was the one, that was it. I wanted Kaga's acceptance, her friendship, and inside I wanted more."

"Sounds like Kaga needed the same from you," Aidan observed, "to be seen for who she was as a woman."

"Exactly," Mima replied. They rounded the corner and approached the apartment building. "It was so right…"

* * *

The scene was one lovers of *Yuri* literature would have paid to see. Two girls, one tall, thin and athletic, the other smaller and of thicker body lay together on the bed in their uniforms. Mima was curled up in Kaga's arms. The bedding was askew, as were their clothes.

Her body fit perfectly with Kaga's. Mima slid her fingers along the girl's bare thigh, and felt as well as heard Kaga sigh with contentment. Both were secure within each other. "I didn't plan this, you know," Mima said quietly.

Kaga chuckled as she ran her hand through Mima's hair and kissed the top of her head. "I'm sure you didn't," she replied, "and I didn't plan on kissing you, or doing any of this."

"I hope you've no regrets," Mima said as she reluctantly moved her head to the large body pillow to be face to face with Kaga. "I don't."

The smile Mima received was as genuine as the kiss Kaga gave her lips. "None at all," she replied. "I have to wonder though, Meem--are you attracted to girls?"

"I don't know," Mima told her, and she kissed Kaga back. "I've never been interested in anyone, until you. I'm not sure what that means either, but I just knew you were special, Kaga. I've wanted to be close to you; this was more than I dared hope for."

Kaga's arms tightened about her again, and a powerful leg locked around her own. Mima drew in her breath. "You made me want you, Kaga," she whispered.

"I do want you," Kaga replied, "but I'm not sure what I am. I like boys, too, but most of them don't have any respect for me. They just want to sleep with me or hang around me."

They lay together, kissed and touched one another a few minutes more. The TV was on in the living room, and Mima's mother did not come down. She tended to leave Mima alone when her daughter was home.

At length, Kaga drew away with reluctance. "I need to ask you this, Meem."

Kaga raised herself on one elbow, and Mima took the opportunity to sit up and fix her blouse. "Ask whatever you like."

"Do you want this kept quiet, Mima?" Kaga's voice was quiet, yet earnest. "I don't worry for myself," she went on, "most people think girls who play sports are lesbians anyway. That means nothing to me, but I don't want you to be treated badly. I can keep a secret, believe me."

Mima pulled one leg to her chest. She rested her chin on her knee and again took in Kaga's body. "Normally, I would not care," she replied, "but I'm worried about what certain people will say. Not our friends or teammates, but my father and mother."

"I get that." Kaga now sat up. She passed Mima's glasses over to her from the nightstand and resituated her skirt and legwarmers. "I gather your family is rather conservative about things like this, huh?"

"Okasan's not so bad," Mima admitted, "and I know she likes you, Kaga. Otousan doesn't like things out of the ordinary. He's old-fashioned, and I'm afraid he would be against us. I don't know what to do about that."

"Then," Kaga replied as she placed her arms around Mima, "we shall keep it quiet. We can be together at my place. It's small, but my family's cool. They want me to be happy." She then smiled and rubbed her nose against Mima's. "You make me happy, Meem," she whispered.

Mima felt her face turn red. "You do the same for me, Kaga."

They kissed again. "I'm sure I love you, Mima," Kaga said. "I can keep a secret, and we can leave things as they are at school. It won't be a problem."

Mima could hear the familiar sound of her father's car pulling into the driveway. "He's home," she whispered, though she tried not to sound urgent about it. "We'd better make this look good."

"Sure." The girls quickly straightened out the rest of their clothes, brushed out their hair and set the bed comforter and pillow aright. They'd not gone that far; if Mima's parents suddenly knocked on her door, they would not have been the wiser.

Once more, Mima and Kaga embraced. "Love you, Meem," she whispered, and followed it up with a kiss.

Through it, Mima replied, "Love you, Kaga-chan..."

* * *

"So your father was kind of old-fashioned, then?" Aidan lit another Gitanes. The two now stood on the deck, Mima huddled in her jacket.

"Old-fashioned, conservative, traditional, antediluvian," Mima replied, "call it what you will. My father liked things ordered; he expected order from Mom, from me and from his subordinates at the office."

"What did he do?" Aidan realized that Mima almost never talked of her father, apart from the estrangement. He'd never even heard his name mentioned.

"He worked as a senior accountant for the Japanese division of Exxon," Mima said. "You may have noticed the old 'Esso' signs here."

Aidan chuckled. Despite Exxon changing its name in the seventies, the original moniker remained in Japan. "It's like that in Canada, too."

There was a pause, and Mima turned her head. "Hey, can I have one of those?"

Aidan was stunned. "But you don't smoke," he replied.

"I do now." Mima helped herself to one of Aidan's cigarettes and accepted a light. After a clumsy drag, Mima exhaled. "I don't know how you smoke these things," she said, "but there's more to tell you."

Aidan went over to one of the chairs and seated himself. "You've my attention as always..."

* * *

Mima smiled as she walked alongside Kaga, hand in hand. Saturday meant only a half-day of class and no afternoon soccer practice. The two were headed to the latter's home for a study session and stay-over. Mima carried an overnight bag along with her school briefcase and sketchbook. Only a couple of days had passed since Mima and Kaga made their pact. Their physical contact while at school was minimal, though both admitted that was hard to follow.

"This is nice," Mima commented as they walked. "I've never felt the need to make a show of things."

"Me neither," Kaga said. "It's sometimes hard to watch your friends with their boyfriends or whatever, but I realize this is one thing we need to keep private." She pulled Mima's arm closer and added, "I kind of like it this way."

Mima leaned against Kaga as they walked, the hands closest to their bodies laced as one. No one took undue notice of the pair; girls holding hands was not that uncommon.

Kaga's home was a simple, one-floor affair with minimal space: a sitting room, kitchen, bathroom and two bedrooms. Kaga's parents were a few years younger than Mima's and knew hers. They were so impressed by the painting of their daughter, they immediately went out and had it framed. It now hung in Kaga's room, above the bed.

Ironically Mima had never visited Kaga's home. She noted Kaga barely had room to turn around. The futon, dresser, and desk left only a narrow lane for movement. They started to undress.

"Hey," Kaga suddenly said, her voice hushed.

"Yes?" Mima asked. She watched as Kaga removed her uniform blouse to reveal a black lace bra.

Kaga smiled. "I can't help but admit it," she said, "I kind of feel the need to be close." Her voice and expression contained polite guilt and embarrassment.

"That's fine." Mima removed her glasses and set them on Kaga's dresser. She then went to Kaga and slid her arms around her waist. "We've seen each other this way before," she asked, "why should it be strange now?"

Kaga shrugged. "I guess," she replied as she searched for words, "I don't want you to think we have to do this all the time."

"If you want," Mima said as she stood on tiptoe and kissed Kaga's lips, "I want."

They shared more kisses, and Mima felt Kaga's fingers work the hidden buttons at the top of her miniskirt. A moment, and Mima felt it slide over her hips and to the floor.

The pair kissed each other again, long, deep kisses as they slowly undressed one another. Mima's fingers slowly slid Kaga's skirt off and felt the narrow strip of the thong beneath it give way to Kaga's bared buttocks. Mima's hands moved over them, and squeezed them a little as the skirt fell away.

They were now down to their underwear. Mima felt Kaga take hold of her, and slowly lead her to the futon. Mima closed her eyes as Kaga pressed her down into the pillows and comforter.

Her hands reached for the hooks that held Kaga's brassiere in place. Mima felt those lips kiss her, down to her neck, teeth in contact with her skin. Mima gasped as she felt her bikini being slid down her thighs. It was time…

* * *

"Blah!"

Mima buried her borrowed smoke in the ashtray and sat down heavily in the chair beside Aidan.

Aidan burst out laughing. "Now that killed the mood!" he exclaimed.

"So sorry!" Mima replied with a huge dose of sarcasm and laughter in her voice. "Did that titillate you, Aidan?"

"It did, yes," Aidan admitted, "but in a good way. So you and Kaga were lovers," he went on. "It sounds wonderful. More than the sexual thing, you enjoyed each other's company."

"That's right." Mima shrugged. "We explored, tested and experimented the way all young people do the first time they're in love," she said. "I won't give you all the details, but we went to a number of places, and Kaga was fantastic. Her strength, her power, they were there, but she never hurt me – at least not intentionally."

The two chuckled again, and Aidan asked, "So what went on? How did it come to a head?"

"A series of incidents," Mima explained. "The first was frightening…"

* * *

The team was again under the hot sun for afternoon conditioning drills. The season opener was only a week away, and the final cuts for varsity were to precede it. Mima was certain she was on the bubble; the team could only carry a set number of defenders, and her position was going to be a target.

Mima kept her mind off the oppressive heat and the monotony of wind sprints by thinking about the situation: as a third-year student, she could not go back to juniors as only first and second-years could play on that squad. Her soccer "career" would end if she were left off.

No loss to the team, Mima thought, or to herself. She had a full course schedule, and preparations for the college entrance exams were another matter. Mima knew she might be able to forego them because of the potential opportunity in America.

Mima's artwork won rave reviews from her teachers over the previous two years. Some of her paintings were displayed at the school's cultural events during this period. Mima planned to submit four new ones to this year's festival. Atop this, her guidance counselor encouraged Mima to apply for a foreign exchange scholarship.

Except for a trip to Hong Kong when she was little, Mima had never been out of Japan. The possibility of seeing the U.S. and getting a specialized education was exciting to her. Mima's parents, especially her father, supported the idea; both agreed to travel abroad would be good for her.

The prospects excited and scared Mima simultaneously, something she confided only to her closest friends. Mima's greatest fear was how Kaga would take it.

They talked it over at Kaga's one afternoon following school. Mima often went there on the days they didn't practice. Ostensibly it was for homework, which was partly true, but so they could be together.

In the afterglow, Mima explained what was occurring. "That's great news, Meem," Kaga told her, "you should do it. That will be an awesome experience."

"I know," Mima replied as she cuddled against Kaga's body beneath the comforter, "but at the same time it frightens."

"Why?"

Mima explained how hard it would be to go away. She admitted that while all the factors toward doing so were positive, Mima feared one thing. "It would mean leaving my family and friends," she said, "and you, Kaga. That worries me."

"I hear you." Kaga held Mima closer and kissed her. "I don't know where I will go, either," she replied. "I'm trying for a scholarship as well, an athletic one. There are a couple of schools that are interested in me, but they're not in Tokyo. I feel the same as you, Meem. I'd have to leave, but I don't want to do that because I fear I'd lose you."

"We don't have to lose one another," Mima offered. "We have each other as friends, and that will never change as far as I'm concerned. We can work out the rest."

Kaga agreed, and the two resumed their time together. Mima wondered about that conversation and how they would deal with it. Then Mima saw something else.

The defenders finished another series of sprints. Some of her teammates stayed loose at the edge of the pitch by stretching, while a couple of others went down to one knee to rest. The heat was even worse now, and one of the student volunteers circulated with two metal carriers of sports drink bottles.

As Mima accepted one, she watched Kaga. The midfielders were sprinting in their direction, but Kaga lagged behind. She was sweating more than the others. Then Kaga's hand went to her chest.

Mima began to move towards her, but everything went in slow motion. Kaga gasped for breath and keeled over.

13 - Incidents One and Two

Mima screamed Kaga's name as she ran across the field. Others were closer, but Mima was first to Kaga. She had fallen face first into the turf and didn't move.

"Kaga-chan!" Mima cried as she rolled Kaga onto her back as the rest of the team crowded around. Kaga's eyes were closed. Her face was bathed in sweat, her hair saturated with it.

Coach Usami, a short, stocky man pushed his way through. "Stand back," he said, "give her air!" He shouted for the trainer and issued orders to one of his assistants, who pulled out his cell phone.

Mima held Kaga's head in her hands and put her ear close to Kaga's mouth. "She's breathing, but it's shallow," she reported.

Usami knelt beside them and felt Kaga's pulse. His face turned grave; Mima saw it. "What is it, Sensei?"

"Her pulse," he replied, "is very fast, and it's skipping."

Mima slid her thighs under Kaga's head as a pillow, and the trainer laid a wet towel over her forehead. He then opened a second one and draped it around Kaga's neck.

Usami carefully opened one of Kaga's eyes. "Her pupil's not dilated," he said, "good. Keep her still," he told Mima. They heard the approaching ambulance siren; a station was only two minutes' distance from school.

Mima gently stroked Kaga's face. Their teammates took off their jerseys and fanned them in Kaga's direction to give her more air. Frightened, Mima set her teeth so no one would learn what she wanted to say so frantically. *Kaga-chan,* she silently transmitted, *please don't go, please hang on… I love you… I need you here…*

The Emergency Services ambulance drove onto the field, and the five-member crew took over. Kaga was placed on a stretcher and whisked away in a blur of flashing lights and sirens. Practice was called, and the team slowly made their way off the field. Two of the girls were in tears; others shook their heads in disbelief.

Mima left the field at a dead run. She was first into the locker room and didn't bother to shower. She hurriedly dressed, then called Kaga's mother as she rushed out of the building for the bus stop.

The ride to the hospital was not a long one, but Mima felt it would never end. She gripped the arm of her seat and tried to figure out what happened. Always the picture of fitness, Kaga never intimated she had a health problem; her stamina was higher than anyone Mima knew.

Did Kaga push herself too hard? Mima wondered. *It can't be a heart attack; younger people usually die outright from those. I hope it's just heatstroke, even though that too is dangerous...*

Mima finally made it to the hospital. After navigating her way past the Emergency Room desk, she found Kaga in a bed surrounded by a curtain. She was dressed in a green hospital gown, and an IV tube trailed to a bag of saline solution hung beside the bed. Kaga was awake, and she smiled weakly when she saw Mima. "Hey."

Mima went to Kaga, took her hand and kissed it. "Kaga, how do you feel?" She asked. "Do they know what's wrong?"

Kaga sighed. She looked pale, even with her dark skin, and her eyes remained half-closed. "I don't know, Meem," she replied. "What happened? I woke up in the ambulance; I don't remember anything."

As calmly as possible, Mima described what she witnessed. "I felt so tired," Kaga said, "I've been all day. I thought it was because I didn't sleep well last night."

Kaga sighed with some discomfort, and adjusted the oxygen tube in her nose. "My chest got tight," she explained. "I don't know what this is, Mima, but I think it's my heart."

Mima caressed Kaga's forehead. "It's going to be okay, Kaga," Mima assured her as she tried to maintain her front. "They'll get you well."

Kaga smiled, again with effort. "Can I tell you something?" she asked.

"Of course."

Another slow breath. "I'm afraid, Mima," she confessed. "I'm the same age as you; this kind of stuff happens to old people, doesn't it? What'll I do if I'm sick? What if I can't play soccer anymore?"

"Don't worry about that now," Mima told her. She gently pulled Kaga's head to her chest as she leaned over the bed. "Kaga, your health is more important than a game," she said, "please, let go your fears. I'll be here for you."

The curtain slid back, and Sora and Eko hurried in, breathless. Mima had texted them from the locker room. "Kaga, are you all right?" Sora asked as they came to her side.

"We had to sneak in," Eko admitted. "We pretended we're related."

"I have more relatives than I ever knew," Kaga joked.

Everyone had to laugh, though it hurt for Kaga. Sora and Eko were updated on Kaga's condition. The three did their best to make Kaga comfortable, and encouraged her to relax. Not long after, Kaga's parents arrived. They were worried, but like Mima, kept their emotions inside. A doctor followed moments later. He apologized, but told the girls they would have to leave.

Kaga's hand reached out to Mima. "Meem," she whispered, "one moment more."

Mima took her hand and came close. "Yes, Kaga?"

"I love you, Mima," Kaga whispered, "I'll do what you say. You're the smart one."

Ignoring what anyone might think, Mima leaned over and kissed Kaga's lips. "I love you," she replied, "and you are smart too, Kaga. We'll be here for you…"

* * *

Aidan had lost track of time but didn't care. "What did happen to Kaga?" he asked. "She obviously survived."

"Kaga suffered from an erratic heartbeat," Mima explained, "It was genetic; an aunt had the same problem. They put her on medication, and Kaga's health improved, but she couldn't play competitively any longer. I remember how I learned…"

* * *

Mima entered the locker room. She skipped out of her mid-morning study hall and hurried to the basement level. Kaga texted she was here, and could Mima come down?

Two days had passed since Kaga's collapse on the field. She now sat on the bench in front of her open locker, her equipment bag beside her. She was dressed in jeans and her team jacket. Kaga smiled and rose when she saw Mima, and the two embraced and kissed.

"How are you feeling?" Mima asked.

"Better." Kaga held the embrace a moment longer, then turned and continued to remove her personal items from the locker. "I do feel better," she added, "but I've gotta take it easy. The doctor's ordered me to stay out of class the rest of the week, and I'm excused from gym."

Kaga then removed the black and gold soccer uniform, and the two sat down. Both stared at the jersey in her lap. "Oh," Kaga said, "I heard you were cut yesterday, Meem. I'm sorry."

"Don't be," Mima replied. "I knew it would be close, and I was not good enough."

"That's not so," Kaga returned. "You are a good player. Usami's wrong this time." Her eyes then averted to the uniform. "I have to go turn this in," she said. "It's over."

Mima put her arm around Kaga, who continued to stare at the jersey and the gold number ten on the left breast. The previous wearer had graduated the year before. "I remember," Kaga said quietly, "the day I was assigned this number. I was honored, yet I was nervous."

"I know," Mima replied. "Your face got so red."

"I was afraid of what the seniors would think," Kaga explained, "I didn't request it. When you see this number on a player, it usually means they're the best--a Pele, a Sawa, an Ozora..."

The two shared the quiet laugh. Homare Sawa led the Japanese women's team to gold in the World Cup and was

Kaga's idol. Ozora wasn't a real person, but the lead in a sports anime who also wore number ten.

Kaga's smile faded again. "It's a responsibility," she said, "to wear this number."

"That is so," Mima said, "but Usami-Sensei always liked you. He knew you could wear that number and carry it."

"I might have even been elected captain this year, too," Kaga went on, "but there's no way I can play, not now. The doctor says I can do light exercise for the time being, but I have to be careful while they get this under control."

She sighed. "There goes my scholarship, Mima," she whispered, "and any chance of me getting into university."

"Kaga, don't think that way," Mima urged. "You can take the Center Exams, your grades aren't that bad."

"But what am I gonna study?" Kaga kept her eyes lowered, her voice tremulous. "All I know how to do is play soccer, Mima. I'm not good at any other sport or anything else. I haven't got it in me..."

Tears traveled down Kaga's cheeks and dripped onto the nylon of the jersey. "I don't know what to do, Mima," she sobbed. "I'm sorry, but I can't deal with this right now. I don't want to."

Kaga leaned forward, but Mima pulled Kaga's body to her as her friend broke down. For one who played it tough both on and off the field, Kaga did have a sensitive side. She rarely permitted anyone to see it; Mima was one of the few.

"It's okay," Mima said as she consoled Kaga. "You have all year, Kaga. You have the time you need to decide," she said, "and I will help you. It's okay to feel this way. I know how much soccer means to you. I'll help you, I promise."

Kaga regained control of herself after several moments. She wiped her eyes on the sleeve of her jacket and sniffed once more. "Thank you, Mima," she whispered. "I do love you, you know."

They kissed, and the two stood up. Kaga closed the locker and said, "Okay, I'm gonna drop this off, and I have to go home. Doctor's orders."

"I'll go there with you," Mima said. Usami was not in his office, so Kaga left the uniform on his desk, and the two walked through the halls to the front entrance.

In the courtyard, Kaga turned to Mima. "I can have visitors, you know," she said, and her smile returned. "Can you come over after school?"

Mima grinned. "I will, gladly." The two embraced again, and each stole a kiss on the cheek. Kaga gave Mima one more wave, then set off across the yard for the street.

* * *

"I remember…"

Mima stood and stared at the moon, shrouded in cloud cover. "…I felt so sorry for Kaga. Yet I knew she would recover and find herself." She looked over to Aidan. "And she did; Kaga went on to college. She earned her certification, and now she's a P.E. instructor and coach. Kaga also got married, so she's doing well."

"Was the breakup a bad one?" Aidan asked.

"No," Mima replied, "but there was one blow in between. The devastating one…"

＊ ＊ ＊

The fall term was in its second week, and Mima walked up the street toward home, Sora in tow. Normally Kaga and Eko would join the two after classes to study and hang out. Today, Kaga was at the doctor's office for a checkup while Eko joined her parents for a shopping trip.

Sora skipped along the sidewalk like a small girl as she discussed her recent art project. Two of her oil works would be presented at the Cultural Festival, as would two of Mima's projects. "I'm so happy for that," Sora said, then abruptly changed the subject. "So how are you and Kaga doing?"

"Oh, we're fine." Mima had to smile. Though they'd never "come out," most knew Mima and Kaga were an item. There were the typical catty comments from some students (the "jealous ones", Eko called them), but the school's policy against hate speech, bullying and related behavior was strict. Neither suffered any real backlash.

"Kaga is an awesome girl, you know," Sora went on, "and she's made you more outgoing too, Mima."

Mima smiled. "You think so?"

"Yeah." Sora took Mima's arm and said, "You were so closed up. Not to say you weren't nice to us Mima, but you were so quiet. Eko thinks the same thing. You've broken out; you smile more and look so happy. I see it in your works, too."

"Kaga has made me more confident," Mima admitted. "I feel prouder, more content. It's not just our friendship or the love we share. She's helped me grow."

"That's for sure," Sora replied as they turned the corner. "Hey, your dad's home."

Mima looked. The Toyota was in the driveway, backed in with the wheels straight, the way her father parked his car. "That's odd," she said, "he's home early."

The two entered the house and slid out of their school shoes. Mima was suddenly aware of the quiet; even the air felt thicker.

"Mima," her father's voice called from the living room, "come here. We want to speak with you."

Mima's heart stopped. Her father was talking in the voice he used on the lower ranks at work or over the phone. He also used it on her mother and Mima when he had something to say.

They entered the living room, where her father, in his tie and white work shirt sat at the low table. He looked as if still seated behind his desk. Her mother was beside him; a calm woman, Mima saw she was anxious.

After a polite, but brief greeting to Sora, Mima's father said, "Mima, sit down. We must have a discussion."

Mima nervously did so, and Sora joined her. "What is the matter, Otousan?" Mima asked. "Sora is my friend, you can speak before her."

Sora nodded in agreement, but she looked terrified. Something was about to go down, and it wasn't good.

"I want to know the truth, Mima," her father began as if he were addressing one of his underlings. "I have heard about a situation involving you and Kaga-san. Now I know her father; he is a fine man, but that is neither here nor there. I want to know of what you two are engaged in."

Mima went cold, the way she felt when her father was displeased with her. She had never divulged the extent of her relationship with Kaga to her parents or anyone but her small circle of friends.

"Our relationship," Mima stammered in reply, "is one of close friendship, Otousan. Yes, we are very close."

"Close' is hardly the proper word." Her father was now angry, and he leaned across the table for emphasis. "Did you not think this matter worth mentioning to me? Or to your mother?"

Mima was shaking internally. There was no way out of it. "What Kaga and I have, Otousan," she said, "is personal."

"Personal?" Her father's face was red, his cheekbones now more accentuated. His short, black hair seemed to rise from his scalp. "How can you refer to such a thing as this personal? You are far too young to engage in such behavior. What is worse, it is with another female!"

"Kaga is my friend," Mima maintained. "I don't know what behavior you are thinking of Otousan, but it is nothing like that."

"I have a very good idea," he replied, "of how these things are!" He moved himself from under the table and placed himself between them and the entrance to the living room; they were cut off from escape.

Mima and Sora fell backward over the table's cushions and got to their feet. Sora clung to Mima's arm; she was frightened, but not more than Mima was.

"If Kaga's parents permit her to act in such a manner, that is their business," her father went on. "My concern is with you." He pointed his finger at Mima. "You will cease this relationship with Kaga," he ordered. "Have you no shame with regard to your mother or this family?"

Mima looked to her mother. The woman sat there, placid and submissive. Then she looked away. She would be of no help.

Somehow, Mima faced her father and his withering glare. "No, Otousan," she declared, "I will not break off my friendship with Kaga. I am sorry, but Kaga is one of the dearest friends I have. She has helped me more than you can ever know. To do so is to betray her—I cannot do it."

"Then you must go!" Her father started toward Mima, and there might have been a physical confrontation, if not for Sora. The first of the group to retreat from contentious situations, Sora instead put herself between father and daughter.

"You are making a mistake, Sasaki-san," Sora protested as she backed Mima toward the door. "You must not do this!" Mima's mother finally got up; she grabbed her husband's arm and pleaded with him, too.

He would not hear of it. Angrily, he pulled away from his wife. "Get out of my house," he shouted at Mima and Sora, "both of you! You have shamed us, leave!"

Mima fled the house at a dead run with Sora at her heels. They didn't have time to gather their shoes or any other items, but her father solved that problem. Shouting a string of insults, he threw their shoes, jackets and book bags out the front door at them. He also flung Mima's sketchbook as if he were throwing away something distasteful. Some of the papers came free of the book and fluttered in the breeze.

The shock overrode any humiliation Mima might have felt by this point. She pleaded with her father to stop his exhibition. Neighbors and people in the street had stopped to watch.

"Come on, Mima!" Sora had already gathered up her things. In shock, Mima managed to grab her own and the two rushed from the property as an entire neighborhood looked on.

They ran up the street several blocks. Once they were sure Mima's father was not following them, they sat at the curb and put on their shoes. Mima shook so badly, she couldn't do it.

Sora was on her cell talking with what sounded like her mother. Mima was barely aware of Sora's words. Her insides were knotted. Instead of putting on her coat, she wrapped it around her body.

"Mima," Sora said, "Mama-san's coming to pick us up. You can stay at our house." She then pulled Mima to her. "Your father is a monster!" she exclaimed. "I don't know how you've put up with him."

Mima buried her face in her hands. "Have I lost my family, Sora?" she moaned. "Did he mean for me never to come home ever again? Is that what he said?"

"It sounded like it," Sora replied, "but I don't know for sure. Either way, we will take care of you, Mima."

Mima melted into Sora's arms. She didn't care if people saw her or heard her crying like a child; this was no worse a spectacle than what her father made of himself. "I can't give up Kaga," she cried, "I can't! My father is wrong, he's just wrong!"

"Of course he's wrong," Sora told her, "he's out of his mind. But Mama will be here soon, and she has already said you can stay. And Mima…"

Sora's hands lifted Mima's face up, and their eyes met. Despite the circumstances, Mima saw something in Sora: her face was as composed as she'd ever seen it.

"What you did back there," Sora told her, "was courageous, Mima. You stood up to your father. That's incredible; you stood up for Kaga and yourself. I know I could never do that."

"But," Mima sobbed, "at what cost?" She again threw herself against Sora and cried out again as her world went black…

* * *

"Christ." Dawn was breaking in the East, or what could be seen of it from here. "I'm sorry, Mima," was all Aidan could think to say.

"Not your fault," Mima replied. She swallowed hard and continued, "Long story short, I ended up at Sora's. I spent the night in her room, crying my eyes out."

"What happened with your family?" Aidan asked.

"Nothing. Yuzuki-san spoke to my father later," Mima said. "He had calmed down since then, but refused to let me back in the house except to get my things. He made sure he and Mom weren't around for that. The only goodbye I got was a note that requested I leave my key in the mailbox."

"Class act." Aidan found himself angry. "So what did happen?"

"Sora's family took me in," Mima replied. "They gave me the room next to Sora's, and they became my foster parents. Later they filed to be my legal guardians. If Mom had a say in the matter, she chose not to speak. She always did whatever my father said anyway, so I was cut off, disowned. They're dead now; dead to me."

Aidan put his arms around Mima. "I'm so sorry," he said, and he meant it. "No wonder you were as you were in Boston."

"That wasn't the half of it." Mima looked up at Aidan and said, "There was one last nail in the coffin of what was once my life."

Aidan held Mima to him as she put her index and middle fingers to her face. "Tears," she whispered.

14 - The Final Disappointment

The girls were a trio any fellow student would have immediately recognized. Mima, Kaga and Sora walked across the courtyard; the first two held hands while the other floated along beside them. She swung her legs this way and that, and playfully ensured to step on as many cracks as possible.

Kaga wore her team jacket (though no longer on the squad) as it kept her warm in the winter months. Mima's outerwear was a plain black wool coat while Sora's was black and red plaid with fake fur trim. All three had pulled their legwarmers up for maximum coverage, though some bare thighs remained exposed.

Life returned to normal for Mima, or as much as possible. Since moving in with Sora, the pair grew closer, and those who didn't know them might have thought they were sisters. They often called one other Nee-chan, though Mima kept her surname.

The story got around about Mima and her family. Fortunately most of her schoolmates were sympathetic. Some, including her and Kaga's former teammates offered help, such as a place to stay if needed or a friendly ear. The school also offered counseling and related services, if Mima wished them.

Mima quickly adapted to having Suemi and Yuzuki as "parents". House rules were more flexible, and Mima found it easy to call them by familial terms. They were there for her, as was Sora; for that Mima was thankful, though it of course was not the same.

The hardest part for Mima was that which she told her companions and Eko--but no other--about the total loss of her parents. To them, Mima ceased to exist, but she realized that there wasn't a lot of contact with the rest of their relatives.

Now and then, Mima would run into former neighbors. They reported her mother, always quiet and unassuming had become more withdrawn. As for her father, Mima heard little about him. Kaga's father saw him on rare occasion due to their related occupations, and he appeared not to have changed at all. Any attempts to bring up Mima were deflected; he would not speak of his daughter.

Mima squeezed Kaga's hand as they walked on, and Kaga reciprocated. Her voice now broke Mima from her thoughts. "Are you two doing the paint-off?" She asked.

Mima and Sora laughed. "Yes," the latter replied, "and I love the competition."

"It is not a competition," Mima corrected, "we do better when we work off one another." The subject revolved around how the two created of late: in either Sora or Mima's room, they would paint, sketch or work on the computer separately. The creative results produced works that earned high marks and higher praise from their instructors; some were being adapted for the school yearbook.

"Well, that doesn't matter," Kaga told them. "You both do such amazing stuff." She pulled Mima closer and kissed her. "Love you, by the way."

Mima smiled back. "Love you," she replied as she returned Kaga's kiss.

Sora giggled as the three walked on. "You are both so cute," she remarked but said nothing more. There came an awkward silence, which both Mima and Kaga understood. Eko was not with them today as she was on a date. Sora had no boyfriend; anytime she hooked up with someone, it didn't last.

"I know what you're thinking," Sora continued, "and it's okay. I'm over it. Like you said, if he's not man enough to say it to my face, he's not worth it."

"Didn't seem that way at first," Kaga countered.

Mima drew an involuntary breath, but Sora handled the quip. "True," she admitted, "I didn't, but then that's how I go. Down into the abyss…" Sora bent her knees and crab-walked several steps, "…and then up again!"

Sora leaped into the air, which made her companions laugh. "Stuff with me," Sora went on, "gets magnified, both my happiness and my melancholy. For me, taking to my bed for three days is nothing; to others, it's madness."

"It is how it manifests," Mima replied, "but you have done better, Sora. We all have, despite what we've been through."

"That's true," Kaga said. "Our grades are all good. Well," she added, "yours always were tops, Meem. Mine are better, and I made it through the Center Exams."

Sora twirled about, her arms spread wide for balance. "Exactly," she replied, "we're all headed for good places."

The lot of Mima and her friends boded well, academically speaking. Sora's grades were marginally better over the past year, and she was in the running for a scholarship to a local art institute. Kaga made it through the National Center Test the month before and was accepted to a municipal university in Osaka, her former hometown. Eko also scored well and was considering a couple of local colleges.

Mima's own future was secured, too. After the summer, she would head for Boston and the Butera School. Though months away, both girls knew Sora dreaded this.

Sora herself brought it up: "I am gonna miss you so much, Mima," she said, "but you've got the chance of a lifetime. Don't worry about me, I'll be all right."

They came abreast of a small convenience store as Sora said this. "I need something to drink," she added, "you want anything?"

Both begged off and waited outside; they left Sora alone as she would have trouble making up her mind. They knew enough not to push her, or she'd get frustrated.

Grateful for the moment, Mima pulled Kaga to her, and they kissed. "Are you feeling okay, Kaga?"

Kaga nodded as she held Mima. "Yeah, I'm fine. Not so sure about Sora, though. She seems out there today, more than usual."

"I know." Mima rested against Kaga. "She's been on a rollercoaster, and not just because of the breakup. Her medications may not be working again; Sora knows it, but she's tired of going back to the doctors. Some of the medicines have side effects."

"Must be tough," Kaga replied, and she leaned against the brick wall of the shop. "I know my heart meds were weird for me until my body got used to them."

"That's part of it," Mima agreed as she appraised Kaga's body in that position, "but Sora is getting scared. It's true, we work on art together, and she is a sister to me now. I love her dearly, as I love you – not like that, though."

Kaga laughed at Mima's quick addition to her statement. "I didn't think that, Meem," she said, "but yeah, she and her folks are fantastic. To take you in – I would not have hesitated one moment to bring you to my place, but we don't have the room."

"I would never have imposed," Mima replied, "but thank you. It worked out for all concerned; I feel so comfortable there. Sora is the best, even when she's off on one of her tangents. When it comes to me, she returns to Earth. Okasan says I 'stabilize' Sora."

"That's cool," Kaga said, "but yeah, I can see where Sora would be worried. I mean, going off to the US? Not coming back for a long time either? How will Sora take that, now that she's so used to you?"

"Sora has always been used to me," Mima said. "I've known her since we were six years old. In a lot of cases, because Sora was often a little wild, I was her only friend."

"Then Sora had you for support?"

"We've supported each other, yes. I could calm Sora down," Mima explained, "and Sora could draw me out. We were good like that."

Kaga looked down at the pavement, in thought. "I wonder," she asked, "what does Sora think of us? I mean, is she resentful of my place in your life?"

"No." Mima shook her head and took Kaga's hands in hers. "She is happy for us," she said, "and you can believe it. She's never minded our friendship or our love. Please don't be worried about that."

Kaga's face reddened a little. "I'm sorry," she replied and looked away. "I didn't mean it like that. I just wondered."

"It's okay to wonder." Mima turned her lover's face to her own and leaned her body against Kaga's. Pinned to the wall, Kaga smiled, and they kissed.

Mima pushed herself against Kaga. She leaned up, rested her hands on Kaga's shoulders and continued to share those kisses. She felt Kaga squeeze her, arms locked together around her lower back. Mima felt herself escape once again, from the negative, cynical things her father said, or implied by his looks of disdain. From her mother's placidity, and words of sympathy that gave no comfort. There also was the flight from detachment; despite a home and friends, Mima could not feel anything but lonely.

Her kisses and the ones Kaga returned were not desperate ones. Mima felt the softness of Kaga's lips, the warm breath from her mouth, the tongue in contact with her own. Each time the two were this close, Mima felt that she and Kaga were making love for the first time. Mima could fall into it, when she so required it…

The click of Sora's shoes informed them of her return. Mima's eyes opened, as did Kaga's. They smiled and kissed once more.

"Sorry I took so long," Sora said, cup in hand. "Went for the chai."

Mima smiled as she walked on with her friends, her right arm hooked into Kaga's left. There was nothing to be worried about…

* * *

"…or so I believed." Mima watched the sunrise. Already they could hear the vehicles below, their owners getting a head start on the morning commute.

"How did it end?" Aidan asked. He needed sleep, but Mima had to let this go.

"The rest of the year was a beautiful, and happy time," Mima said. "We graduated on time, all of us."

She turned for the door. "Come with me, I want to show you something."

Aidan followed Mima inside to her computer. Seating herself on the stool, Mima opened a file, and after a quick search found a folder. "Pictures," she said.

A slideshow crossed the screen; there were graduation photos of Mima, Sora, Kaga, Eko and several other students. All were holding their diplomas, smiling, grinning and making the "V" sign to the camera. Mima provided the back-story and added the names of a few others in the pictures.

There followed a series of shots from a beach. "A bunch of us took a trip to Niijima, to celebrate," Mima commented. There followed more shots of the girls in bikinis –- Mima wore a black one-piece –- but that interested him less than the closeness he saw between Mima and her friends.

Mima stood between Sora and Eko in a shot, their arms about one another. Then there was one of Kaga on her knees in the surf. Her hands were in her hair, in a classic model's pose. That one was dead sexy, Aidan thought, but he kept his mouth shut.

There was another of Mima with her arms about Kaga. Then more pictures of them in the surf, dripping wet, their hair damp…and a distance shot of the two standing on the shore in silhouette, kissing.

Aidan smiled at that one. "Nice one."

"Sora took that." Mima was smiling, too, hers a sad one.

"Those were all good pictures," Aidan replied. "One of those fine times, right?"

"Yeah." Mima closed the file and leaned back in her seat, hands in her lap, her expression pensive. "That was the best summer of my life," she said. "We celebrated our last free time before university and the real world took our lives over. I was about to leave for America," she added, "when Kaga let me go."

Aidan leaned against the table. "Why did she do it? What was her reasoning?" He tried to make his questions as gentle as possible.

Mima sighed. She adjusted her glasses, then returned the hand to the other and laced her fingers together. "It wasn't over someone else," she replied. "It was a practical consideration, which I understood, but…"

* * *

Kaga sat beside Mima in her bedroom. The former was in jeans and a cropped t-shirt. She looked so good to Mima, as always; but she knew Kaga wanted to discuss something serious. Mima knew what was coming.

"I need to talk to you about something that's bothered me, a lot," Kaga began. Before Mima could answer, Kaga took her hands in her own and said, "Mima, it's nothing you have done. You are one of the few close friends I have. And," she added as she looked Mima in the eyes, "I love you dearly. I always will."

"I love you, too." Mima felt numb. She knew what she was about to hear.

Kaga took a deep breath, then looked Mima in her eyes. "The way I feel for you," she said, "will never change, Mima. I will always love you, and I have no regrets about any of it. I hate doing this, but," Kaga inhaled and added quickly, "I feel we have to call an end to our relationship."

Mima reached out and ran her hand along Kaga's hair. The girl's head lowered; she was trying not to lose her nerve.

"Tell me why, Kaga," Mima prompted her. "I will listen, and I will not judge you."

Kaga's head rose; tears had formed in her eyes. "It is like this," she whispered. "You're going off to the States and I'm going back to Osaka. You will be gone for a long time, and I understand you won't be able to come home too often. I don't know when I'll be back in Tokyo. Long-distance relationships don't work, Mima. I think it's best for us to go our own ways."

Mima pulled Kaga close and rested her head on her shoulder. "It's all right," she said over Kaga's quiet sobs, "I understand. I don't want to do this either, Kaga, but you are right. We're going to meet different people and experience new things. But we will always have our friendship."

Mima's hand was wet as she lifted Kaga's face to hers. "And Kaga," she added, "I will never stop loving you as a friend. We'll always be together in our hearts."

They kissed and clung to one another, one last time. After a goodbye to Suemi, Kaga put on her sneakers and jacket, walked down the drive and passed out of sight.

Sora joined her at the glass exterior door, her hands and an old sweatshirt covered in paint. "Did what I think happened," she asked, "just happen?"

"It did." They went into her room, and Mima described the breakup.

Sora wiped the excess paint from her hands on the sleeves of her shirt as she listened. "I don't know whether I should be angry with Kaga or sad for her," she said.

"It's all right." Mima slid onto her futon and curled herself up against one of the pillows. "Don't be mad at her, Sora, please; she is correct. If Kaga and I tried to stay together, there's no way we could be faithful to one another, no matter what we did. An open relationship would not be good for me anyway; too many problems would crop up. I can only love one at a time."

Sora looked at Mima; she was feeling worst of all. "I'm sorry, Mima. Do you want me to leave you alone?"

Mima shook her head. "No."

Sora removed her sweatshirt, then slid onto the bed beside Mima. At times like this, Mima noted that Sora's manic phases would go away. She would get serious, focused and attentive. Especially where Mima was concerned.

Mima felt Sora's arms encircle her, and her head was pulled to Sora's chest. She clung to Sora and closed her eyes. There were no tears to come; enough fell within.

* * *

"The final disappointment," Aidan commented.

"I don't know," Mima replied as she brought up the desktop's design software. "A disappointment, yes, but not as tragic as it seems. We each had to live our own lives, and I know that I grew. Kaga did, too."

"That wasn't the last time you saw her," Aidan asked, "was it?"

"We saw each other a couple more times before we went off to school," Mima said, "and after. Since her marriage, Kaga rarely comes back to Tokyo."

Mima turned to her screen, prepared to resume work. "How do you feel about seeing Kaga again?" Aidan asked. "It's difficult to consider, isn't it?"

"It is," Mima replied, "but I have that in hand. Sorry Aidan," she went on, "but I need to finish this."

"Sure." Aidan shed his top clothing and picked up his sweat pants as he headed for the bathroom. He was beat; a long night had turned into a longer morning. He could sleep anywhere at this point, even on the Hercules.

As he turned into the bathroom, Aidan looked back. Mima was hunched over her stool before her screen. She was back at it; this was Mima's method to block out what she confessed to, but also what Aidan was certain she had not.

15 - War

The woman stared at the bare, white canvas. Two desk lamps were rigged to shed light upon it; this was all she would need.

Her hands went to her hips. Naked but for a gray tank top and bikini, Sora tightened the strap that held her iPod. She plugged in her headphones and hit "play". Overproduced dance music with a series of auto-tuned female voices "harmonized" over a synthesized track; she was ready.

Sora fell to her knees, into the drop cloth before her easel. Two dozen tubes of oils lay in the folds alongside a series of long-handled brushes and a plastic palette. Her hands grabbed a tube, twisted off the top and squeezed its contents out, then another, and another. She tossed the caps and tubes aside once done with them.

Soon all the colors Sora required were represented on the palette. She rose and stood before the easel, staring at it as she mixed the colors. It wasn't the most orthodox method, but Sora didn't care; this was how she painted.

In time to the beat of the music, Sora feverishly made changes to the hues of the mixtures. Six different brushes hooked into the fingers of her left hand, Sora set the first in her teeth and pulled another. They were almost ready.

The night out with the others was fun, but Sora couldn't go to sleep. The picture formed in her mind during the evening, and she had to produce it.

She felt the sweat seep out of her, and she had only been at it a few minutes. That was good. Sora picked up a broad brush, and dipped it in the pale green she'd formed in a thick mound in the center of the palette. Sora began to brush the canvas as if she painted a fence. She battled the white and forcefully made it disappear into the green. A second coat; now, Sora could paint.

Time meant nothing to Sora; she hadn't slept since the night before, and though tired this would not wait. Sora's method was to paint when the idea was in her head, or it would be lost.

She selected one of the thicker brushes, stabbed it into the palette and went to work. Focused, the female J-Pop group keened in her ears as Sora attacked the canvas. She switched brushes on the fly, remixed colors, and she painted; a quick scrape with a knife and she painted; a little more white to mix in, and she painted.

Sora did not allow anything to interfere. Long ago, her parents learned they should not enter the room unless in an emergency. They understood "artistic temperament". Food, drink nor Sora's medications took precedence; this was her work and no one would stop her.

A good portion of the canvas was no longer that shade of green, when Sora went to the floor. She needed more paint. Sora searched in the cloth for the tubes. These found, Sora furiously pushed more onto the palette. She remixed and again leaped to her feet. It was on; more detail in the corner, now carefully down the side.

The music reverberated off Sora's eardrums. The work was taking shape, a bright, angled abstract in sea green. *It's working*, she allowed herself to think, *I see you…I'm going to get you…*

A fan-shaped brush in hand, Sora jabbed the pale background with a darker, forest green. Now this far, Sora thought of other things. She thought of last night, and of Mima.

Last night's meet-up with Eko intrigued but also concerned Sora. Eko hit it off with Aidan; that was easy to see. Mima seemed not to like that…was she jealous?

That could not be. Mima always maintained that Aidan was no lover, nor a boyfriend. He was that male friend, the one Mima never found at home. *He strikes me at times as brash, but he is a gentleman, as Mima said.*

More of the dark green; another strike against the canvas. Eko's attraction to him would have been seen as natural, but not so. Eko did not throw herself easily at men, at least not anymore…

Her legs shook, and Sora's hands began to as well from exhaustion. Sora kneeled and wiped her face with her paint-spattered hand. She wasn't done yet. Sora wondered what time it was. The music was too loud to hear, but Sora detected Yuzuki's heavy tread in the hall. *It's morning; Papa-san's getting ready for work.*

She stood again. *This is my work… this is war.* Another brush in hand, Sora again painted. The shakes over for the time being, Sora attacked once again. She thought of Van Gogh, who supposedly had the same affliction as she. Did he paint this way? It sounded like it from what Sora read of him, and what she'd seen of the one-man show of his life on television. His works had a brilliance Sora could not find in any other artist.

Sora painted on. She was no Van Gogh, but her work was of a Modernist persuasion. It didn't matter what people called it, and what was said of Van Gogh was true of Sora: she painted what she wanted to see. *I am an artist, damn you…!*

The canvas heeled back but remained clamped to the easel. Lip between her teeth, Sora concentrated on this part using a brush she had modified: a tiny wisp of bristle remained in it.

She dotted, dashed and slashed down the edge of the canvas. The detail for this area looked good, but a little more…

Her thoughts drifted again to Mima. She remembered the days in this room after that frightful one with Mima's father. Mima slept in the room next door, but she often came to this one, and the two painted or drew side by side.

Their styles were as different as their personalities. Mima was slow, deliberate and mindful with every stroke; what power went into her works was controlled. Sora was a storm; paint flew from her brushes, the palette and canvas itself. Eventually, the two had to turn their easels back to back so as to protect Mima's work from Sora's battle with her own.

Mima's product was rarely finished; she would agonize over every detail, and spend hours getting it "right". To Sora, perfection was when she took one look at a project and knew, in that moment, she was done.

They would end, their clothes covered in sweat, paint or whatever they used. The two would critique one another's works and offer words of praise or advice. Then they would look at one another, laugh out loud and embrace. Kaga came up with the term "paint-off", and it was fitting; both ended looking as though they'd been in a fight, Sora more so than Mima.

Detail work done, Sora picked up the knife from the floor and began to carve again. Some of this needed to go. Bonus mixes of one of the girl group's hit singles thumped in her head, and Sora fought off the urge to stop. The opponent showed no mercy… *neither will I…*

Sora's eyes opened to the scream of one of those nameless singers. She lay on her back in the folds of the drop cloth.

The easel rose above her, as a victorious fighter over a vanquished opponent.

Sora pulled herself to a seated position. Her body shivered from cold plus lack of food and sleep. She peered up into the lights and looked at the work; Sora could do no more.

So not to disturb the easel, Sora felt around the floor and looked for her tools. She stacked the brushes and knife in a pile, and then gathered the tubes of paint. The caps were another matter; Sora crawled about the floor, searching out each one in the shadows.

Fingers twitched as Sora forced the caps onto the tubes. Each had to be reconciled with the right color. Sora felt her temper rise as she tried to match them up. Finally, she laid the tubes out in a row and found the corresponding caps. She screwed them on tightly, then took these and threw them into a drawer. The brushes went into a plastic tray for cleaning. Sora pulled a plastic bottle of Turpenoid from the shelf and carried these into the bathroom.

Sora cleaned her brushes and tools; she then scrubbed her hands, face and body free of paint. One accord Sora did not have to make with her parents was to clean up after herself. The tools of her trade had to be ready for the next time, the next battle…

Tasks complete, Sora returned to her room and put things away. She shut off her iPod and cast it and her belt to the floor. Off came her paint spattered underwear, which she threw at the laundry basket in the corner. She stared again at the painting on the other side of the room, and approached if not stalked it.

She regarded the canvas and ardent shapes set into the field of green. Other than that bit of detail, it was all right. Sora managed a smile; she had fallen, but rose up to win this fight.

Sora switched off the lamps. In the darkness, Sora's shoulders sagged, and her hands went to her mouth. Eyes closed, Sora gave a stifled cry, then another. She turned and stumbled for the bed.

She crawled naked beneath the comforter, and wrapped herself in it. Her arms found one of the pillows and Sora disappeared into the cotton and down. Tears broke from her eyes, and Sora cried aloud.

This was Sora's release from the force that held her talent hostage. The creative process was to Sora exhilarating, sensual and erotic. At its end was the comedown; weakened physically and mentally, Sora crashed. Now the rest of her was freed.

Sora wailed and held to the bedclothes with the last of her strength; she would not sleep long, but just enough. She willed the pillow and comforter to surround her and to become human. She did not wish for Suemi or Yuzuki to hold her as they once did; Sora wanted another, that one that never stayed.

Beyond her parents, the only arms that held her right belonged to Mima. Sora wished she were here.

16 - The Bluest Blues

Aidan awakened to find Mima packing her laptop into its case. "I have to deliver the new layouts," she said, "so you are at liberty."

The two chuckled at that. Aidan was ready to go out once more. He waved goodbye to Mima as she sped off into traffic on her bike. Aidan shook his head; cyclists were no different here than in Boston, though motorists had their own views on the matter.

He slid on his shades, shouldered the Minolta and walked in the other direction. Time to get back to business, and Aidan worked alone. He blanked his mind out with respect to time and slowly walked the streets of Tokyo. This was Aidan's method: one didn't know when a photo opportunity would present itself, and Aidan did his best to play the role of a casual tourist.

Tokyo bustled as almost every other city Aidan visited, but for once he tried to see this place. Soon Aidan saw how the natives moved in a flow uniquely theirs. Aidan could never explain this in words; the pictures would have to tell the story.

Aidan paused now and then to take snapshots of things that took his fancy. Strange vehicles, people walking along the street, a sidewalk café that looked no different, apart from the signage and odd-looking drinks the customers consumed.

One photo that would have seemed a waste of film to anyone else was of a row of those vending machines. Aidan came across an impressive line of them, and kneeled to take a long shot. He read somewhere Japan boasted one machine for every two dozen citizens, a figure confirmed by Mima. Another reason these conveniences caught Aidan's eye: they dispensed everything from soft drinks to anti-acne creams, the name of the last a familiar one.

Aidan paused to get a cup of coffee from the one that offered it. He exchanged most of his dollars for yen upon arrival in Tokyo, but Aidan found he could use his Amex card to pay at these machines. For fun, Aidan did so; he smiled at the thought of what might appear on his statement.

The "coffee" wasn't bad, considering the mechanized muck he'd drunk elsewhere (roadside rest areas, in particular). Later, Aidan wandered into a park whose point of interest was a shrine. This he needed to have.

Today was not a holiday, so there were comparatively few people here, unlike the masses Aidan saw on Youtube. Those who came to pray or make their devotionals, however, took the trip here seriously.

Aidan took different angles on the approach and snapped a number of pictures. He was intrigued –– most were in everyday dress, though a handful chose to wear traditional kimonos and other such garb. Aidan made a point to take his shots from a distance, though he did find an older couple that spoke some English and were delighted to pose for the Minolta.

By and large the other folks didn't seem to mind either. Tourists were a regular thing, but Aidan made sure not to get too close to people. He didn't want paparazzi shots, not unlike what he took of Callie. The thought of that bothered him.

Aidan put his camera away. He climbed the steps to the place where offerings were made and watched as citizens of all ages dropped their coins and bills into a receptacle. They clapped their palms together, bowed and rang the bell atop the long rope before them.

Fascinated, Aidan joined one of the lines. He reached into his pocket and found a 100-yen coin; only about a dollar in equivalent US funds, but that would do. When his turn came, Aidan tossed it in and followed the example.

Though Boston Irish and Protestant, Aidan's family was not that religious. He, Katie, and Stephen were sent to Sunday school until they were twelve, and that was the extent of their spiritual training. Aidan understood what he witnessed here; it wasn't much different.

What did people pray for here, Aidan wondered, and how did they ask? "I'm not good at this," he spoke half-aloud to whoever was listening. "If there's anything I'd like to happen, it's to find peace for my friends. I could use some too, but I find it hard to ask for anything for myself. My father used to say if it's meant to be, so it shall be; if there's anything like that for me, I'll gladly accept it."

Aidan took the rope in his hands and rang the bell. This done, Aidan descended the steps. He wasn't sure what prompted his action or those words; either way, he felt better for it.

"Aidan-san!"

He looked up. There on the walkway were Sora and Eko along with two small children, a boy and a girl. The former rushed up to him and grabbed him in a big hug. "Good to see you!" she exclaimed. "What are you doing without Mima?"

Sora was dressed in a purple skirt, a long affair with black tights beneath, a denim jacket over the outfit and a striped knit cap. Her eyes were extra large today, and Aidan saw the dark circles the woman's makeup did not hide.

"She's at a meeting," he explained as Sora led him over to Eko and the kids.

Eko looked quite good, Aidan had to admit to himself, in jeans, a black t-shirt of some band whose name he couldn't decipher and a short leather coat. Her blorange hair was tied back in a long ponytail and flowed from beneath a floppy black cap. "Very nice to see you again, Aidan-san," she said and offered her hand. After bowing, she added, "These are my sister's young ones."

She introduced the two, both of whom politely bowed in return. They were obviously brother and sister and couldn't have been more than four or five years old. They had gone quiet at the appearance of this strange foreigner, and they stuck close to the women.

Aidan realized he was still wearing his shades; Mima told him children here were taught to avoid strangers who wore sunglasses. Supposedly, anyone who did not reveal his eyes had something to hide. Aidan quickly removed them and smiled in the direction of the kids. That made them a little less nervous.

"We made our offerings a few minutes ago," Eko continued, her eyes on Aidan, "and we wonder if you are in a rush. Perhaps you would join us."

God, she's forward… but I find I don't mind. "I'm in no hurry," Aidan replied, and talked of what he was doing on his own this day.

The little boy asked a question of Eko in Japanese. Eko replied, but didn't talk down to him. Sora of course understood; she seemed as pleased as the kids were.

"There's a place for the children to play," Eko explained, "and we promised to take them there if they behaved. Why don't you come with us?"

"Sure." The five went further into the park. Aidan watched how both Eko and Sora walked and held the hands of the children. Both seemed comfortable in charge of the siblings, and Sora was as animated as they were.

"I know," Sora offered, "I'll take them down there." She motioned to a large, well-appointed play area. Several others, supervised by a few adults were there. "I gather you'd like a break, Eko."

Sora didn't disguise the wink she gave her friend, and Eko laughed. "Okay," she replied, "be good…the three of you!"

There was laughter from all as Sora led the siblings off. "They adore Sora," Eko commented, "and she's wonderful with them. I suppose if they were American, they would call her 'Auntie Sora' or something of the sort."

"They might," Aidan replied as the two seated themselves on a nearby bench. "You seem good with them, too."

Eko smiled as she watched the three. "Thank you," she said. "I love being around any children." Her smile faded, and Eko turned to Aidan. "I hope you don't mind my changing the subject so abruptly, but might I ask about Mima and how she is?"

"She's fine," Aidan replied, "though I'm not sure of how you mean. Is there more behind your questions?"

Eko nodded. "I suppose I should not," she admitted, "and forgive me if this is out of order. You see, Sora and Mima are among my oldest friends. Kaga is another who is dear to me."

"Mima told me about her last night," Aidan replied.

"She told you?" Eko asked in surprise. "That's good," she said, "that shows how much she values you, Aidan. Mima talks nothing but words of praise for you. I have wanted to meet you for a long time, and I am glad to see you now."

"I'm honored." Aidan nodded politely.

"You helped Mima more than you know," Eko said, "while she was at school. She needed someone like you at that time. Mima changed during her years in America; we saw that upon her return, but we all changed."

Aidan said nothing. Eko gazed off in the direction of Sora and her relatives again. Satisfied all was well, Eko turned back to Aidan. "I worry a great deal about Mima," Eko explained, "as I do about Sora, though for different reasons."

"How so?" Aidan asked.

"Mima is a very hard worker," Eko said, "and she is a brilliant artist. She and Sora are both supremely talented. It is wrong to compare them, for their styles are so unalike. They are also different people; it is not possible, nor is it fair to try."

Eko sighed; her eyes scanned the park once more. "As for Mima," she said, "she is a person whom I admire and respect. She has traits and strength I do not possess. That said, Mima's whole life is her work, and the need for independence takes priority. She is trying to show the world that she can make her life alone. Mima does this as well, to throw off her past."

"What happened with her family, you mean?"

"Yes. Mima has no connection with her blood family," Eko went on. "Her mother passed away two years after Mima was cast out of the home. The feeling amongst those who knew her was the lady died of a broken heart. Did you know," Eko asked, "that Mima was not permitted at the funeral?"

"No," Aidan replied, surprised. "I didn't."

"That is what occurred," Eko went on. "Mima was barred from attending the service by her father. She had to grieve at the temple on her own."

Eko looked at the ground. "We all have scars," she continued, "from the things that have happened to each of us."

She again turned to him. "Aidan," Eko said, "I do not profess to know about your life, but I sense you have an understanding of this. Mima bears scars; Sora has scars of her own, and I have mine. These are the things that have made their respective marks across our lives. Out of all of us Kaga has the fewest, though I know how painful it was for her to leave Mima.

"You," Eko continued, "have a reason to be here, Aidan. Mima will not say so, but she has needed a friend such as you to come around. She remains on the journey to find Mima. While some say returning into the past is not good, at times you have to look back. You do this to find things you remember, and to be reminded of them."

She placed her hand on Aidan's arm. "I hope that makes sense to you."

"It does." Aidan placed his other hand on Eko's and looked directly at her. "I've my own scars," he told her. "I have a reason to be here, but I thought for myself. I see now that Mima is in need. Sora perhaps, as well."

Eko smiled with relief, and she put her other hand over Aidan's. It felt warm, and the small, slim hands had deceptive strength in them. "Thank you," she replied. "We three that stay here are friends can trace our lives back to school, but I'd like to think we left there. I cannot say what I have faced in my life is worse than what Mima or Sora did, but that is what binds us together. Sora has her health issues, and she remains closest to Mima, though God knows she tries not to depend upon her."

"How about you?" Aidan asked. "You live at home, but I am not judging that."

"My reasons are my own," Eko replied, "and not all of them do you know. I'll make my move when the time is right, and not before."

She looked across the green. Sora and the children were chasing one another. They were laughing, Sora the loudest of all. Eko smiled at them, but as she looked back to Aidan it faded again. "I don't like being called a parasite, Aidan," she continued, "and it's not how it appears. I try to ignore it because I have to do what I must do."

"I don't think it's a fair assessment of all people," Aidan said. He kept hold of Eko's hands. She appeared comfortable with his grip. "Some do that, sure," he continued, "but there are reasons for all things. I don't know them all, but I don't care to."

He again met Eko's eyes. "Mima is my friend," he said. "I've needed to see her and talk to her. I like you, Eko; I like Sora, and I think I'd like Kaga, should I get to meet her. I can see the love you have for one another. You hold to your friendships, you don't let them go. That's something I don't know about, sad to say."

Eko's hands squeezed his own, and she smiled. Aidan was falling into her.

"We are all we have," Eko said quietly. "I want to know you more, Aidan. I want to talk with you more like this. I like you, too."

There was a moment where the two looked at one another. Aidan felt a closeness, a real one had just been cemented.

He could hear Sora and the children approaching, and the two carefully disengaged. Aidan drew out his camera and easily convinced them to pose for a few pictures.

Once done, Sora embraced Aidan again. "We'll see you soon."

"I hope so," Aidan replied.

"Indeed," Eko added, her own wink none too subtle.

There were bows and farewells, and Aidan watched as the four walked away. Eko turned back and smiled in his direction, then flashed the "V" sign with her free hand.

Aidan gave it back, and watched them leave. As he returned toward the street, a strange song entered his mind. *"It's the bluest blues… and it cuts me like a knife…"*

It was an Alvin Lee song. Stephen turned Aidan on to Ten Years After, and he'd caught Lee with his solo band in Majorca a couple years before his death. Lee seemed to write songs so he could play rock guitar, but this one was deep blues, and became a favorite of Aidan's.

The song applied. From what Eko said, and from what Aidan had heard and seen since arriving here, there were cracks in everyone's facades. The song was like glue; it caulked together everyone's individual stories. *"It's the bluest blues… since you walked out of my life…"*

He thought of Philippa. Aidan loved her: her irreverence, her brains and dedication to what she loved. Hell, he loved everything else about her, too. Aidan was also aware he could not blame the attack, Mansur's death, Stephen, Callie, none of them for their end. Philippa wanted more than he could give. That whole thing was the send-off.

The wind blew colder, and Aidan dug out a fresh pack of Gitanes and his lighter. Shielding the flame of his Zippo, Aidan considered the thoughts that simmered within. Mima's losses, her family, Kaga, Sora's travails, and the allusion Eko had her own to contend with. Then Aidan had his – Eko saw directly into Aidan and right through him.

Aidan exhaled and walked on as he thought of his peculiar disposition. He was an American traveling in Asia with the strains of a song by a British rocker burning through his mind. *"It's the bluest blues…when you can't find your way home…"*

17 - The "L" Word

Aidan looked up from the couch as Mima stepped into the apartment, sweaty from her ride. "How did it go?"

"Great." Mima kicked off her sneakers, threw her coat on the bed and headed into the bathroom. "They like the ad design," she called through the closed door. "A few more tweaks and I get paid."

"Good for you." Aidan folded today's *Japan Times* and set it aside. Mima soon returned after a stop at the fridge. "So where did you end up?" she asked as she opened a bottle of iced tea.

Aidan told of his travels. Mima returned to her table and listened while she powered up her computer and downed the first third of her drink with a belch in the bargain.

"Charming," Aidan returned with mock dignity.

"*Nyah!*" Mima shot back.

They shared the laugh and Aidan finished, "I ran into Sora and Eko today."

"Yeah?" Mima scanned her emails. "Tell me about it."

Aidan described the meeting and discussion with Eko. Mima remained focused, but said, "Eko adores kids. Her sister's little ones are sweet. Sora loves them, too."

"Yes," Aidan replied, "rather a big kid herself."

"That's right." Mima closed the screen and re-wired her laptop to the hub. "Sora was up all night painting," she added. "She texted me about it. It's good she went out. After an all-nighter, Sora usually sinks into a puddle of plasma."

"What do you mean by that?"

"Sora drives herself into her work," Mima explained. "When she paints, Sora does not stop until either the work is done or she physically collapses. I'm not on a limb when I say that's what happened to her this morning."

Aidan remembered the look of Sora's eyes. "She was in a good mood," he replied, "but I understand it, though. I can go for hours on a project myself; I get that caught up in it. Philippa is the same way."

Mima brought up the project up on her screen. "We all do it in some form," she said, "but Sora does not know when to stop. Though she looked well enough to you and Eko, I'm afraid the pendulum is about to swing in the other direction."

"How so?"

"Sora's text came after she awakened; she was in one of her moods." Mima went over some detail with the mouse. "You can't detect tone of voice in a text," she continued, "but Sora has expressions she uses when she's down. I think the medications are giving her trouble again."

"More of the up-and-down effects, then?" Aidan suggested.

"That, and one other." Mima drank down more tea, while she examined her work. "Sora goes to her therapist once a week," she said. "Today, in fact. Of late she's dreaded the visits because he wants her to start on lithium."

"That's heavy stuff." Aidan and Stephen had a close friend in high school that used it to treat epilepsy.

"Yeah." Mima saved her work and continued to trace. "Sora has resisted for some time. She won't call the drug by name; she calls it 'the L Word'. Sora's afraid of what it might do to her; she doesn't want to become part of the 'Lithium Generation'."

"I've heard the saying." Aidan leaned on the arm of the couch so he could look in Mima's direction. "People all smacked out like they're zombies?"

"That's what she's terrified of." Mima's hand moved the mouse slowly. "Sora can get manic, sure," she said, "but I don't think it's that drastic. I can't imagine the effects of lithium are the same on each person, but Sora will not have it. She also fears being put away against her will."

"Her parents would never section her, would they?"

"No," Mima said, "but a doctor might." Mima saved her work again, and turned to face Aidan. "I don't think they would be able to," she said, "unless Sora did something that was a danger to others or herself. Sora is frightened of being put into a hospital and having to take those kinds of medications."

"I gather Sora's been close to that before?" Aidan asked.

Mima nodded and took another drink. "Sora used to have these meltdowns when we were in school," she said. "She would lose it and cry without stopping. You had to know how to let Sora run down until she calmed herself enough that you could talk to her. One of them during our first year of high school was so severe, she was hospitalized."

"No fun, I'm sure."

"Not at all," Mima replied, "but Sora was finally examined, and her mania diagnosed. She's been on medications since then. Sora fears the worst of things. I do as well."

Aidan noted the seriousness and sadness behind Mima's glasses. "How do you fear it?" he asked.

Mima removed them, sighed and rubbed her eyes. "Nearly 25 percent of all bipolar sufferers kill themselves," she said.

"Sora is not one of those people, not in a conscious manner, but if she goes too deep into the darkness, Sora might no longer know what she's doing. I'm afraid she could take her own life if she falls that far."

"It doesn't sound like she's disposed in that direction…" Aidan was about to say more when the buzzer went off.

Mima crossed to the intercom and pressed the button. *"Hai, who's there?"*

"Mima-chan!" Sora's voice distorted through the cheap speaker in response. "Let me in! I need to talk to you!"

Mima quickly pressed the button to allow Sora entry, then opened the door. Aidan followed her into the hall.

Distraught, Sora rushed up the stairs. No longer the child-like, elated person Aidan saw a short time ago, Sora was now what Mima intimated. The tracks of tears stained Sora's face, her chest heaved from running.

Mima brought Sora into the room and steered her toward the bed. "What is it, Sora?" she asked calmly. "Tell us what's wrong."

Sora took several moments to catch her breath, and then reached down to unzip and remove her boots. "I just came from my therapist," she managed to explain, "after we saw you, Aidan. He wants to change my medication again. He wants me to go on the drug. I got angry and walked out." Sora put her face in her hands. "I will not do that!"

"Lithium?" Aidan asked, and then realized he'd said the wrong thing.

Sora's head snapped up. "Yes," she replied, "that one! He's so fixated on it, he will not listen anymore!"

Sora looked ready to blast off, but she gripped the edge of the futon in an effort to control herself. "I won't have anything to do with that drug," She went on, "I know what it does to people, I've seen them. Shuffling up and down the halls, staring at the floor, talking out of their heads. I won't do it," Sora finished, "I will die first."

Mima took her by the shoulders. "Sora," she said firmly, but with a calmness born out of practice, "that will not happen. Mom and Dad won't allow it, and I won't either, but you must not go off like this."

"I know…" Sora balled her fists into her hair and pulled at it. "I can't do this, Mima," she cried. "I'm sorry. I'm sorry to have to lean on you all the time. I can't control these things like I want."

"It's all right." Mima secured Sora in her arms. "Let it go, Sora."

Aidan stepped onto the deck and pulled out his cigarettes. He continued to watch through the glass. Though only a matter of a minute or so, Sora was already "coming down" under Mima's touch and encouragement. Aidan had seen depressed and manic individuals before but never on the scale Sora displayed.

As he lit up, Aidan observed Mima's "therapy". He couldn't hear the words Mima spoke into Sora's ear, but these plus the gentle yet strong embrace she held her friend in helped bring Sora back. Her limbs stopped shaking, and she melted into Mima's arms.

By the end of his smoke, Sora was becalmed but exhausted. Mima laid her on the bed and wrapped the comforter about Sora's body. She then joined Aidan on the deck. "That," Mima said, "was a meltdown, though a lot less violent than others."

"I've not witnessed anything like that before," Aidan replied. "So this is what you and Sora's parents contend with?"

"Yes," Mima said, "but all of us are aware that Sora takes it the hardest. No matter what stress it puts on us, believe me, Sora places even more upon her own self."

She leaned against the rail and kept her eyes on Sora. "Sora knows what she has isn't her fault," Mima went on. "All the same Aidan, she tries hard to be 'normal', and composed. Sora feels so ashamed when she can't do it."

Aidan watched as Sora turned to face the wall and hid her body in the comforter. "The comedown must be pretty harsh."

"It is," Mima said. "You remember how I had to go in and wake her the other night? Same thing here –- it might take a while for Sora to awaken. Until then, I'll have to watch her."

"I can tell Sora is proud to have come this far," Aidan replied, "but how long can she go through this without hurting herself? For that matter, how do you deal with it?"

Mima gave her slight smile. "I deal with it," she said, "as we do any such incident in life. Sora and her family stood by me when I was in need; I do the same for Sora, but not in return for those kindnesses. I do it because she is my friend."

She looked again through the window. "Sora needs me, Aidan," Mima continued, "as she needs her parents and Eko. Sora will and has done the same for each of us. At the darkest hours in our lives, Sora rose to the occasion."

"I know about what happened with your father," Aidan replied, "Eko, too?"

"She saved Eko's life a couple years ago," Mima told him. "That is the kind of person Sora is; when things are most urgent or at their worst, Sora forgets her illness and she acts. We owe her that."

Aidan heard the sincerity and determination in Mima's words. "I am impressed," he replied with all honesty, "at your devotion to Sora. I never experienced that in my own family."

"We are different," Mima replied, "yet we are bound by circumstance, fortune and misfortune." She put her arms around Aidan's waist, and Aidan slid his free arm about Mima's shoulder. "We are this way," she went on, "because often all we had was each other. Sora, Eko, and Kaga were my true friends when we were younger. You became the one friend I needed in Boston. When I came home, Sora and Eko returned to their places at my side. I had to do the same. I will do anything for them."

Mima then disengaged and said, "I must be with Sora. Sorry if this gets involved."

Aidan shook his head. "Don't worry."

He watched as Mima went back inside to tend to Sora, and checked his cell. There was a text, and despite what just occurred, Aidan had to smile.

18 - Stuck in the Moment

The woman with the long hair and dye job leaned forward. Chin level with her Cosmo glass, the woman's upturned lips were a succulent, liquid red. The dark eyes focused across the table at her western companion with the five o'clock shadow, Asahi in hand. "While I am concerned over Sora," Eko said, "I know she is in good hands. I am interested in why you are now before me, Aidan."

"To see you," Aidan replied. "Your text indicated you wanted the same."

"Yes." Eko sipped her drink and set her glass to the side so she could take Aidan's non-beer holding hand in both of hers. "I admit," she continued, "that I enjoyed your company the other night, and seeing you today was good. I like you, Aidan; you are the man Mima made you out to be."

Aidan smiled and nodded. "Thank you."

"That said," Eko went on, "while I know you are not thinking this way, I want you to understand I am not promiscuous. It may seem to some that I carry on, but I am honest when I tell you that I do not share my bed with any man."

Eko was not being sanctimonious or in any way exclusive. "I'm not looking for, or expecting that either," Aidan replied, pleased he could say it with a straight face.

"I am sure." Eko nodded politely. "I appreciate you allowing me to say this," she said. "When a woman stands up for herself, it is at times taken the wrong way."

"I understand." Aidan drank, thought then asked, "Can you tell me about the way you and the others are so entwined?"

Eko's eyes widened, and she gave an inscrutable smile. "Entwined?" he asked with faux-mysteriousness in her voice. "I don't believe I comprehend the question."

"Perhaps I mean," Aidan could not find the right word without effort, "*intertwined*. Mima has spoken," he went on, "of the closeness she feels for Sora. I can see all the reasons why; it is there with you, Eko. Mima also experienced it with Kaga, though more intimately."

Eko calmly sipped her Cosmo and placed the glass on its coaster. "We have indeed maintained that friendship," she said. "Sora and I remained close friends with Kaga after the breakup, and after she went back to Osaka. I know Mima still loves and cares for her, but it is as friends. We do share a most unusual relationship, the four of us."

"There is an attachment," Aidan observed. "That's not a bad thing, but I've been led to believe such attachments are not always so in Japan."

"Families are close, that is so," Eko replied. "Roommates, as you would know them do not exist here. My living at home with my parents and Sora with hers is not so unusual as neither of us is married.

"The problem," Eko went on as she took another sip, "involves our ages. We are older than the average young adult at home, Aidan. That is where the 'Parasite Singles' term comes in. Sora has her reasons, and we know what those are. I have mine."

Aidan did not mention what Mima told him earlier. "You have every right to them," he said. "At home, with the economy as it is, there are many adult children living with parents or relatives. Things have gotten tough over there for some. We have our own version of such folks. They're called a lot of things, like 'Cellar Dwellers'."

"Ah," Eko chuckled, "the stereotype of living in the parents' basement? Or in the case of Sora, living in the room she grew up in as a child?"

"Something of the sort." The concept of grown men or women living in a darkened basement was a running joke, but Aidan didn't know anyone who lived like that. Sure, there were friends of his who had to move back in with their parents for a while after college, but those were temporary things. "I never had to deal with that," he admitted, "but then, my folks are both passed on."

"Oh, I'm sorry." Eko removed her smile. She reached out and once more took his hand. "Do you miss them?"

"Yeah." Aidan found he could answer so. "My dad died nine years ago of cancer. Mom passed on four years back. She had heart problems, and her health failed slowly."

Eko nodded sadly. "Still I am sorry," she replied. "How did your siblings take it?"

"We did okay," Aidan explained. "Stephen never talked about it, he kept those things to himself. Katie, our sister is the oldest. She was like that, too. We all held it in, I suppose."

"I see," Eko assessed, "reserved. Is that a common trait for Americans? It does not seem so here, with the way your countrymen sometimes present themselves."

The sounds of this dimly-lit bar faded out. Aidan didn't hear the music, the clinks of bottles and glasses, or that loud group at the next table. He was looking into those eyes. Eko was deeper, more thoughtful and questioning than he imagined.

Aidan tried to regain himself, but Eko had him and her smile confirmed it. "Perhaps it is our error," she went on, "but we tend to see Americans as a loud, aggressive people, often impolite. You, Aidan, are the opposite of that."

"It's a New England thing," Aidan explained. "Northerners tend not express their emotions or feelings too well, apart from anger. When it comes to things like crying," he added with a shrug, "we're not good at that. It comes off as soft."

"That is familiar to me. You know," Eko asked, "how Mima simulates her tears?"

Aidan made the gesture with his fingers. "Like this?"

"Yes. Her sorrow is buried deep within," Eko said. "Mima once admitted to me she has not wept openly since the day her father threw her out. She did not even do so when her mother died; that's far too long."

Eko ran her index finger along the top of her glass. "I was aware of Mima's blading," she continued, "and I came to understand the blood she spilled was her way of spilling the agony out of her. I had to experience something similar before I could do the same, but it is what one goes through."

She drained her Cosmo and signaled for the bar girl. "Another, Aidan?"

Aidan slid his empty bottle next to Eko's glass. "I should say so," he replied, and again took Eko's hand in his. "I hope you know," Aidan said, "that I am extremely interested and intrigued by you, Eko. Your company is something I appreciate."

Eko's white teeth shone under the hanging lantern light. "That is good," she replied, "for I appreciate yours as well, Aidan. Perhaps I do know what you mean by 'intertwined'. You mean that Mima, Sora, Kaga and I are intertwined by our pasts and experiences, correct?"

"That is what I mean, yes." He'd had only one Asahi, but Aidan was already intoxicated.

"We have gone through much," Eko said, "but you have as well, Aidan." Her expression turned serious. "Mima has as any real friend would do, said nothing that would give the wrong impression. I do detect a strong desire in you to unburden yourself. I will not press you, but know that you can trust me."

The two hands squeezed each other in the moment, as the server stepped up to deliver refills. She silently took the empties, bowed and stepped aside.

* * *

The light over the computer cast shadows against the two women across the room. Mima sat on her bed and watched as Sora, wrapped in the comforter peered out. Only her forehead and strands of hair could be seen.

"I'm sorry," she whispered.

"You have nothing to be sorry for, Sora," Mima told her. "You mustn't think that."

"I know," Sora replied, "but it is all the things that weigh on me. When they fall like this, it is so hard to deal with. I know I'm sick, and while it is not my fault, it is my responsibility."

Mima reached inside the cover and brushed her hand along Sora's hair. "Is it harder," she asked, "in these days as opposed to when we were in school?"

"I feel like such a child," Sora said in a small, tired voice, "a grown-up child that cannot decide anything. I get so hung up on decisions that I can't make them. The only ones I can make are when I paint; those I can do, but then that fails me."

Sora reached up to take Mima's hand, and held it to her face. "I lean on everyone," Sora continued, "my parents, Eko and you. It seems like I have to be around you to stay together, or when I have to let things go. I'd rather stay home, so no one sees me."

"Is that why," Mima asked, "you don't leave your room at times?"

Sora nodded vigorously. "If I had not promised Eko and the children I would go out with them today," she said, "I would not have left. I worked all night on the new one, Mima, and it's good, but I could feel myself going. I was afraid to keep any of it inside me, so I threw it all on the canvas."

"I have never been able to ask this," Mima said, "but I must now." She put her arms around Sora and asked, "What causes you to hide away in these moments?"

"It is pride," Sora replied, "and I get trapped by it. I take to bed and try to ride out the storm within, so you don't have to deal with it. It's worse when I become delusional -- then I have to hide."

"You are aware of it, though," Mima said. "I have seen you that way."

"And I must hide away," Sora finished with a deep sigh. "I so want to have a normal life, Mima," she said. "Mama and Papa-san won't be around forever, and I can't have them taking care of me the rest of their days. I should be watching over them, that is my obligation."

Mima needed to move the subject forward. She slid alongside Sora and gently pulled the cover off Sora's shoulders. Mima then took Sora's upper body into her arms. "You are thinking properly, Sora," she said, "but your illness has other ideas. The medicines need to be changed again, am I right? I understand why you're scared of the lithium. I would be, too."

"But I don't want to be like that, Mima." Sora buried her head against Mima's shoulder and said, "One of the girls in my old support group, Noboku, she was on that stuff. She hated it, Mima. She told us about it, and how it made her so sick."

This was news to Mima. "You never told me about her."

"The rule was," Sora explained, "that whatever was talked about in the group, stayed in the group. There were six of us, during that time last year."

"You are no longer in it," Mima said. "Can you tell me about Noboku, and the others?"

Sora sniffed and rubbed her eyes as she clung to Mima. "I suppose so…."

* * *

The meetings were held in an old office building in Shinjuku District. By day, this was a conference room, but at night various non-profits took it over. The walls were painted white, and the overhead fluorescent lights further brightened the interior. The blinds were drawn, and a large dry-erase board sat in the corner, the official name of the group written in red.

Sora looked around the rectangular conference table. At its head was the facilitator, a mental health professional in his fifties. Seated in the plush chairs were the people Sora had come to know over the past several months: a construction worker in his forties, a musician of about thirty, a housewife, a retired office executive, and the one all knew as Noboku.

She was the youngest, a tall, painfully thin but attractive woman. Noboku's hair was long, her eyes black. She dressed fashionably and with careful taste. Her favorite color was brown, and Noboku usually wore a lot of it. Tonight her outfit included a brown dress, knee-high boots and a brimless felt cap. Of those she'd met here, Noboku was Sora's favorite.

* * *

"Noboku was more anxious," Sora explained. "She used to have hallucinations, these trips where she believed she was a goddess. Noboku said during these periods she believed her first child would be the child of God. Our meetings went this way…"

* * *

The facilitator opened the session by asking how each person was feeling. There was no need for introductions; they knew one another. Everyone took their turn, though members did not need to speak if they so chose.

That was no problem for Sora, but here she kept her remarks brief. Some of them went on forever. With tactful prompting, all would get in their report about their health, their feelings, medications and so forth. The facilitator then asked more general questions, and encouraged the group to join in the dialogue.

Meetings of any kind bored Sora. It felt like being back in a classroom, but Sora knew she had to listen as well as speak.

* * *

"The older people were the quiet ones," Sora said, "I think they were embarrassed to be there. They needed to be helped, to bring them out and let them know that it was okay to be there and talk about it."

Mima's voice echoed in Sora's mind as if from deep space. "And the others?"

"The musician guy was off the wall," Sora explained. "He just talked and talked and slurred his words. Nice person, but his attention span was messed up. Most of his medications were to bring him down. He could be that way a lot, too; he'd lost his band and his family."

"How about Noboku?" Mima asked. "You bonded with her?"

"Yes, we did…"

* * *

Noboku stood up. Sora had tuned out most of the conversation this week, but now she paid attention.

"I think…" Noboku had restless hands, and she used them to make her point. "…I have to consider the possibility of trying lithium once again. I have spoken in the past of its effects on me; at the same time, I fear I don't have a choice."

"I'm on it now," the musician replied. "I don't like it either, but it does slow things down enough for me to function."

Others made sounds of agreement. "All the same," Noboku went on, "I fear what it will do to me in the long run. I am doing well in school, but it is hard to keep things together. I find myself unable most days to get out of bed, and yet I know I must. I drag myself here and there; other days, it feels I am on fire, and I cannot stop moving."

"These are very common moods," the facilitator observed. "Can you tell us, Noboku-san," he asked, "why your doctor feels lithium is required?"

"I've run out of medications," Noboku replied, "and options. It appears to be the only remaining alternative."

$$* \quad * \quad *$$

"The room went silent," Sora recalled. "I saw the look on Noboku's face; it was the look of someone who faced a death sentence. After the meeting, I caught up with her..."

$$* \quad * \quad *$$

Noboku was always first to leave the room. Sora pulled on her coat and threw her bag over her shoulder as she ran to catch up. "Noboku-san, wait!" she called.

The young woman stopped at the top of the stairs. She smiled at Sora, a tense, thin one. "Yes?"

"I was wondering," Sora asked as they descended the stairs together, "if you would like to go out for a drink?" They'd done so in the past, and Sora felt a strong desire to speak more with Noboku.

"No, but thank you, Sora-san," Noboku replied with an apologetic smile. "I do have to get home –– I have a research paper I must finish."

The two walked toward the nearby Metro station in silence. Sora again tried to initiate conversation. "I wondered if you were okay," she said. "You sounded nervous about the lithium. I know I am –– my therapist wants me to use it, too."

"Don't let them!" Noboku's hand shot out to Sora's arm. The woman's eyes flashed, and they looked right through Sora.

"It is a terrible drug," she went on, "you are better without it, Sora. It is not something you want."

Sora could not look away from the urgency in Noboku's eyes. "It's that bad?"

"Yes," Noboku replied, and the two resumed walking. Before they parted at the Metro, Noboku turned and embraced Sora.

"Be strong, Sora-san," Noboku said, and her smile returned. "You'll be all right."

Sora held Noboku a moment more. "How about you?"

"I will be fine," she replied. "See you next week."

The two exchanged waves as Noboku headed for the escalator. *That was the last time I saw her. I quit the group after I learned Noboku committed suicide.*

✳ ✳ ✳

"How did she die?" Mima asked gently.

"Noboku didn't show up the next week," Sora replied. "It wasn't unusual for someone to skip a night; we'd all done it. Then at the next session…" Sora took a deep breath. "…we were told she stepped in front of a train near her home."

"Oh, no."

"Noboku's parents told the group leader she'd gone back on the lithium, then went off it again," Sora said. "We knew she didn't like the side effects. Noboku was thirsty all the time, and it made her sick to her stomach. They were going to put her in the hospital, but Noboku didn't let them."

Sora's words became a torrent. "The day before she was to go," she stammered, "Noboku climbed a fence and hid near the tracks. When an express train approached, she stepped in front of it. There was no time to stop."

Mima held her tighter. "I'm sorry."

"She was only nineteen, Mima!" Sora cried. "That girl was so smart – she was on scholarship to a big university. Noboku had her whole life ahead of her, but for this!"

She burst into tears again and curled up against Mima. "Is this what I face, Mima? Will that be what I turn into?"

"Sora," Mima replied, "you and Noboku are not the same person. We'll find a way for you, but don't think like Noboku," she pleaded, "don't go there."

"I don't want to," Sora sobbed, "but what choice have I? I don't want to die, Mima, but I can't live like that. I'll be living dead. What kind of life is that?"

"I know," Mima told her, "but not everyone will have the same reaction, Sora. Even if you have similar reactions to what Noboku went though, there has got to be ways to make it work. We'll find them."

Mima took Sora's face in her hands and kissed her cheek. "I love you, Sora," she said, "and I promise, we'll make it through. All of us will."

"You mean for yourself, too?" Sora asked.

Mima paused. "Of course," she replied, "I'm in this, too."

19 - Affirmations

The room was so dark Aidan could not see his hand front of his face. That was of little consequence at this point.

He lay on his back, naked. A down comforter covered most of his body, the thinner, warmer one provided by Eko. She was asleep, her legs coiled tightly about his right one, and her hands gripped his shoulders.

Aidan slowly ran his fingers through Eko's long, thick tresses. Her breath was warm against his chest. He kidded himself for pretending this wasn't something he wanted.

They had gone back to her place, and Eko disabused him of worry. "I've done it before," she replied with a grin as they climbed into her car, a Mitsubishi. "Besides, we'll use the entrance which goes into my side. They will not know, at least not tonight."

She turned the key; the car came to life, and some female pop singer wailed over the stereo. "If you are concerned," Eko went on as she pulled into traffic, "it has been some time since I have done this. In any case, my family does not mind, for they hope one of the men I bring home might be the one."

The pair laughed, but in the back of Aidan's mind, he wondered about something Eko said before. As he watched the street traffic fly past the vehicle, Aidan then thought of himself, but in relation to Eko.

Eko was so poised, and Aidan admired that in anyone. She exuded confidence in everything she said and did, yet Aidan focused in on those same qualities. They were the ones easiest for any person to put forward, but they could also mask the most glaring of weaknesses.

"What are you thinking of?" The Mitsubishi was at a stop sign, and Eko turned to look at Aidan.

"Why I'm here," he replied. "My concerns about Mima and others."

Her hand reached over and took the one nearest hers. Eko said, "It is all right to think about yourself, you know."

"I do." Aidan looked forward as Eko put the car in gear. "I feel there's a lot I should say and explain," he added, "but I don't always know how to do that."

"You will," Eko replied, "in time."

The drive into a residential area did not take long. It must be near Sora's place; Aidan recognized some of the buildings and signs in this district. As mentioned, Eko's home was a duplex with distinct separate units. The porch lights for both entrances were on. Aidan could see an SUV in the driveway, a Honda. Eko pulled her car into the open space beside it, and the two alighted.

She took Aidan's hand and led him around the side of the house. She unlocked a door unseen from the street. Up a short flight of steps and they were inside.

The unit was larger than apartments such as Mima's. It boasted a kitchen and small sitting area with a television. Sliding doors hid the bath and bedrooms, and Eko led Aidan inside the latter.

There was no more need to be polite. Aidan pulled Eko to him, and they kissed. Aidan did not think of what Mima would have to say about this. He didn't think of Philippa, either. The only person that mattered was Eko.

The lead-up took a long time, but neither was in a hurry. As their clothes went away, so too their inhibitions.

Aidan was about to remove Eko's blouse when her hands stopped his. Her back was arched, her slender legs spread, her hair about her body. "Turn off the light," she whispered. "I like it in the dark."

What followed was physical. Aidan knew what he liked, and hoped Eko would go along with it. So far, she had. For a woman so small, Eko had surprising strength. The two did not fight – each coaxed, urged and forced all they could from the other.

Eko moved from her knees onto the bed once again, and Aidan followed her. He kissed her mouth, then down her neck and to her small, but well-formed breasts. He lingered there for a short time, and then kissed down her belly.

Her hand suddenly squeezed Aidan behind his neck. "Now, Aidan," she ordered, *"now!"*

At that moment, Aidan felt something cross his lips that didn't feel right, but he thought no more of it. The coupling was swift. Aidan's gasps and Eko's cries must have been heard by her family (if not the whole neighborhood), but neither cared.

There were words hours after all this, but Aidan could not remember most of them. He did remember what he said when their bodies slowed down, and Aidan pulled Eko to him. "I love you, Eko."

From the darkness, Eko's voice, thin but strong returned: "And I love you, Aidan."

Aidan didn't want to move again. He didn't need to know whether this was collective lust between two people or something real. It felt real enough to him.

He slowly drew Eko closer. She gave a sigh, and while asleep Eko pulled herself tighter to Aidan's body. They were all right for now.

* * *

The two-liter bottle of Pepsi Red was half-empty. Mima and Sora were seated on the floor before the TV, on a break from *Halo 3*. "So," Sora asked, "wherever did Aidan-san end up?"

The two giggled like a couple of women younger than their years. They weren't drunk, but the combination of the soda, a bag of chips and half a box of Pocky sticks left them wired.

Their disposition was certainly better than a few hours before. Sora had gone to sleep, the usual result of her meltdowns. Sometime in the night, the two awakened and talked while they held to one another.

"Sorry again," Sora had whispered from beneath the comforter.

"I'm gonna smack you," Mima replied with mock severity, "if you apologize one more time."

Sora chuckled. "I might enjoy that, you know…*Nyah!*"

They laughed and then lapsed into silence. Mima found the courage to ask, "Have you considered what you might do, Sora?"

A sigh expelled from the body beside hers. "I have," Sora replied. She paused, then said, "I will think about the lithium. I'll try not to be so dismissive of it, but I believe the real problem is with the other drugs, or perhaps the combination of them."

Sora rose up on one arm. Her hair hung over her face, her voice rough from use. "I'm almost sure that's what it is," she went on. "The way I feel when the changes come? That could be it."

They sat up, and Mima wrapped the comforter about their bodies. "Tell me more."

"There are certain medications," Sora explained, "that are constant for me, but I am certain it's the others. There's too many, and I'm going to ask the doctors to take another look at them."

"That's sensible," Mima praised. Sora was coming out of her crash; this was the best time for her to think. "What else have you considered?"

"One thing the therapist has brought up but I've resisted it, too: ECT."

Mima knew what that meant. "Electroconvulsive therapy."

"Yes. That could be the ultimate last resort." Sora shook her head. "I remember those horrible images in old films of people convulsing. I read a story about a woman who went through that, too. I could never."

"The treatment," Mima said, "is not like that at all. I've read it is safer than that, though I don't think I'd want to find out."

"It's funny," Sora replied. "Noboku never brought that up in the meeting. I am sure she refused that idea as well." She sniffed and added, "I want to think that before we go there, I might find another way. There is something else I've been wondering about."

"Such as?"

"My thought processes," Sora said, "have never been very straight. I may have to change the way I think. Does that sound right?"

"You mean," Mima asked, "your cognitive thinking?"

"That's it." Sora went over the points by counting them off on her fingers. "I've tried hard to understand things," she explained, "and a lot of it is impulses. I have them -- you know what they are, Mima. I feel sometimes like I'm falling into deep water, and I have to go down with it, though I fear I might drown."

Mima nodded. "That sounds right."

"The other thing," Sora continued, "is the impulse I have to shop--you know me, I can't go past an art store without going into it."

Mima laughed, and Sora joined her. "I'm that way, too," Mima admitted.

"Yeah, but you know what I mean," Sora replied. "I have a method -- if there are things I need like supplies, I buy those first. Then I see stuff I want, and more stuff, and that's where I get into trouble."

"I think we all do that," Mima said, "but you did more than most back then."

Sora sighed and leaned against Mima. "I'm doing better at controlling that now," she asserted. "The problem for me is I get so overwhelmed, and I shouldn't. You take so much stuff in stride, Mima. When things don't work out, you accept it and move on. I can't do that; I feel like a failure and a loser if I have setbacks."

"I didn't used to," Mima admitted.

Sora's fingers caressed Mima's arm, and two of the deeper scars. They had faded with time. Others were thin lines one had to look directly at to see. "Mima," she said, "you've never told us exactly why you bladed."

"I did tell Aidan," Mima replied, "but that was because I had to. The pain came from the losses, the loneliness and my heartbreak. In a strange way, I imagined that when I cut myself, I was cutting my father to make him feel what he put me through."

"What did you do," Sora asked, "to stop that?"

"I just stopped." Mima rubbed her eyes. "After Aidan caught me," she said, "I forced myself to stop. Every time the urge came upon me, I resisted. By sheer will, I found other ways to stop the pain or direct it elsewhere."

"And the paintings?"

"I destroyed them," Mima replied. "I didn't want anyone to see those."

Sora looked to Mima. "You have shown such power before," she said, "I wish I had it, to stand up to what I feel like most of the time, which is a failure."

"It's a human thing, Sora," Mima told her as she held Sora close. "Failure is something we all have to face at one time or another. It does not mean we are bad people. It's also human to feel sorry for oneself. I know; I've been through that."

"True, but too many times," Sora said, "I feel the whole world is coming down on me. I know it's silly, but when I didn't do well in school or a painting didn't come out right I used to feel I was worthless. I would hear the voices of people screaming at me."

"Whose voices?"

"Voices," Sora said, "no one's in particular. I'd hear a million voices shouting at me, calling me names. I would try to shut them out, but I couldn't. This was before they found out what was wrong with me, Mima, so don't think it's happening now."

The two pushed back against the wall, and Sora stared up at the ceiling. "I need to get out of my house again Mima," she said. "I have got to try and live on my own again, and this time I can't fail. Yet I am so afraid of another failure. I know what I must do, but I can't take that first step, not yet."

Mima embraced Sora beneath the cover and kissed her forehead. "Sora," she said, "what you have told me is almost like a revelation, your own. You've recognized the problem, and you may have found the solution with your medications. That's a positive thing, Sora, and I know you'll do it one day. The rest of it is one step at a time."

"I believe in your words, Mima," Sora whispered. "I have always believed in you," she added, "but I have to learn to believe in myself, too. I'll do my best, I promise."

They smiled. Then a moment later, the two kissed one another on the lips. It was a totally conscious kiss; both made the move at the same moment.

"Love you, Mima-chan," Sora declared, "my dearest friend."

Mima blushed and hid her face in her t-shirt, which made Sora giggle. A moment later, Mima lifted her head and kissed Sora again. "You know I hate that 'BFF' term," she said, "but you are my best -- no offense to Eko or anyone else."

"She would understand." They kissed once more and held each another. Mima didn't think there was anything sexual about the moment, yet there was a feeling that came with it, a familiar one.

Mima thought of it again later as she fired up the Xbox. She looked over her shoulder and watched Sora while she rummaged through the kitchen for snacks. Mima had never been kissed by anyone other than Kaga, except for Aidan's attempt. Mima wondered if that counted.

She and Sora then battled it out on the game. During a break, Mima received a text. "Ah," she declared, "a report from our wayward foreign correspondent."

Sora produced a mischievous smile and slopped the last of the Pepsi Red into their glasses. "Ah," she replied, "and just what is Aidan-san up to?"

Mima grinned and showed Sora her Smartphone. "I have a feeling he and Eko are having their own discussion."

"She's captured him!" Sora exclaimed. "I knew they would like one another." There was more laughter, and Sora added, "I know that didn't sound right, but I think Aidan and Eko would be good for each other. Of course, how they'd ever have a real relationship, I have no idea."

"That's true," Mima said. "Aidan lives in Washington, when he's not running around the world. Eko is a Tokyo girl. This is her home, and I can't imagine her moving away, let alone to another country."

"I know, but wasn't it the same with Kaga?" Sora asked. "A distance thing?"

"Yes," Mima replied, "but in the end, Kaga was right. I grew up, and I changed over there. Kaga did when she went away to school. Without that parting, neither of us would have grown the way we needed to. I don't think we would have been able to stay together anyway."

She took a deep drink of the soda. "I am grateful to have had Kaga in my life as I did," Mima went on. "I felt so honored to be loved by her. To feel that close to someone I admired and respected, and to have that given back in a meaningful way…"

Mima raised her hand to make her point, and let it fall. "How glorious that was. I had what all people dream of, the things that are expected when one falls in love. I can never hope for that again. At least I had it once."

Sora slid over, put her arms about Mima's neck and kissed her. "You did have it," she replied. "Kaga loved you, and while I was envious, you needed each other. Friends like you two were, and I hope are -- we all need them. Though far apart, to know the other is there for you is heartening." She then leaned against Mima and whispered, "You are that friend for me, Mima."

The embrace was their affirmation and the kiss they shared bound them together. Mima drew breath as she held Sora to her.

"I am the luckiest of all," she said, her words muffled by Sora's face and hair. "I have had two, all this time."

20 - Healing Ground

"I do have to go to work," Eko said as she ran a brush through her hair before the mirror, "but not till later."

Aidan watched Eko's thin frame from the bed. She had donned a black silk bikini and matching tank top; a sultry female voice sang from the stereo on the dresser at low volume. It made for a striking picture. "I don't mean to hold you up," he replied.

Eko turned to face Aidan and smiled. "You do nothing of the sort." Then a remarkable change came over Eko. Her eyes flitted to the side, and she turned away.

Aidan sat up. "What's wrong?"

Eko took the two steps to return to the bed. "Aidan," she said, "there is something you need to see. It will help you understand."

She went to her knees before Aidan, and he had to smile. He regarded Eko's breasts as they pushed beneath the top, and of course the rest of her. Aidan took in the remnants of her perfume, and ran his finger along her bare thigh; Eko enjoyed that, but she remained resolute.

"My point," Eko continued, "is you have a hard time letting things go. I do as well, but I must now. I also hope what you are about to see does not upset you."

Aidan was confused. "Why would it?"

"You will see." Eko's face fell. She vacillated, one moment confident, now uncertain. Hesitantly, she reached down for the hem of her top and pulled it over her head.

What Aidan saw made him gasp. Across Eko's belly, above the navel were two deep, jagged scars. One was about eight inches long, and parallel to it was a second one half that length. The cuts were fused, irregular rivers across Eko's torso. Aidan had seen enough casualties to know what these were. He also knew what his lips came across while kissing Eko down there.

He looked to Eko. Her face was now of a woman ashamed, but not of her nakedness. "What happened?"

"Three years ago," Eko replied. She crawled to Aidan's side, propped up her pillows and sat back against them, legs drawn to herself. Her head lowered, Eko's hair washed over her small body. The assured and forthright woman Aidan knew existed no longer.

"In this bed," Eko whispered, "I was attacked. I brought a guy back here. He seemed attractive. Anyway, he wanted to do things I wasn't in the mood for, and he got angry."

Aidan cautiously put his arms around Eko; she did not pull away. "I'm not sure I can tell you this, Aidan," she said. "It's why I live at home. I need the safety of this place, even though I almost died here."

"It's all right," Aidan replied, "you don't have to tell me."

Eko huddled against Aidan. "No," she replied in a halting voice, "I have come this far. You must know. He pulled out a knife..."

* * *

Eko felt she'd been punched in the stomach. The small, stocky fellow with the short, spiked hairdo drew his hand back. In the light of the bedside lamp, Eko saw the flash.

Her reply to the second blow was of surprise. Eko didn't feel any pain, but knew she was in danger.

The only weapon at hand was the lamp. Eko grabbed it by the base and lashed out. The cover flew off with the first blow; then Eko thrust for her assailant's face. The bulb smashed in a shower of sparks.

Her assailant screamed and rolled off the bed. After swearing and hurling other words in Eko's direction, he staggered from the room. Eko could not follow him; her hands went to her stomach as she felt the dampness there.

Without the light, Eko couldn't see anything. She heard her attacker's flight, the door thrown open, heavy tread down the stairs and into the night.

Eko was blacking out from the blood loss. She reached for one of the pillows and tried to hold it against her stomach. Then came the pain.

The adrenaline was gone, and Eko cried out. Her voice was weak, and she floundered on the bed. Eko crawled for its edge, and her hand splashed in the widening pool.

She reached for the night table and grabbed her cell. In her confused state, Eko managed to flip it open and speed-dialed a number. Sora was near…

* * *

"I was dying," Eko said, her voice now level. "I couldn't think straight. I couldn't call out loudly enough, and I dialed Sora out of instinct. Fortunately she was home and rushed over."

* * *

"*Eko, hold on…*" She heard Sora's voice, but to Eko she sounded a million miles away. Eko could not see. She was floating. *What am I doing in the water?*

Another stab of pain and Eko's cry was cut off. Her cough made it worse.

"I'm sorry," Sora said, "but you've lost a lot of blood, Eko. I've got to stop it."

She sounds so calm, Eko thought. Sora applied pressure to Eko's abdomen. She moaned again, but it didn't hurt now. She thought she could hear her parents' voices. Her mother sounded frantic...*what's going on?*

"Stay with us, Eko," Sora called, "the ambulance is coming."

It was dark, but for a light in the distance. Eko felt herself moving toward it. "I'm coming," she said to whoever was there, waiting for her...

"Stop that!" Sora's voice was angry. "You're not going to die, Eko," she shouted. "I won't let you..."

∗ ∗ ∗

The head lifted, and Aidan ran his hand along Eko's cheek. Her eyes were slits, but Eko granted no emotion. "Sora got a towel and held it over the wounds until the ambulance arrived," she explained.

"Mima told me Sora saved your life," Aidan said, "but I didn't know how."

Eko rested her head on Aidan's shoulder once more. "Sora has the ability to react to things like that; she can be composed under pressure. She's like that with us."

"You did survive, though." Aidan lifted Eko's face to his and kissed her lips. "What happened after?"

"I was rushed to the hospital," Eko replied. "I underwent surgery, and they stitched me back together. I was in shock due to losing so much blood, but I survived."

Eko shook her head and went on, "The police never caught him. His name and description didn't match anyone they were after. I had enough to contend with at that point."

"How?"

"The trauma." Eko stretched out her body and lay alongside Aidan. "It took a long time to get over it," she said. "Mima, Sora, my family –- everyone supported me. If anything came from it," she added," I learned a harsh lesson: not to trust people so easily."

The warmth of Eko's smooth skin, the curves of her body and the softness of those long tresses aroused Aidan again, but it was not the time. "Do you think you were too trusting?" he asked.

"I was," Eko replied. "I was everyone's friend, I suppose. I lived life the way I wanted to, and that's where the 'Parasite' thing comes in. I told you I'm different, Aidan. After this, I became a different person inside."

Eko moved up against Aidan, her head to his chest. "What that man did to me left me paranoid," she said. "I didn't go out alone for a long time after that. I kept looking over my shoulder; I thought he was after me."

Aidan could sympathize, but he said nothing.

"I also had to deal with these." Eko indicated the scars. "They could be diminished by surgery," she said, "but they'll never go away entirely. I don't wear a bikini anymore, and I can't wear anything that exposes my stomach because I don't like people looking at me that way."

Eko sat up again, her voice now bitter. "I hate being asked about the scars," she growled. "I hate feeling like a whore because some people think I deserved what I got."

"Who said that?"

"One of the cops," Eko spat out. "He said I brought home a man I barely knew, so of course this would happen! I wanted to rip his heart out, but there wasn't one there."

"He's a prick," Aidan said.

"Among other things. I'm sorry, Aidan," Eko continued, "but you needed to know. As painful as it is, I'm okay. I can live with the scars. I can live with the fact I'm lucky to be alive and that I'm not ready to leave home."

Aidan watched Eko's face. If words were tears, Eko wept them. "Part of the reason was the attack," she said, "but I'm not a parasite, Aidan. Only the people closest to me understand because they know me and the things that make up who I am." She added, her voice breaking, "Others say I'm so capable in my job, with kids, other stuff. I am in some ways, but not others."

"As we all are," Aidan told her. He pulled Eko close and kissed her. After a few moments, their eyes opened at the same time and looked into one another's. Eko's smile was a real, but sad one.

"We have time, Aidan," she whispered, "can you now tell me?"

Aidan replied, "I'll have to take you back…"

* * *

The suitcase was packed, with the required amount of space for what Aidan knew he'd bring home. Aidan slid his new Dell Studio 15 inside its home and stowed that in his shoulder bag. These plus the Minolta, a quick check of his wallet and passport, and Aidan was gone.

Aidan took the elevator ride down to the lobby and wheeled his case out to the parking lot. Philippa was waiting for him in her Siouxsie & the Banshees tee, jeans and leather jacket. She blinked through her glasses; it was far too early for her. "Ready to invade Japan?" She cracked.

"As I'll ever be." He tossed his luggage into the rear of the Rover and climbed into the passenger seat. "It'll be a different sort of trip," he added.

Philippa nodded, her ear tuned to WTOP as she pulled out. The traffic report was longer than most stations provided, and she gunned the Rover down the street to line up behind several other vehicles for the Expressway. "Yeah," she said, "and it's a good thing for you to do. Wish I could get away."

Aidan looked over. Philippa was focused on the road, but leaned forward as if this would get the trip over with sooner. "The new guy gonna work out?" he asked.

"Yeah. Bob's a good kid. He's doing alright, but we'll see how long before the network fucks him up." Philippa shook her head. "You know, Callie was like that when she came up: all about the business, straight-edge journalism, the whole shebang. Then the power and the ego trip got to her."

"She thought she was the story," Aidan posed.

"Bingo!" Aidan held onto the *"Oh, Shit"* handle as Philippa floored the Rover and made an expert lane change. "Callie let it go to her head," Philippa went on as she braked to a legal speed, "she started rubbing elbows with all those big names, and she got star-struck. She let her personal politics and feelings get in the way, like most of 'em do. I never gave a fuck about Callie's antics and those blue-nosed assholes she hung out with. Callie didn't care that I was a lefty either. We were friends. We got along, and we worked well together, you know?"

"I do." Aidan worked with plenty of people that he would never have associated with outside of work, but that was the business. You couldn't always choose your colleagues. "Not to change the subject," he went on, "but do you feel as I do?"

"How?" Philippa shot a quick glance over her glasses to him.

"Used."

"Huh?"

Aidan reached for his cigarettes and opened the window slightly. He took his time in lighting up before responding. "I feel used, Phil," he replied after the first exhale of dual smoke trails from his nose. "Despite what Callie did," Aidan asked, "why do I feel what we helped do to her was incredibly wrong?"

Philippa scanned the traffic ahead and thought about the question. "I know what you mean," she replied after a longer than normal pause. "We got used to catch Callie out and make her talk. But God -- she brazenly handed over that info, knowing you would be a target, Aidan. In one way that justifies how I feel about it, but..."

"...it doesn't justify," Aidan finished for her. Philippa nodded, and Aidan continued, "It's wrong to say, but I can't stand that woman, and not only for trying to help get me killed."

He took another, deeper drag. Aidan was on a rare roll. "Callie is an example of everything I was taught not to be," he went on. "She transformed from a good journalist into a cartoon character, a media darling who thought it didn't matter anymore about being fair, or remotely honest! Her betrayal of me is one thing, but what makes me so mad is that Mansur got killed. His was a valueless death, like all the others; and it did nothing for anyone. It just caused more suffering."

Aidan threw the cigarette out the window and glanced at the leaden sky. They were approaching Dulles. A jet took off in the distance, but he didn't see it.

"You okay?" Philippa suffered through Callie's numerous diva fits before; this was nothing.

"No," Aidan exhaled. "I'm burned out," he said, "and it's not over Callie or her ilk. I'm part of the problem too, Phil. I'm causing the same kind of suffering. I'm a party to it all, and I fucking hate it."

"How are you involved in that?" The Rover came to a rolling stop at a red light; then Philippa wheeled right, with a squint at Aidan in the bargain. "Tell me."

"I put myself in those places," Aidan explained. "I'm like a prostitute: I fly around, I do these stories, but nothing ever gets done. There's no resolution and no solutions beyond revealing the things I report. I used to think I was doing good by bringing these things to people, so the rest of the world knew what was going on."

"And that is good." It was now Philippa's turn to finish. "Aidan," she said, "I get it about Mansur -- you and he became friends right away, but don't let his death stay on your conscience. That guy was a pro. He knew the risks, and that story does tell a lot more. Anyone who watched it saw something that needed to be seen. Whether it affects change or not, that's out of our hands. The fact," she went on, "that you put yourself on the line to get that story, and you presented it the right way -- that is your contribution."

Aidan kept quiet until Philippa pulled up to the United Airlines terminal. Once Aidan got his gear out he said, "I think you're right, Phil. You usually are about these things."

Philippa slammed the cargo door shut. "Forgive me," she replied in a sweet voice, "but I am right."

The two laughed hard, and Philippa took Aidan by the shoulders. "Look," she said, "you're my friend, Aidan, and I love you. I am to blame as much as you for us. I violated my first rule of this business, when I let a colleague become a lover. But don't worry, I've no regrets."

Before Aidan could answer, Philippa continued: "This trip will be good for you. You need time to decompress, work on your book idea and enjoy yourself. You'll figure out where you're headed. Just realize," she added, "you are a good person, Aidan. You have always been one."

"As have you." They kissed, and Aidan held her for an extra-long moment. "Thanks for the ride, Phil," he said. "I'll think about that."

He walked inside the terminal as Philippa drove away, like Stephen had. As he'd left his brother, Aidan didn't look back.

* * *

A whispered feminine voice made a familiar come-on through Eko's speakers. Aidan was back in her room. Topless, Eko returned the cordless phone to its cradle. She then slid back into bed and kissed Aidan. "Called in sick."

The voice whispered the next lines, which Eko lip-synced. Aidan grinned. "That's not gonna get you in trouble, is it?"

"No. Aidan, you are indeed a good man," Eko declared, "as Philippa said. I now see why you have come. As I say, you have a reason for others, but also yourself."

Eko slid between Aidan's thighs. Her fingers moved up along his unshaven face. She held it in her hands and said, "You are a brave man, Aidan, to go to places like Afghanistan, and to bring those stories back takes a special kind of courage." She kissed his lips. "Also," Eko added, "a special kind of person."

Aidan locked his arms around Eko's waist, but he could do no more than listen. "You have given up a lot," she continued. "About your life, and the questions you ask of yourself. All of us have to move on, but you do as well."

The song was the one Aidan thought it was; the woman's version of it was as seductive as the original, if not more. "I'm trying," he whispered.

"Do." Aidan closed his eyes and felt himself sink deeper into the bed. He felt Eko's body cover his own, those hands in his hair, her lips against his own. Then that woman's voice, sensually singing about healing of a kind neither he nor Eko had experienced in too long a time.

21 - The Call

They were not passing ships as Aidan and Mima did find one another at the apartment. The former got quite the appraisal from the latter as he returned in the early afternoon.

"Well, well," Mima called sarcastically from her worktable, "what has the cat dragged in?"

Aidan chuckled as Mima turned in his direction. While in last night's clothes, Aidan felt better after a few hours' sleep and a shower with Eko. "Draw your own conclusions, Mima," he replied with a sheepish grin, "I'm sure you will."

"Your hair is damp," Mima noted, "but you have not shaved. Hmmm," she went on, index finger against her chin, "might I surmise Eko had her way with you last night and this morning?"

"Please!" Mima rocked on her stool with laughter while Aidan took off his boots and removed his jacket. "First," he replied, "Eko sends her best. Second, I am sure you know exactly what happened. Your personal grapevine has the longest of tentacles."

"Oh, not for everything," Mima replied. She was dressed for going out, in black skin-tight jeans (which showed off her curves quite nicely) a matching t-shirt and blue denim vest. "I'm off to close," she added, "sorry I can't stick around for the gory details."

Aidan shook his head. "They were not gory," he replied, "apart from what Eko showed me."

Mima slid her laptop into its case. She gave no surprise in her reaction. "I'm impressed," she said. "The stabbing was one thing, but Eko is extremely self-conscious about the scars. She definitely likes you."

"Is that a bad thing?" Aidan asked as he sat on the couch. "I got the feeling you were upset that Eko showed interest in me. The signals were pretty obvious."

Mima shook her head. "No," she said. "If you and Eko have hit it off, then good. Eko didn't socialize with anyone except us for a long time after she was attacked. She protected herself behind the 'Parasite' label, in spite of her dislike of it. Eko had to work through a lot of pain, and not only the physical kind."

"I can believe that," Aidan replied, "but Eko was very forthright about it all." Aidan related some of the discussion, then finished, "As for the two of us, Mima..."

He paused, shrugged and then plunged ahead. "I have to admit, I love Eko," Aidan said, "and there's a lot to love there. Is it like Philippa and me? No," he answered himself, "that was different. I wonder can Eko love again after what happened?"

"With you," Mima said, "she can." She carried her bag to the bed and sat to put on her sneakers. "Eko has always been the woman you see on the outside," Mima explained. "You're the first new person she's opened up to since then, and I hope you can make it work. Eko needs time, but we all do."

"How is Sora?" Aidan asked.

"She's okay." Mima tightened the laces and stood up. "Sora made a forward step last night. She's identified part of the problem and pledged to take it in hand."

"Good news, then." Aidan crossed to the door and helped Mima get her backpack on over her jacket.

"Thanks. I'll be back in an hour or so." Mima then turned to Aidan. "Sounds like everyone's coming to terms with stuff, huh?"

Aidan didn't understand the question, nor did he get the look Mima gave him. A sad expression appeared momentarily, then was gone.

He made a point to give Mima a hug, which she returned. "Good luck."

"Thanks again!" Mima was out the door, and Aidan heard her quick steps on the stairs fade away.

He closed the door and thought for a long moment. That was a strange statement, and an equally odd stare. Aidan wondered what it meant.

After a needed shave and a smoke on the deck, Aidan began to re-organize what of his life existed here. He straightened out his suitcase. There was a laundry in the basement of the apartment building, and Aidan would need to deal with his. An inspection of his emails and texts followed. There was another update from Philippa and a forwarded story from a rival network that took Callie to task.

Aidan only read the first part. He knew the reporter who wrote it; he was as big a hack as Callie, only in the opposite direction. Aidan's name did not come up.

His mind wandered back to Eko. After their shower (a tight fit, but neither complained), Eko gave him a ride home. "I have enjoyed our time together, Aidan," she said as she drove, "and I'd like to have as much as possible before you leave. When will that be?"

"I don't know," he admitted. "I do have to return to Washington." Aidan explained he was a likely candidate to testify before the grand jury. Senate hearings were being talked about as well, but Aidan did not expect to be subpoenaed for those.

"And will you return to your work?" The corner of Eko's left eye searched his own.

Aidan leaned back in the seat. "Actually, I should get to the reason I am here. I've only taken a few photos, and that is something I need to do. As for the selections for the book and the editing, I can do those anywhere."

"Ah, so desu ne…" Eko's mischievous smile carried over as she made the turn onto Mima's block. "Then perhaps you will be around."

She switched on the flashers and brought the car to a stop. "Aidan," she said, "I don't want to force you into something you are not ready for. I'm not sure I am, either. But while you are here, I want to be around you. I am uncertain about all of my feelings for you, but know that I do have love and great affection for you."

They kissed, and Eko added, "Whatever direction you choose, Aidan, it must be yours. Don't make one that will please me; please yourself first. Do you understand?"

Aidan nodded as he took Eko's face in his hands and kissed her again. He took in her scent, and his time.

"I do, and I will, Eko," he replied. "I promise you that."

One last kiss and Aidan was out of the car. This time, he watched as Eko drove away. Her right hand waved out the window as she pulled back into the street. Aidan waved back and watched until the car vanished into traffic.

He thought again of that conversation. Where did Eko fit into his life, and he into hers? Aidan could not expect Eko to pull up stakes and follow him to the States, but Eko was as close to a westernized woman as he'd met here, next to Mima. She'd adapt to that way of life easily.

Then he had another thought: what about here? Tokyo was an expensive place to live, but was it any worse than DC? Both cities had their traffic issues, though Aidan guessed Tokyo had the edge due to the crush of population. Aidan would also need to work on the language; he was fluent in French, and had a working knowledge of Spanish. Japanese shouldn't be that hard. Aidan knew well if you were immersed in a nation, you learned fast.

Aidan shut down the laptop. He plugged in the charger and reached for his cigarettes. The book concept could be assembled here, but while he was back home Aidan would have to pore over hundreds of photos he'd never scanned. That would be a long job unless Mima knew some trick to that.

Then Aidan realized something more: while he'd been abroad throughout his career, Aidan never lived abroad. Perhaps that was part of the change he needed to make. All the same there was Eko's admonition… *please yourself first.*

He finished his smoke and was back inside just as the phone purred. Out of habit, Aidan picked up and remembered this wasn't his place. "Good afternoon," he greeted.

The caller converted to English, which was heavily accented. "Good afternoon," an official male voice responded, "this is Detective Fukuda of the Tokyo Municipal Police. I am trying to contact a Mima Sasaki. Is this her place of residence?"

"Yes," Aidan replied, "but she is not home. Might I help you?" The voice of the detective was correct and professional, but Aidan was more concerned about why the police would be calling Mima.

"Would you please have her contact us at this number?"

"Certainly," Aidan replied. He moved with the cordless handset to Mima's table. He found a pen and replied, "I am ready. The number is?"

Aidan wrote down and repeated the name and number. "What is the nature of this call, sir?" he asked. "Mima, I mean, Sasaki-san is a friend. Could I help in some way?"

"I should not say," Detective Fukuda replied, "as this is a personal matter."

"Would this be of an urgent nature?" Aidan asked. His journalist training kicked in; this was not routine. "If so," he went on, "I can contact Sasaki-san directly."

By the man's light breath through the receiver, Aidan could tell Fukuda was considering the offer. "Yes," he replied at length, "that would be helpful. Would you please inform Sasaki-san that her father has passed away?"

Aidan allowed too long a silence. "Hello?" The detective called.

"Oh, um…" Aidan stammered, then recovered, "…yes, sir. I will have her call you back as soon as I can reach her."

A thank you from the officer later, and Aidan said goodbye and hung up. Aidan stood in silence, and remembered what Mima said about her parents…*dead to me.*

Aidan would need help. A text to Eko was soon answered. The former told Aidan she was near Sora's house and would pick her up. Meanwhile, Aidan smoked on the deck and tried to figure out how he was going to break the news.

He deduced that unless Mima had reason to be involved with the police, then they would not have her cell. If they did, Mima must not have responded. She probably shut her phone off for the meeting.

The larger problem gnawed at him, and he hoped the others could help solve it. Mima never said much about her family, and nobody brought them up in her presence. Was that so as not to upset Mima…or didn't they know, either?

He didn't have long to wait. The apartment buzzer sounded, and Aidan let Eko and Sora in. After brief hellos at the door, the two hit Aidan with a series of questions.

"Did Mima ever tell you about her parents?" Sora asked.

"Only certain things," Aidan replied, and he related what Mima told him at Sora's house. "She's also said her folks were dead to her."

"Mima was dead to her father," Eko said, "that's how it really was."

"Did they say how he died?" Sora asked.

"No idea," Aidan replied, "they didn't want to tell me anything."

The three assembled on the deck so Aidan could smoke. "It's true," Sora said, "Mima's mother died about two years after she was thrown out. It's also true that Mima wasn't allowed at the funeral."

"Mima is the only direct next of kin," Eko noted, "so I can see why she was contacted."

"Mima almost never mentioned her natural parents to me," Aidan said. "I know being separated from her mother hurt Mima, that's one of the reasons she bladed."

"She told me more about that last night," Sora replied. "It now makes sense," she went on, "Mima was erased from their lives. Mima was close to her mother, but that guy ruled the family like an emperor."

"Authoritarian father?" Aidan suggested.

"Yeah," Eko said as she sat on one of the deck chairs. "The house, not to mention his family had to be his way and only his way. I don't think he ever hit his wife or Mima, but he didn't need to. He had such a hold over both of them."

Aidan shook his head. "I can imagine Mima being in for a lot of abuse, considering her nature."

Sora took the other chair. "That's right," she said, "Mima was so closed off and shy when she was young, and her father was not good at encouragement. The only way for Mima to communicate for a long time was her art," Sora added. "She opened up that way, and later to us."

"The subject of Mima's parents was a sensitive issue," Eko said, "and was rarely brought up. We tried never to mention them, out of respect for Mima and what she went through. That may have been a mistake. Mima denied their existence in an effort to shield herself, and we went along with it."

She stood up and joined Aidan at the rail. "When Mima was thrown out over her relationship with Kaga," she went on, "the split from her father was complete. It was the loss of her mother that nearly killed Mima. The woman was so under her husband's control, she couldn't break away."

Aidan stubbed out his cigarette. "I have no idea," he said, "how I'm going to explain this. If Mima has lived like this all these years, the last thing she needs is to have it brought back. And yet, Mima had to recognize this day would come."

"It makes me think…" When Eko didn't continue, the others looked to her. "Something still doesn't add up," she finished.

"Okay," Aidan broke in, "she's coming." He could see Mima now as she weaved her bike through traffic.

The three headed inside. "I should break it to her," Aidan said. "I took the call."

"We'll back you up," Eko replied. The women sat on the bed, Sora more nervous than Eko, but both were. Aidan was too as he headed into the hall. He could hear Mima stow and lock her bike in the foyer downstairs. He headed down the one flight.

"Hey," Mima called when she saw him, "it's a done deal."

"Congrats," he replied, "glad to hear it. Sora and Eko are upstairs."

"Cool," Mima said. She removed her helmet but noted Aidan's look. "What's the matter?"

"Let's go upstairs," he said quietly, "there was a call while you were out…"

There was no way to break it to Mima gently, but Aidan tried. Mima sat on the bed between her friends and Aidan took up the stool from Mima's worktable. Placing it in the center of the room before the three, Aidan passed her the note, sat down and detailed the conversation between himself and the detective.

Mima stared at the piece of paper, then looked up at Aidan. Though she showed no reaction, Mima seemed to shrink by the moment.

"I'm sorry, Mima," Aidan finished, "to tell you like this. I should have let the phone take the message."

"No, don't be sorry about that." Mima's hand went up to stop Aidan. "It's better you told me."

Aidan kneeled before her, and Sora and Eko rested their hands on Mima's shoulders. She stared at the note again. Her fingers trembled, and the paper slipped to the floor.

"Mima, we're sorry," Sora said. "What can we do?"

Mima removed her glasses. She could barely hold them in her hands, so she set them on the bed between her and Eko. "I don't know."

"Why," Aidan asked, "did you always represent your father as dead, Mima? I'm sorry, but this is hard for me to understand. If we're to help you, we need to know."

"He saw me as dead," Mima whispered as she looked up at Aidan. "I had no reason to consider him as anything other than that. I'll never get over what he did to me and to my mother."

Both Sora and Eko now put their arms around Mima. She leaned forward, her breaths heavier.

"What did he do?" Aidan asked. "I know about Kaga, but what else was there?"

"He…" Mima struggled to speak, "…never wanted me. He cut me off from all support. He forbade Mama-san to get in touch with me, though she knew where I was. She just did what he said. It was easier for her to keep the peace."

Mima swallowed. "Then," she went on between gasps, "he forced the rest of the family to forget about me. He drove them away, convinced them to ignore me, and I had no one."

Mima wrapped her arms about herself and set her teeth. She was headed full speed for a breakdown.

"Let it go, Mima," Eko urged.

"I can't!" Mima's voice was a cry, but to Aidan it sounded like one of the female characters on an anime show. "He took my mother away," she cried, "and he left me alone. He forced me to become a nomad, living wherever I could find a place. I had no home to go to, and no family that was mine!" She turned to Sora and said, "I know that sounds wrong…"

"…that's all right," Sora assured her, "I know what you mean."

Each word struggled to leave Mima's throat. "When Mama-san died," she said, "she died because her heart was broken. I know that – she was deprived of me, and so gave up. I wasn't even allowed to mourn her passing!"

"Look," Aidan said, his hands on Mima's quaking shoulders, "he is gone from your life. Mima, I'm sorry, but you need to let it go. There's anger in you –- I can feel it. I remember how upset and angry I was," he hurriedly went on, "when I found out what happened to me. It's never easy, but these things have to leave us. You can do it, Mima. Do it now."

Mima's reaction was more than the three were prepared for. She lunged forward into Aidan, and sent him, Sora and Eko to the floor.

Mima grabbed the stool Aidan was sitting on, and with a scream, threw it across the room. It smashed against the wall. The impact sent two of Mima's works to the floor in a shower of glass.

Aidan grabbed Mima's ankle and took her down. On her back, Mima shouted unintelligible words, swung and kicked. Aidan had to use his weight to keep her on the floor. The others each grabbed an arm and struggled to hold her.

"For God's sake, Mima," Sora shouted, "stop!"

"No," Eko said, "she has to let this out."

The three held Mima down as she screamed again, this time one long, loud shriek from deep within.

22 - Crossroads

Aidan lit another smoke as he stood on the deck with Eko. Both were well into the pot of coffee the latter put on. They watched through the door as Sora sat on the bed with Mima curled up in her arms. "Classic role reversal," Aidan commented.

"Classic?" Eko asked. "In what way?"

"Last night," Aidan indicated with his Gitanes, "Mima was comforting Sora in the same manner. Now it's turned around."

"It is how they," Eko observed, "and we are."

"So Mima's father was alive all this time?" Aidan asked.

"I didn't learn a lot," Eko said. After Mima calmed down, Aidan and Sora swept up the debris from her eruption. Eko meanwhile impersonated Mima over the phone in order to obtain more information from Fukuda. "The officer says they don't know when he died."

Aidan's brows rose. "They don't know? You mean, they can't tell?"

Eko sighed. "It seems Sasaki-san died alone," she explained, "but authorities can't be sure when it happened. His utility bills went unpaid for several months. That's how they found out he was dead."

"That would make sense," Aidan mused. "Mima's father sounded like a very ordered guy. He wouldn't let that slide, unless something happened to him."

"That's right. I know he had health issues of his own," Eko said. "The way he was, I'm surprised he didn't implode. The detective told me Sasaki–san took early retirement about three years ago. No one appears to have had contact with him since."

"So he cut himself off, too?"

"It's called '*Kodokushi*'," Eko explained, "a lonely death. It has become prevalent here in recent years. The elderly, having no family or close friends just die in their homes. Sometimes their bodies are not discovered for years."

"But he wasn't that old," Aidan asked, "was he?"

"No, but it does happen to men of Sasaki-san's age." Eko sipped her drink and said, "A lot of men never marry in this country because they devote themselves to their jobs and careers. They don't make time for a wife and family. Then, in middle age, they get laid off or lose work. They don't know what to do and have no one to turn to. They become reclusive and eventually die alone."

Aidan tried to imagine such a scenario, but couldn't. "I've heard of people dying alone, but never anything like you describe."

"Mima's got a tough job ahead of her," Eko said. "She has to go back to that house. The authorities need to figure out what to do with her father's body, and what his last wishes were." She again looked through the window. "For now, we have to leave it up to Sora. She's the only one that can get through to Mima at this point."

"There's a lot I don't understand," Aidan replied, "and I hope you can help me."

Eko looked to him. "What is that?"

"Mima," Aidan explained, "always struck me as a saddened person, despite her outward happiness. Is Mima bipolar too, like Sora? Is that how they understand one another so well?"

Eko moved her head in the negative. "No," she replied, "Mima is not. She does not have the mood swings and tendencies you've seen from Sora."

She motioned with her index and middle finger, and Aidan produced his cigarettes. "What you suggest," Eko went on after she selected one and Aidan gave her a light, "is true: Mima has never felt completely happy in life, though she had her good periods. When she creates, when she is with friends, Mima is okay. When she's alone, it is another story."

"Has Mima ever sought help for that?"

"No." Eko exhaled and shook her head. "Mima is too proud," she explained, "but Mima is also strong. She prides herself on her ability to work through things, but now..."

Eko took another drag, then stepped over to Aidan. "I knew this was going to come about one day," she said, "because her father denied her existence, so Mima did the same to him. The people you have met -- Sora, her parents, me? We are her family, Aidan. But now she has to face her real family, or what's left of it."

She rested against Aidan, who put his arms around her. "I want to believe she can."

"Whatever happens," Aidan replied, "I will help her. Mima is family to me, too."

* * *

Sora sat against the wall in the dark room. Mima was silent. She had not gone to sleep but remained attached to Sora, her head rested in her friend's lap.

"I know," Sora said as she stroked Mima's face and hair, "you would not speak of him because of what happened that day and afterward. You must have realized that one day he would pass on."

Mima shuddered. "Yes," she replied, "but I didn't think it would matter. I thought I was finished, and I wouldn't have to have to deal with him ever again. But I have to now, and I don't want it."

"What don't you want?" Sora asked.

Mima sat up and ran her hand through her hair. "I don't want anything," she explained, "from him. I don't want the house. I'm sure I was cut from the will long ago."

"We can't say that," Sora said, "until we know."

"I know." Mima leaned against the wall beside Sora. "All my life," she whispered, "my father resented me. I don't think he ever wanted children. I know Mama-san loved me, and she did her best. She was also traditional, and did whatever he said. He saw me as a hindrance, a pain."

Sora pulled Mima back to her shoulder and held her. "I recall," Sora replied, "your father was a stern man. He was correct, but I hardly ever recall him smiling. I got the strong feeling he didn't like kids. Maybe he just didn't like people."

"That's so." Mima's hands slid up and around Sora's shoulders. "No one was ever good enough for him," she said, "and his standards. His own were extremely high. He expected everyone to be as efficient, as hardworking, as goal-oriented as he was. Mama-san used to say his father was a lot like him: an emotionless man, sometimes difficult. He died when I was about two years old, so I don't remember him.

"When it came to Mama-san," Mima continued, "I believe he loved her; but he didn't show it well, and I never felt it from him."

"Mima-chan," Sora whispered, "we're here for you. You always backed us up, and we'll do whatever you need us to do."

"I wish," Mima sighed, "that Aidan didn't have to see this."

"Why not?"

"He's my friend," Mima said, "and he's got his own problems. What happened to him in Kabul -- that's changed his life. Aidan doesn't know where he's going now."

"Do any of us know?"

There was a pause. Sora hadn't meant the question to be such a deep one, but it made Mima stop and think. "What do you mean?"

"Look at all of us, Mima," Sora posed. "Aidan has his issues; Eko is not the same since she was stabbed, you have had a rough go, and we know about me. We're all in the same place, Mima. We don't know what's next in our lives or where we're going. We are all at a crossroads, and we don't know which turn to take. Better we go together as friends, don't you think?"

Mima didn't answer. Sora caressed Mima's cheek and whispered, "Mima, we've been through so much of each other's lives together, we know one another. We see in each of us the things that drive us, and make us whom we are. When I'm around you, things are good. I feel I can make headway in my life. I want to think I've helped you, and that I can now."

Mima's eyes fluttered. "You have, Sora," she whispered back. "You recognize me."

"What?"

"You recognize me for the person I am," Mima explained. "You've known me, when I didn't know myself. I've also seen the real you, Sora."

Sora felt Mima draw closer, and she tightened her arms about her friend. "You are an artist, Sora," Mima went on, "in the purest sense of the word. You paint the things you see, and the things you wish for others to see. That's what an artist should do. I'm also proud of you, for trying to break out of what holds you. You did it for me; you broke me out of that shell I was in."

"Seems like we're stuck with one another," Sora kidded, "aren't we?"

Mima smiled in the dim light. "I have never minded that," she said.

"Nor have I." There was a moment's hesitation, and the two kissed. Sora felt Mima's lips hold to her own.

"I love you, Mima," Sora whispered, "and I'll support you in anything and everything."

"After Kaga," Mima replied, "I believed there would never be another; but you were here the whole time. I love you too, Sora."

"We are together," Sora observed, "due to circumstance, but because we also recognize one another."

"And we make up for one another's differences."

The two chuckled and kissed again.

* * *

"I think," Eko said in the glow of her cigarette, "Mima will be all right. With Sora, she always has been."

"I think so, too." Aidan leaned over and kissed Eko. "I have an idea," he said.

"Oh?" Eko looked up with expectant eyes. "Tell me of it."

"It's going to sound weird," Aidan warned her.

"I like weird," she returned. "Try me."

Aidan grinned back. "Do you own a video camera?"

* * *

Once recovered, Mima resolved she would go to the house after she spoke to Fukuda, and all agreed to accompany her. Aidan also brought up his idea, which was received well.

"So how about your book?" Mima asked.

"I will do that," Aidan replied, "but there's something I've missed until now. There's a project here worth exploring."

The meeting then broke up. Aidan would stay at Eko's while Sora would spend the night with Mima. Mima embraced Aidan and Eko before they left. "I so appreciate you being here," she said. "I will see it through, and I'm glad I have friends with me."

"We've been right here," Eko told her as she kissed Mima. "If there's one thing we don't do, we don't give up on our friends."

At Eko's Aidan familiarized himself with her camera, a Sony Hi-Def with enough features to make a professional smile. "What do you have in mind, Aidan?" She asked as they sat on her bed. "What exactly are we going to be shooting?"

"I think," Aidan explained, "there's a real, human story to the world you three live in. Here's the thing: each of you have talked about the 'Parasite' term, and how some see you that way, right?"

"Right," Eko replied. "We try to ignore it, but it is painful since no one knows our situations."

"That's precisely what I'm getting at," Aidan concurred. "I would like to shoot your stories, and interview people like Sora's parents, her therapist, and Kaga, if she is willing. It'll make for an extraordinary inside look at your society, but also your personal lives."

Eko warmed to the idea. "That is a good concept," she replied as she leaned across the bed to kiss Aidan. "Are you thinking of selling this to your network?"

Aidan smiled as he kissed Eko back. "Well, it's not my network, but I've dealt with others. I'm sure I could find one that would air it."

"Well, then," Eko replied, "if they won't take it in America, NHK might. However, I would suggest a step beforehand."

"Which is what?"

Eko grabbed Aidan's shoulders and pushed him onto his back. "You should put my camera down," she ordered, "now."

Aidan carefully (under the conditions offered) set her camera on the floor beside the bed and pulled Eko down to him.

"Yes, Miss," he mumbled as their lips found one another's.

23 - Kodokushi

Eko's car pulled to a stop before the house. Mima and Sora were seated in the back; Aidan rode shotgun, camera in hand, and he continued to shoot until he had enough raw footage.

Aidan was first out of the vehicle. He stood back and shot again as Mima and the others emerged. The lens took note of how the women gazed at the home, and Aidan zoomed in on Mima. Her face was impassive, but Mima's posture showed she dreaded the coming experience. She looked over the site more like a prospective buyer rather than a person who lived the first 16 years of her life here.

The property itself looked like many of the others on this suburban block, apart from evident decay. Structurally, the place looked sound. There were no broken windows, and the roof appeared solid. A gutter hung at a bad angle on the left side of the home, and water dripped from it due to blockage. The lawn was overgrown with weeds and looked to Aidan like a small hayfield. The garage was closed, the windows for these too high and small to be looked through. Spooky was the one word Aidan could think to describe the place, but kept silent as he shot.

In the carport, its pavement cracked from the elements and age was an unmarked police vehicle and a white van from a cleaning service. Three young men in blue coveralls stood nearby. One talked with a small, older man in a gray suit.

"I know this place," Mima commented, "and yet I don't. I haven't set foot in there since I moved out."

Sora took Mima's arm and replied, "We're here, Mima. If it's too much, say so."

Mima shook her head. "It's cool," she said, "let's do this."

They headed up the walkway. At the garage, the man in the suit showed his identification and introduced himself as Detective Fukuda. Once proper introductions were made, Fukuda said, "First, Sasaki-san, may I express my sincere condolences at your father's passing."

Mima nodded in response to Fukuda's polite bow. "Thank you."

With Mima at his side, Fukuda preceded the others up the weather-beaten steps to the front door. "Based on what we were able to determine," he said, "Sasaki-san withdrew from society in the wake of his retirement."

"How did you find out he passed on?" Mima asked. She then recalled Eko pretended to be her with the detective. "I mean," she added, "how exactly?"

Fukuda paused at the front door. "A collector came by the other day," he replied, "because the electricity bill was overdue. Sasaki-san could not be reached by telephone, and a man was sent out. The collector noted the state of the lawn and took the initiative to walk around the house."

The delicate nature of what Fukuda then said was made clear by his hesitance. "The collector was able to look through Sasaki-san's bedroom window as the blinds were parted slightly. He had seen this kind of thing before; that is why we were called in."

"I see." Mima motioned to the door. "I am ready."

The door opened, and Fukuda stood aside. Aidan and the others hung back to allow Mima to be the first in. Mima paused, nervously. She took a deep breath and entered the foyer. Aidan focused over Mima's shoulder. The aim was to shoot through her eyes.

To the right of the door was a space for shoes. There was only one pair, obviously Sasaki's. Aidan immediately noticed a significant detail and zoomed in on it: a thick coating of dust covered the shoes. They had rested here for a long time.

He was also aware of a musty smell. "We have taken the liberty of ventilating the home by opening some windows," Fukuda explained.

Aidan sniffed the air. In addition to the smell, he became aware of how cold it was.

"This is eerie," Mima commented. "It's like walking into a mausoleum, it's so quiet."

The others didn't respond. Aidan shot and watched through the lens as Mima removed her shoes, then stepped into the living room. Eko took over shooting while Aidan removed his. She then returned the camera to him.

Mima stood in the room and looked down at the table. This had to be where the drama went down, Aidan thought. Sora stood by Mima as she examined the room. "Everything is so dusty," she said. "My father would never have permitted this."

"From his bank records," Fukuda replied, "it appears Sasaki-san paid ahead on his bills and insurance for a period of three years. That is unusual, but it was not until recently those went into arrears."

"That long?" Eko asked. "I can't understand how nobody noticed the lawn, and suspected nothing was the matter."

"I have questioned the neighbors," Fukuda replied. "According to them, Sasaki-san rarely left the home. There was no newspaper delivery, and he seldom received visitors. A local market delivered foodstuffs and supplies on occasion. The manager said Sasaki-san would call in occasional orders, but he stopped doing business with them some time ago. When he was seen, Sasaki-san did not speak to anyone. If he did, it was only to return greetings. He seemed to wish to be left alone."

Mima motioned to the room at large, then the walls. "Everything looks the same," she said. "Books are in place, the furniture has not been moved. These pictures," Mima added, "are as I remember them, but those of me are gone."

"We contracted for the cleaners," Fukuda mentioned, "as a matter of safety. They are ready to take charge at your word."

"That's fine," Mima replied, "but I should like to look around before they come in."

"Certainly." Fukuda nodded politely. "Please take your time." He then returned outside.

"Come on," Mima told the others, "I need to see this." She led them through each room of the darkened house. The mats crackled under their feet, they were so old. In the kitchen, there was a distinct odor from the refrigerator. They noted that appliances, utensils and related items were in order.

"This is like a time capsule." Sora noted the calendar on the wall, some three years out of date.

The bathroom was in the same, orderly alignment. Aidan and the others watched as Mima went down the hall and slid open a door. "This was my room."

All looked inside. The area had long since been converted to storage. Plastic containers and cardboard boxes were neatly stacked on one side of the rectangular room. Several plastic bags were piled on the right, and there was a narrow walkway to get through. Any indication a person once lived in here was gone.

Mima went to the next room. The door was open, and she looked in. "This was their bedroom," she whispered, and led the others in.

There was nothing unusual about this room either, except for the dust, and the spot on the floor at the foot of the bed. Blocked out by yellow police-line tape, there was a discoloration in the wood.

This might be dismissed as a stain or spill of some kind, if not for its size and shape. The shape was that of a man, but there was no man. All that remained of Mima's father was an outline. Whatever clothing he might have worn, that was gone, too.

"*Kodokushi,*" Eko whispered.

The body had dissolved; it lay there that long. From the taped outline, Sasaki must have died where he'd fallen. Heart failure, Aidan guessed.

There was a long silence as Aidan shot the scene. He found it hard to keep his hands steady. Angered as he was before, Aidan could not but feel sorry for the man. To die like this, alone; for what he'd done to Mima and by extension his wife, Sasaki atoned in some way for it.

"Sasaki-san's death," Eko declared, "was a lonely one." She put her palms together and bowed, and Aidan watched as Mima and Sora did the same.

Mima's eyes became attracted to something. Aidan followed them with the camera.

"Now this is strange -- look!" Mima walked over to the dresser. There were items any man would have on it: a comb, hairbrush, nail clippers and a round black container of some sort of hair product. There was also a framed photo of a couple, obviously Mima's parents.

The figure beside this was what caught Mima's attention. Gingerly, she picked up a little stuffed cat and held it in her hands. White with black spots, it bore the nub of the Japanese Bobtail breed. It sat in the famous "Beckoning Cat" position, on its haunches with one paw raised. Aidan knew the cat was meant to be a bringer of good fortune.

Mima showed the cat to them and indicated a small knob on the side. "This was a musical toy," she explained. "Mom used to put this in my crib when I was an infant. It played 'Sakura', and the music would help me go to sleep."

"That's so cute," Sora noted, but without joy.

She sat on the bed, and Sora and Eko joined her while Aidan continued to shoot. "My sister had a stuffed animal that made music, too, only it was a pig," he said. "Stephen and I each got it passed down to us."

"This is so odd," Mima said. "I can't imagine my father keeping this in here. Mama-san must have done so."

"Does it still work?" Eko asked.

Mima's fingers shook as she turned the knob and wound it up. Once more, the cat sang. The traditional melody of spring sounded as it was being played on a toy piano. No one spoke for several seconds as the song played, then slowly wound down; one note, then another, and another…

Aidan watched through the viewfinder. Mima held the tiny creature in her hands, and her head came up.

Tears fell from her eyes.

24 - Recognition

The four sat on the hood of Eko's car or stood around it. They had remained in the bedroom, for it took some time for Mima to regain her composure. One she did, Mima gave the go-ahead for the cleaners to begin work. Mima also conferred with Fukuda about the ongoing search for her late father's will and legal documents.

They watched from here now as the staff donned gloves and protective facial masks. To Aidan they looked like Haz-Mat workers. "I'll have to figure out how to get the house in order," Mima commented, "and make it ready for sale."

"We'll help you," Eko said. "I have a feeling it's going to take a lot of work."

"Do you have any other relatives?" Aidan asked.

Mima shrugged. "There may be a distant aunt, or a cousin or two," she admitted, "but I don't know if any of them are alive. My father was the youngest in his family. I don't know where the others are, it's been that long."

"The police can track them down," Eko assured her. "Right now, let's see about getting this taken care of."

Mima reached into her coat and drew out the stuffed toy. She held it gingerly and stroked the cat's head as if it were alive. "I think Mama-san kept this out as a way of having me close," she said. "It showed she still loved me, even if she couldn't tell me."

"Your mother was sweet," Sora agreed. "Look, whatever it takes to get this done, we'll help. You shouldn't have to do this alone."

"My uncle's an attorney," Eko put in, "if there's anything that needs to go to court."

Mima smiled. "Thanks, all of you," she said, and she leaned her head on Sora's shoulder. "I know now why I've put up with you two all these years."

The four laughed in spite of the circumstances. "Okay," Eko asked, "why?"

Mima rubbed her eyes behind her glasses. "Because," she replied, "in one form or another, we instinctively have come to one another when in need. It's never asked for, but done."

She reached out to Aidan and took his hand. "This goes for you too, Aidan," she added. "There's a reason we're together after all these years. You said it best last night, Sora. We recognize each other. So few people take the time to do that within their own families. We have that here."

Aidan brought out the Minolta. "Need a shot of you three," he said. "I know what you mean, Mima."

Sora and Eko threw their arms around Mima, and they leaned against the front of the car. The smiles were not overjoyed ones, but of three friends secure in their bond. Aidan clicked the shutter; a perfect still shot, and even better to see.

* * *

"Okay, we're rolling."

A pair of white sheets hung from the ceiling and walls in the corner of Mima's room. The remainder of the fabric lay in a cautious but casual fold, on top of which Mima's stool rested. The owner sat on it now and looked past the camera.

Mima's camera was on a tripod, which Aidan stood behind. To his right was Sora, the subject Mima was to "speak" to during the shoot. Moving about the room with her own hand-held was Eko. Her task was to take different angles of the "interview".

Mima sat up straight in her black jeans and a *Last Airbender* t-shirt. Speaking in Japanese, Mima answered the questions Aidan passed to her.

"My name is Mima Sasaki," she began. Mima stated her age, where she lived and her occupation. "The saying 'Parasite Single'," she continued, "is used to describe young adults, mostly women who stay at home longer than the average adult..."

Aidan prompted Mima with a further series of questions. He kept these open-ended so Mima could expound on her answers without direction. Edits could be made later.

"The term is insulting," Mima went on, "and I am offended by it. Technically I'm not one of these women because I do live alone, in my own place. I pay my bills, I take care of myself, but sometimes I feel as if those words are extended to women like me who don't get married or who don't choose to have children."

Eko was zooming in from Mima's right. Aidan smiled; for someone who described herself as an amateur, Eko was at home behind the camera.

"For me," Mima said, "it's hard. I was estranged from my family for many years. I recently found out my father passed away, and we're not sure when that happened. It is called a 'lonely death', and it is another of those subjects we as a society are not prepared to talk openly about. We must, though..."

Mima took a deep breath, and continued: "This may sound off the subject, but we need to be more open with each other, as people. We mustn't be afraid to talk about things that are personal or hurtful, no matter what some might say about them."

Eko took another angle to Mima's left and raised the camera above her. Mima carried on without notice: "My father kicked me out when I was in high school because I was in a relationship with another girl, a classmate of mine. After my mother died, he appears to have cut himself off from the rest of us. I don't know why…" Mima paused and scratched her head. "I wish I could know why."

Mima lowered her head, swallowed hard and looked up again to face Sora. "He let himself go lonely, for whatever reason," she said. "I have been lonely all my life. I was an only child, and were it not for some real, true friends, I would be more so."

Aidan slowly zoomed out. Eko moved around him to get another angle. "I am lonely," Mima confessed, and not without emotion in her voice. "I realize my life is a path that must be walked alone, and I've made my choices. I do not regret them, but it is difficult, very difficult…and painful."

Mima had no more to say, but Aidan let the camera roll. *We'll fade that segment out right there…*

* * *

"Aidan," the distorted voice sounded over the computer speakers, "I knew you were gonna come up with something exotic, but this takes it!"

The sound of Philippa's laughter was delayed by about a half-second, and it made her body language over the Skype hookup even funnier. Phil looked the same in her glasses and kinky hair, now dyed auburn red. She sounded like her mouth was full due to the new steel ring in her lower lip.

"Is it a good enough idea, Phil?" Aidan posed. He stood before Mima's worktable in her wireless headset. "What did you think of that footage?"

"Different," Philippa replied, and she turned the ring in her lip. "I don't speak the language, but I could tell from the questions you asked that it's pretty personal stuff. Mima's got a real, sensitive nature," she went on, "people will get that. I'd say film all you can, Aidan."

"This is gonna take time to get together," Aidan said, "but no one's checking my time card. At least I didn't think anyone was."

Philippa put up her hands. "Far be it from me," she shot back, "to push you in any direction, dude! It's your package; bring it when you have it. I think it's a good story, at least for some kind of human interest. But I gotta ask, what about your book?"

"I'll get to it eventually," Aidan assured her. "Right now, this has gotten my attention in a big way."

As he spoke, the women crowded around him and stuck their faces in the camera. "*Konichiwa*, Phil!" they shouted, waved and gave the "V" sign.

Philippa howled with laughter, which made her lean back in her chair. "Hi," she finally returned, "I can see that! Just like you, Aidan; you get all the good lookers, you animal!"

There was more laughter, and Mima pulled Sora and Eko with her out of shot. "As you say, Phil," Aidan said. "Look, I have to go because there are a number of issues before us. I promise I'll get on it quick as I can."

"You're on your own, as you like it, Aidan," Phil replied, "and good luck with that little blonde...*animal!*"

Aidan stuck out his tongue in response. "Love you, Phil."

"Love you too, man. Out!"

Aidan signed off and returned to the table where the others were gathered over cups of coffee and a series of documents. "Where do we stand?"

Mima looked up from the table. "My father's affairs," she said, "were not surprisingly simple. The will was in his safe deposit box at the Bank of Tokyo, along with his insurance papers and deeds to the house and property."

She then took up a series of bank records and continued, "His checking and savings accounts were in order. The police found his wallet and identification in the house; no unusual activity, and no signs of foul play."

"Do you know what the will says?" Sora asked.

Mima removed her glasses and looked around. "The preliminary examination is he left everything to my mother. However," Mima continued, "in the case of her death before his, everything would pass to me." After Mima let that sink in she added, "By the same language, I am also the beneficiary of his insurance."

"That's excellent news," Eko said. "The house is yours, Mima. At least that makes it easier to dispose of."

"A surprise," Aidan noted, "considering he ran you out of your family's life."

"Did he forget?" Sora asked. "My family's got a will, too, but they haven't touched it in years. Maybe that's what happened."

Mima thought about it. "I don't know," she said. "I'd like to feel relieved or happy over this. I'm not, though."

She rose and went over to the stool on the "set". "I don't want to sound ungrateful," she explained as she sat on it. "The money will be welcome. I could probably pay off debts, my loans, whatever else..."

Mima then rested her hands in her chin. "I am not trying to think about what I may receive. I'm just conflicted."

Sora moved to her and put her arms around Mima's upper body. "How?"

Mima rested her head against Sora's shoulder and replied, "I want to be rid of that house. The tenseness of my life there, and that one memory -- I want it all to go away. I need closure, yet I yearn for some connection to them. I wish I could have seen my father once more -- to ask why."

"I don't think he knew," Sora said, and she kissed Mima's cheek. "He had a way, and some people can't get out of that way, you know what I mean?"

"I do." Mima sighed and said, "I'm going to see Fukuda-san tomorrow. He is ready to wrap up the investigation. I will have to go to the bank, and I need to get the house ready to sell..." She then closed her eyes. "I'm so tired."

"That's why we're here, Mima," Eko replied. "Delegate. We'll help you get things in motion, and you approve or disapprove, okay?"

Mima opened her eyes and smiled up at Eko. "Okay."

The group broke for the night. Aidan would stay at the apartment as Eko had to work in the morning. She would take Sora home, and they agreed to return in the afternoon for more taping. There was also the issue of meeting up with Kaga. "Kaga promised to call when she hit Tokyo," Eko said.

In the hallway, Aidan embraced Eko, and they kissed. "Until tomorrow," he said.

"Yes." Eko kissed him again and replied, "Aidan, you have a brilliant plan for this story. Like the one in Kabul, it is another that must be told. I know I'll need to get in front of that camera too, but I rather enjoy the other side of it."

"You're not being forced to, you know," Aidan reminded her.

"No," Eko said as she held to Aidan, "but I must. Mima has shown her courage, but she has it. The recognition she spoke of is an important matter -- we recognize one another. That has sustained us all the years of our lives."

She ran her hand through Aidan's hair and added, "I recognize you, Aidan, as a man I am quite in love with."

Aidan smiled. "And I'm in love with you, Eko."

"That," she replied, "is all I need to know." The two kissed again, and through the cracked door Aidan could see Mima and Sora engaged in a warm embrace and kiss of their own.

Recognition…that word had a whole new meaning for him.

25 - Confessions

Sora sat before the low table, now situated on the drop cloth. Nervously, she checked her hair in a hand mirror while Aidan focused the steady cam.

For variation, he had Sora use the table and set the tripod at its lowest level with a downward angle. Eko would again move about with hers. This time, Mima stood off to Aidan's left as Sora's target. "Ready?" Aidan asked.

Sora looked up, nodded and put the mirror in the pocket of her sweater. She looked to Mima as the cameras rolled, and began to speak.

Her nerves showed, but Sora spoke a little faster than her friends anyway. "I was diagnosed with bipolar disorder in my first year of high school," she explained after her introduction. "I had always been energetic, a little hyperactive as a child, and that's what most people thought it was. I'd grow out of it, you know? Well, I never did."

She giggled slightly; then Sora visibly controlled herself. "I knew I was not right much earlier in my life, though," she continued. "I went through mood swings; I would feel indescribably happy, and then right after that in despair. Things that were amusing became hilarious to me. Things that were a little sad upset me to tears. I never knew which way I would feel, from one moment to the next. It could be very embarrassing."

"How would you feel about the highs and lows?" Aidan asked from off-camera.

"I would feel ashamed," Sora replied, "because no one around me was acting like this. Yet I didn't always know that I was different. Sometimes I might do or say something strange, but it wasn't that way to me. Then people would stare at me. Their faces always seemed to say, 'What the hell was that?'"

"The disorder has become more understood in recent years, though," Aidan said. "There is more to it than say, depression in itself."

"Yes, that's so. There is a neurological component," Sora explained, "a defect. I've had it explained to me, but I could not repeat all the terms for you. The short explanation is: something in us does not work the way it does for 'normal' people, but we're not abnormal either. I'm like everyone else; but I think differently, and the illness allows me to explore things in another way."

"Do you mean the creative aspects?" Aidan asked.

Sora knotted her fingers together on the table. She looked down at them, and then to Mima. "Yes. I have always loved to create things," she said. "I love to paint especially. Art is my outlet. I have a couple of hundred works completed. I've sold a few. Some I think are good. I have never felt that I am a great artist…"

There was a long pause, then Sora added like an afterthought, "…but it's all I have."

"When you say, 'all you have'," Aidan asked, "does that mean it is your one talent, the one thing you're good at?" He'd heard similar comments from people who were closely identified with their careers, either as writers, artists or musicians. He could think of one, but Aidan wondered what else was behind Sora's statement.

Sora took a deep breath and tried to focus on Mima. Almost immediately, her hand went to her face, and she tried to hide it. The other hand knotted into a fist. Eko zoomed in from his left. To his right, Mima stood where she was, but looked concerned.

Sora reached into her sweater for a tissue. Her other hand dug into the opposite sleeve of the garment as she tried to control the emotion. "That is it," she finally said and looked down at the table. "It's all I can do. I cannot hold a real job-- I've tried. I can't live away from home because I can't stay focused on things."

Less than a moment later, Sora became angry. "And I hate being considered a parasite," she muttered, "because I'm not! There's a reason I'm like this. You're looking at it now!"

Aidan never liked to film subjects in these situations. His colleagues too often exploited people for their emotions, especially their sorrows. This time there was something compelling about it: Sora seemed near the edge of either elation or depression all the time. Perhaps, Aidan thought if people actually saw such a moment, they might understand.

Her shoulders turned inward, Sora wiped her eyes again. "This is what I live with," she said, "every day of my life. I'm either like this, or about to be like this. My medications keep having to change with me, and dying sounds like an escape.

"The only friends I had," Sora went on as she wiped her face on her sleeve, "were three people: Mima, Eko and Kaga. They let me be Sora, and didn't judge me all the time. Without them and my family, I'd have jumped in front of a train years ago. One of my other friends did that."

"Tell us," Aidan prompted, "about that friend. Why do you think she did that?"

Sora dried her eyes. She told the story of Noboku, her place in the support group, and how she had taken her life. The recollection seemed to steady Sora. She then explained Noboku's fear of lithium.

"Have you ever tried that medication?" Aidan asked.

"No." Sora shook her head firmly. "I refused it. Noboku didn't like what it did to her, and I didn't want to experience it." There was a pause, and Sora added, "That sounds silly, not to want to at least try something, but I don't want to."

"Would you be willing?" Mima had asked the question on the spur of the moment, and Aidan continued to watch Sora's reaction. Eko moved around to the other side of the room and took a shot that was level with Sora.

"To do what?" Sora asked, this time specifically to Mima.

"We spoke of this earlier," Mima replied. "We'll help you, Sora, as you have helped us." Mima then moved into the shot and slid to her knees beside Sora.

Aidan and Eko looked to one another; the former nodded. This wasn't planned, but it was good. They continued shooting as Mima put one arm around Sora's shoulder and took her hand with the other.

"Sora-chan," she went on, "I love you. We all love you. If you have problems with the lithium, if you don't feel right, tell us. There is no shame in telling the truth."

Sora's lower lip trembled, and her eyes watered again. "You will?"

"Yes." Mima nodded and added, "I promised. It's what friends do."

Sora allowed Mima to rest her head on her shoulder, and she melted into Mima's arms. Aidan slowly zoomed out and let the camera roll for several seconds to allow time for a proper fade.

* * *

The tall woman's hair was now straight. It fell to her shoulders and naturally curled inward under her jaw line. In a brown suede jacket, a white turtleneck, blue jeans and sneakers, Kaga caught people's eyes. Her smile was bright, her movements graceful as she entered the restaurant.

Sora was first to greet her, with Eko a close second. The trio laughed with delight as they exchanged embraces, kisses and comments on how each other looked. Kaga's eyes then looked over at the table from where Mima and Aidan had risen.

"Meem," Kaga called as she came over, "I'm so glad to see you."

"Me too." The words, the movements and the show of affection were genuine, and Aidan smiled as the two old friends politely kissed each other on the cheeks.

"You look great, Mima," Kaga declared, then looked to Aidan. "And this must be Aidan-san, the intrepid reporter?"

Aidan laughed as he was properly introduced. "And you have to be the oft-mentioned Kaga."

Kaga's laugh was as easy as the rest of her nature, and the party sat at the rounded corner booth. Aidan watched and listened as Kaga caught up with her friends. Mima chose to sit beside her, but there was no physical need between the two former lovers. Mima was as easy around Kaga as the rest.

An update of Kaga's life was the women's first order of business. "Masato and I celebrated our second anniversary last month," she said, "and it's all good." She passed around her iPhone, which showed a photo of Kaga with a slim, bearded fellow in a tie and collared shirt. "Masato teaches science at my school," Kaga explained for Aidan's benefit.

"How's the team doing?" Eko asked.

"My girls are awesome," Kaga gushed with understandable pride. "We tied for the district title last season, and I've got most of them back for the coming year. They're my kids, what can I say?"

"How about your health?" Mima then asked.

"I'm okay," Kaga said. "I take my meds, I stay fit, and I don't miss my checkups. I'm fine," she added, and Aidan noted the movement of her hand for Mima's. Mima accepted it, and the two women grinned. The friendship, and love remained.

A double order of steamed clams and a second round of drinks later, Kaga declared, "I'm done talking about myself. Tell me about all of you," she added and nodded toward Aidan, "especially you. I've heard good things about your work, and I'd love to see it. I'm staying with my cousin another day or two, so I'll be around."

The others deferred to Aidan. He explained his reasons as well as the new project, which intrigued Kaga.

"Would you be willing to take part in the shoot?" Mima asked her. "I'd never done anything like that before."

"We agree you'd have a lot to add," Eko put in.

Her glass of Kirin halfway to her lips, Kaga froze; she then carefully returned it to the table. "Whoa," she replied, "I honestly had no thoughts of getting involved. I'm honored to be asked, but what would I say?"

"You have a unique perspective," Eko said, "of us, and yourself. I often have said you emerged from our earlier life with fewer scars than the rest of us."

There was a chuckle around the table, but Kaga didn't take part in it. She stared at her hand, connected to her glass. After a moment, Kaga looked up. "Sure," she said, "I'll do it. Perhaps then I can say what I wish to."

Aware all eyes were on her, Kaga went on: "I don't think I've always been entirely open about things regarding the four of us. Maybe I could explain some of it better in that way. It's nothing bad," Kaga added, "but I watched each of you, sometimes from a distance as you tried to cope. I wish I could have shown you more consideration." She cast a sideways glance, a guilty one at that, toward Mima.

"Kaga, don't feel that way," Mima replied. "You were always considerate of me, even in the hard times, and I don't forget that."

"Yeah, you were," Sora put in, "don't be down on yourself, Kaga."

"And that's coming from you?" The rejoinder and the way Kaga said it caused all four women to laugh and Aidan joined in. Some things never did change.

After a meal involving one of the chefs cooking at their table, the group headed back to Mima's apartment. Aidan found Eko on one side of him, their inner arms linked, with Kaga on the other. Mima and Sora walked a few paces in front, hand in hand.

He noted Kaga's smile. "That's very cool," she commented.

"They found themselves once again," Eko said.

Aidan guessed Kaga wanted to say more, but she kept silent. At the apartment, Aidan lit a smoke on the deck and Kaga joined him there. "Do things feel the same to you?" he asked.

"That's a tough question." Kaga leaned against the railing and looked at the building across the street. "In some ways, yes. I was worried about this meeting," she added. "It's been a few years since I've seen them face to face, other than Eko, who came to my wedding."

She turned to Aidan. "Believe me, I'm happy to see them again," she said, "especially Mima. I am proud of her, and I'm glad to see Sora and her like they are. I somehow knew they'd end up together, like an old married couple, I suppose."

Aidan laughed, and Kaga did as well, but it was forced. Her eyes now fixed on the street below, Kaga continued, "I know you were instrumental in keeping Mima together when she was in Boston, and I thank you for that. That time was so hard on her, and I've felt like a real bitch for a long, long time about it all."

"How so?" Aidan leaned closer so Kaga could keep her voice down.

"I know I should tell Mima this," Kaga replied, "but I have felt so guilty about how we broke up. Then I heard about her cutting herself and using the blood to paint with..."

Kaga shuddered at the thought. "That shook me," she went on. "I felt kind of responsible for driving Mima to it, breaking up with her and leaving her all alone."

You shouldn't feel guilty over that," Aidan told her. "That was years ago; and there were the other factors."

"It's gonna sound stupid," Kaga sighed, "but I broke up with Mima, right when she needed someone..."

The door slid open. "Hey," Mima said, "we've got the video ready..." Her voice cut off when she saw how close the two were in conversation.

Aidan seized the moment. He crushed out his smoke and said, "You're right on time." He turned to Kaga. "Sorry," he added, "but you need to say what you were about to say to Mima. It won't be like you think." He winked as he passed Mima and returned inside.

Aidan joined Sora and Eko before the monitor. "I had a feeling," Eko said, "that Kaga needed to talk. She's been holding back all night."

"Her guilt over Mima," Sora observed. "We've suspected it. It's time."

* * *

The two women stood before one another. Mima pulled down the sleeves of her old Butera sweatshirt due to the nighttime cold and looked to Kaga. "What do you want to say to me, Kaga?"

"I guess I should be direct about it," Kaga replied, and she took a deep breath. "Mima," she said, "I'm sorry."

Mima's hands went to Kaga's forearms, and she felt the prickly sensation of the jacket's material in her fingers. "About what?"

Kaga looked down at their feet momentarily, then at Mima. "About dumping you as I did," she replied. "I am sorry because I didn't tell you the full truth about things. At first I didn't think it mattered, but in recent years, it has in my mind."

"Kaga," Mima replied, "you told me the truth, and you were right. We could not have carried on a relationship half a world apart. We both had to become the people we would be."

"I know," Kaga said, "but I was not fully honest with you, Mima."

Kaga took Mima's forearms in her hands and held them. "It was true," she continued, "that I felt the relationship could not go any further, but that wasn't all of it. I was scared of something, Mima, and I couldn't face it."

In the streetlight shadow, Mima saw it cross Kaga's face. Her expression was the willful, determined one Kaga had when getting herself up for a soccer match, but the words were different this time. "I saw," Kaga said, "the way Sora struggled with her illness. Then you: I saw how down you got, how sad you were. I knew a lot of it had to do with your family, but there was a lot of darker stuff there."

Kaga inhaled and tightened her grip on Mima's arms. "I could tell how difficult things were for you," she said, "and I was scared for you at times. I was afraid of what would happen, but I resolved to stand by you. Then I realized…" Kaga's voice trailed off. "…I couldn't do it."

"How did you know you couldn't help me?" Mima asked.

"Your dark periods," Kaga explained, "the ones when you got so quiet and sad, and when you and Sora painted together. I knew you had to go through whatever was going on. For me, the decision to break up with you was the hardest one to take."

Kaga took another deep breath, and her voice rose. "I didn't want to let you go," she said. "I wanted to protect you, to be your friend and your lover. I don't regret one thing we did, Mima. I loved you then, and I still do. I'm just sorry I couldn't face up to it."

"Kaga, don't." Mima's arms slid around Kaga's neck. "You don't have to feel sorry Kaga, there's nothing to be sorry for. Listen," she continued, "you ultimately made the right choice. I had to discover myself on my own, and I had to do it away from everyone, including you. I would never have grown, matured or learned what I needed to. No matter how hard things got, I had to go through that process.

"I was fortunate," Mima continued, "to have Aidan there as someone I could talk to. I am the luckiest woman alive. I had Aidan when I needed him, but I had Sora, Suemi and Yuzuki, Eko, and yes, you, Kaga--all of you in my life."

She clung to Kaga and buried her head against the woman's breast. It felt like it did the first time. "You must not feel sorry, Kaga," she urged. "If there is anything to forgive you for, I already have. I forgave you years ago."

Mima felt those arms go around her shoulders. She felt Kaga's hand pass through her hair as it had done so many times before. The arms that held Mima were as strong, the touch as tender as in years past. "You mean that?" Kaga asked.

Mima looked up at her. "When did I not mean something I said?"

The shell around Kaga's face dropped, and it was replaced by a huge grin. "I do love you, Meem," she whispered, her throat tight, "so much."

"Love you, too..." Mima replied, "...Kaga-chan."

One final time, the two kissed.

26 - What Never Dies

The shades across the sliding door were drawn, and Mima switched off the light. In a t-shirt and her underwear, she slid into bed beside Sora.

"Mima," Sora whispered, "are you sure this is something you want to do? I don't want you to do it for my sake."

"It is for me, too," Mima reassured her. She moved into the woman's arms, and her head found Sora's chest. "The change," she went on, "will be a good one. Once the estate is settled and the house taken care of, I want to find a better place, a larger one. I need the space, and I've lived here far too long. Besides, someplace we can be together? That will be better."

Sora sighed. "I agree, but," she asked, "are you certain you can handle me?"

"I've handled you all my life," Mima replied, "why not now?"

They laughed, and their lips found one another's. "You have had to deal with me, Sora," Mima added.

"True." There was a pause, and then Sora said, "Mima, I think I will try the lithium. I shall at least talk with the therapist about it."

"That's good," Mima praised, "and don't worry. What I said earlier, I meant."

Mima felt Sora hold to her more tightly. "I'll do my best," Sora promised, "as I will to love you, Mima. I think we are stuck with one another."

"And I," Mima replied before their kiss, "will take that."

* * *

Aidan's thoughts were of many things, but mainly the one before him.

Eko slid out of her silk robe in the dark. "Are you enjoying this?" she asked as she turned in silhouette by the window. "I would hate to think I am interfering with your projects."

He laughed. "No, Eko, you've my undivided attention."

Eko's smile was the bewitching one she'd used on him before. She then joined him in bed and locked her body around his own. "Your decision," she asked, "have you arrived at it?"

"I think so," he replied. "I have to return to Washington next week." Aidan described the text he received from Philippa: an order to appear before the grand jury was coming.

"How long will such a proceeding take?" Eko asked.

Aidan moved his head down to kiss Eko's lips; they remained sweet from her lip color, even after the bath they shared. "For me, perhaps one day of testimony," he replied. "I should be free to travel again after that." Aidan added, "And I shall return, believe me."

"I should hope so," Eko told him, "or I would search all over Washington until I found you!"

There was a conspiratorial chuckle from the pair. After several kisses and other maneuvers, Aidan said, "Well, the video, editing, and photography must be done, and I can do that here. I don't care how long it takes, but I need to be here."

"It best not all be for me," Eko cautioned him again. "You have more to go through, as well as do, Aidan. I am aware of this, and I'm more than willing to wait for you. I don't know if I am ready to leave this house, let alone my homeland, but I want to go where you go."

She kissed him again and added, "I am in love with you, Aidan. I have seen all of the reasons why Mima held you in such esteem. I'm honored to be this close."

Aidan's eyes involuntarily closed. He was exhausted, and Eko's body next to his own took him away from his world. The projects, the testimony, all that shit in DC. He didn't want it to happen, and he didn't want it to take him away from this land, his friends, and Eko.

"I'm the one who's honored," he whispered, "and I'm in love with you too, Eko. I would stay here if it made you happy."

He felt Eko's body climb astride his. The ends of her mane tickled his face and chest. Her fingers caressed his cheeks while his felt the taut curves of her hips. Eko's breath was warm as it approached his own and she said, "It is what makes us happy, Aidan. It's all right to include yourself in such things."

The lips came closer, closer. Then Aidan reached and found the back of Eko's neck. He pulled her lips to his.

Yes, he thought: all right, indeed.

✳ ✳ ✳

The body that lay on the bed was not skinny, though its intent and position were prototypal. Mima's curled position and the placement of her hands revealed nothing that could be considered offensive.

Three sets of overhead lights, including two brought from Sora's room, hung from above. The white cloths used for

Aidan's video project were now set for another purpose; they covered her bed and the floor around it. Her hair was draped about her shoulder, the contours of her slightly Rubenesque body in plain sight.

Sora sat on the floor in front of Mima, though the latter would not see her. A large sketchpad open on her crossed legs, Sora sketched with a dark pencil the nude woman before her. Above her, Aidan quietly moved about the room with the Minolta. He took a series of photos, first from one angle, then another. Eko and Kaga stood by to change the lighting, and to mark out places on the floor for the photographer and the "model".

"I've never done this kind of work," Aidan calmly noted as he changed rolls.

"I've always wanted to do Mima," Sora replied, then drew her pencil away from the paper while she and the others laughed.

"This is a major stretch for me," Mima admitted. "Sora has been fascinated by my body for years, but I could never bring myself to do this."

"You are shedding your old skin," Eko suggested, "as I did when I told Aidan what happened to me."

"We have all done that to some extent," Sora noted as she resumed sketching, now with a second, lighter pencil. "Like snakes, we get rid of them over time."

Aidan reset the Minolta, checked the battery life on his flash and continued to shoot. There was nothing obscene about this: the photos were not meant for publication, unlike the collection Aidan resolved he would make a book out of one day. These were models for Sora to use, and for Mima to shed that skin.

He smiled and exchanged one with Eko. Aidan had no idea where they were headed, only that he had to be around her. Be it Tokyo, Washington or elsewhere, it didn't matter.

As he looked over the four women, one a friend for life, one a potential love of his life and the others, Aidan thought of the shoot made right before this session. For someone who hadn't been around, the last member of the group said everything Aidan, Mima, Sora and Eko tried to for so long.

* * *

Kaga sat on Mima's stool against the white backdrop. In a casual cotton blouse and jeans, Kaga looked comfortable in front of the cameras, and had no problems with the shooting as she spoke to Mima via Aidan's questions.

"I never considered myself a parasite," she said, "because there was no need. When I left for university, I knew what I would do for a living. Following graduation, I was fortunate to find work as a coach. Since then, I have had no reason to be worried. Getting married happened, I think as it does for most people. So really," Kaga added with a chuckle, "I'm the *tsukkomi!*"

Kaga's joke referenced the "straight man" of Japanese comedy teams. Aidan waited for the laughter to die down, and asked his next question. "Aside from the 'Parasite' term, is it still hard for women to take their place in Japanese society?"

Kaga thought for a moment. "Yes," she replied. "I always felt that if I did marry, it would be to a man who was like myself, a teacher or someone involved in sports. Who else would understand how I have conducted myself in this line of work? I have to set an example for the girls I instruct and lead onto the field. That sometimes does run counter to what men expect women to be. But this is me, and I mustn't deny that, especially not to myself."

"Your friends," Aidan asked, "do you see them differently now, with the passing of years?"

There was a slow, silent nod. "Yes," she said at length, "but the differences are not so great. My relationship with Mima came out of two people who needed some kind of validation, one that cannot be given by one's family. You certainly can't give it to yourself. We would have been friends without that. Sora and Eko, I understood them both because they understood me. What amazed me the most was how none of us had to push ourselves to do that."

Eko moved to Kaga's right and got a profile shot of her seated there. "You know," she said, "we each meet hundreds, if not thousands of people in our lives. What keeps the four of us this close, even when separated by miles, over years?"

She paused. "I think," Kaga said, "it is true friendship. The bonds of friends who are meant to be friends, and are meant to care for and stand beside one another -- that never dies. Those friendships are the special ones, even beyond marriages and families. I wonder if anyone's ever considered it that way; I have to wonder…"

Kaga's thoughtful words, her mood and emotions were captured. Aidan stared at the camera's viewfinder for several seconds, then reached out to switch it off. Eko, who waited for Aidan's cue, lowered hers and did the same.

"That's a wrap," he declared.

Made in the USA
Middletown, DE
23 October 2021